To:
Enjoy!

The Road to
Lancaster Manor

Wes Henderson

Published by:

FriesenPress
Suite 300 – 852 Fort Street
Victoria, BC, Canada V8W 1H8

www.friesenpress.com

Distributed to the trade by The Ingram Book Company

In memory of my parents, Ellen and Jack.

CHAPTER ONE

The cheerful tunes of the songbirds could not be heard today, only the dreadful cawing of the crows and ravens as they peered down on the congregation. The soaring black silhouettes seemed appropriate against the backdrop of tree branches that were already barren of leaves, twisted and looking angry against the charcoal scuffed clouds and the dreariest of skies. The light but constant rain played a tortuous rhythm on the umbrellas of the few family members and a select number of close friends huddled together in an out-of-the-way corner of a five hundred year old cemetery; the mourners peering down onto two ornate wooden caskets as they were being lowered into the soggy ground.

Richard Lion stood motionless except for the shivering brought on by the cold and wet surroundings, aided by the sense of shock and emotional strain he was feeling with the loss of two remarkable souls so dear to him. While the mourners were attentively listening to Reverend Arthur Jameson and his chosen bible readings, Richard was somewhere else altogether staring into a void, recalling with some difficulty and without clarity, events almost exactly one year ago that were to lead to his death and in a sense his rebirth. Richard was as much a son to the Lancasters as he was to the Ramseys, his natural parents.

The formal service having ended, the congregation slowly made their way to the protection of their vehicles waiting at the base of the hill. With a sense of concern, Richard's new best friend Jason said to him, "Come on Richard, it's time to go." Richard, his eyes damp and his lips quivering, replied without looking at Jason, "You go with Monica; I want to stay for a few more minutes."

More tears came to his eyes as Richard's mind tried to control and organize the complex series of extraordinary events imploding within his head – events that were beyond belief and had transpired in only the past twelve months. He recalled that his journey to this point in time began on a beautiful autumn day in September, a significant contrast to this September morning. He could still see in his mind's eye the vibrant golden and fire red leaves of the Maple trees standing in the front yard of his parent's home as he opened the door to let his good friend into the house. Richard was known as Adam then.

"What do you mean you're not going?" Adam hollered in amazement at Jeff. "We've been planning this trip for months. We've saved the money; we've paid for our plane tickets. Damn it Jeff we're supposed to leave in less than three weeks. Now you're telling me that you are not going - why the hell not?"

Jeff had fought with himself for three days trying to get up the nerve to tell Adam that a surprise job offer had made him reconsider whether he really wanted to hitchhike around the world for a year. It was his sister Jodie who finally tore into him accusing Jeff of being cowardly and inconsiderate not letting Adam know of his decision as soon as he had made up his mind to accept the job. Knowing he would eventually have to break the news to Adam and suffer the consequences, Jeff reluctantly found his way over to Adam's parent's house to face him.

"I'm sorry Adam, but a few weeks ago my Uncle Joe offered me a job most guys would kill for. I mean how could I turn down the opportunity to be a part of the promotional team for the Toronto Raptors of the NBA. If I hadn't taken the job at this time, I would have lost the chance of a lifetime."

"I thought we had made a pact," said Adam, "that no matter what, we would hold off our careers until we came back from our trip. You know damn well that I turned down a job with Warner Consulting after we graduated and then Stanton Industries approached me during the summer. I was committed Jeff and I thought you were too. And what's this about you knowing for three weeks? Geez Jeff, I am really pissed."

"I couldn't tell you because I was afraid you would react just as you have." Jeff paused for a reaction from Adam. When there was none, he continued, "What do you think you will do? Will you go on your own?"

Adam thought back to his last year in engineering. He seemed to have an easy time comprehending the most complex concepts of electrical engineering and his professors at Queen's University in Ontario said to him that with his natural talents and his hard work ethic, he should be successful in anything he wanted to do. Professor Hitchcock had even promoted the talents of his young protégé to a number of his friends in some of the largest engineering firms in the country. Adam would have no problem getting a good start on his career. But Adam wanted to travel and when he and Jeff started to think seriously about the trip, his mind was made up. And when Adam set his mind to something, it was difficult to change it.

"I guess I will have to," replied Adam, now in a calm and despairing tone. "I mean I still really want to go."

"You don't know how bad I feel Adam. Will you forgive me?" pleaded Jeff.

"Yeah, don't worry about it," Adam said, his mind already racing ahead to plan B. "It'll work out."

The next few weeks went by in a blur as Adam completed his final preparations for his own chance of a lifetime. Actually his mother was probably as busy as Adam in getting her son ready for his adventure, an even greater adventure now that he was traveling on his own. Joan Ramsey was like most moms who were both proud of and fearful for their sons, especially when they were embarking on some new challenge. It was the same when Adam went to volleyball camp for the first time, when he went off to Queen's, or when he left for a summer job in northern Alberta planting seedlings in the province's remote mountainous back country. She had good reason to be concerned at that time as it turned out. Adam and one of his co-workers came upon a Grizzly Bear one day late in the planting season and were lucky to escape with their lives, but not with all of their skin. The young men had suffered a severe mauling before their supervisor ran the bear off with his rifle. Fortunately Joan had to wait several days before she could see Adam and by that time his appearance was not as gruesome. And now Mrs. Ramsey's son was leaving on his own for a trip across the

Atlantic; a trip that was planned to take the better part of a year "to see the world" as they say. He would start in Europe, travel through Africa, then into Asia and return home in time to seek out a job with an engineering firm a couple of months prior to the date for the next class of engineers to graduate. Well that was the plan anyway.

"Don't worry Mom," Adam said as encouragingly as he could to his mother. "I'm going to be alright. I will likely meet up with some fellow travelers within days of reaching Portugal. I will write often and if I need money I will let you know."

These past few minutes before departure were anxious for Adam and his family. His mom, dad, and sister took him to the airport to see him off. The weather was particularly warm for September 30th. The sun was bright, the sky was blue. In all it was a good feeling day and a spectacular backdrop for his send off. Adam's sister, Joy, was six years younger and so wanted to go with him, or at least go on a trip to Europe. She hoped that if Adam's experience proved safe and successful that she would have a better chance at convincing her parents to let her go next year with her friends Tony and Jill, after she finished high school.

"I know you're going to have a great time son," cheered Mr. Ramsey. "I also know that you will be careful and take measures not to get yourself into predicaments that could be risky. But if you have any doubts or concerns about anything and you want to talk about it, just call me anytime."

Ed Ramsey was very proud of his son and of the many accomplishments he had jammed into his young life. Adam was twenty-four years old, an "A" student and an athlete as well. He participated in all sports in high school and was a conference all-star in basketball three years running. He played guitar, taught swimming, and volunteered at a local centre for children with intellectual disabilities. Golfing came naturally to him and he and his father spent many a Sunday morning together bonding as men do in friendly rivalry. But Adam's greatest passion was fencing. Like many young boys, Adam was a big fan of swashbuckler movies, of pirates and sword fighting. He began taking fencing lessons when he was twelve, mostly to live out his fantasies, but it soon became evident that he had both an interest and skills and his teachers encouraged his parents to continue with more serious training. By the age of sixteen, Adam was attending tournaments across the country carrying home many trophies. He excelled on his university team, leading them to several national championships and would have represented his country in the Olympics if it hadn't been for the incident with the Grizzly Bear.

Adam had a great attitude and he was respectful and considerate of others. These were traits that were demanded by his mother. He was also an incredibly focused young man with a strong will to do things right and to succeed. That trait was passed on to him by his father. Ed was not stubborn or mule headed about things. He simply believed that when he committed himself to a task, whether at work or at home, it was his responsibility to complete his job with professionalism and in the best way he knew how. Adam had learned this work ethic early in life and it had served him well in school, sports, and in the community.

"They are calling your flight," Ed said. "We should get you through security."

Trying to delay her final words she knew would be difficult, Joan said, "If you get a chance during your stopover in Montreal, give your Aunt Trina a call. She would love to hear from you." Finally after all the goodbyes were said, Joan took Adam aside, hugged him tight and whispered in his ear, "I love you so much. Be safe."

With Ed's comforting arms around her, Joan managed a brave smile as Adam walked out of sight on his way to board the plane.

It had been more than a few minutes since Jason had beckoned his friend to join the other mourners and he could see that Richard was getting drenched in the rain with no intention of moving. He said to the young woman standing next to him, "You go speak to him Monica. He needs to get out of the rain and back to the Estate. He'll catch a death of a cold if he stands there any longer." As soon as the words fell out of his mouth Jason had regretted using them in this moment. "The guests will be expecting him at Lancaster Manor and he has a responsibility now."

CHAPTER TWO

Standing alone as a sentinel keeping watch over the graves, this time of solitude presented Richard with the opportunity to search deeper within his mind and reveal images of some of his most memorable experiences during his travels that had unexpectedly come to an abrupt halt after only four months. He wiped away both rain and tears from his face as he recalled his first view of Europe after a devastatingly long plane ride. From his window seat he witnessed millions of angry blue swells of ocean crashing hard and furiously onto rocky outcrops, with their turbulent waves exploding watery mist against the Portugal shores. In stark contrast with the brutal wind off the ocean, the sun shone brightly against a brilliant blue sky. Adam had arrived in Europe via Lisbon. Sitting on the port side of the Boeing 767, he had a clear view of the city and was surprised at the continuous maze of white-walled buildings. Most of these were houses from the old districts of the city. To the east rose the modern-day downtown business centre with its tall, glass fronted buildings which further highlighted the centuries old areas on the ocean side.

Adam had flown on several planes throughout North America when he was attending fencing tournaments for the university, but this was his first trans-Atlantic flight. Even on board a large plane the flight time was still over eight hours and he was tired and stiff. His more than six foot frame did not fit very comfortably in the economy seats. Adam hadn't slept a great deal during the flight primarily because of the physical discomfort, as well as the tortuous snoring from an older woman seated two rows behind him. He remembered seeing her early on in the flight noting that she wore all black, including a black shawl drawn over her head allowing just a wisp of her grey hair to be seen. The trip ahead of him was also on Adam's mind. Of course he wasn't supposed to be travelling alone. He still couldn't believe Jeff had changed his mind about their trip at the last minute. While Adam had some misgivings and concerns about starting out by himself in a strange country, especially when he couldn't speak the language, he convinced himself that he would be alright. He had invested a great deal of thought and planning into this project and he wasn't going to let Jeff's change of heart rob him of this dream.

Richard wiped more tears than rain drops from his eyes as he mapped his way across Europe and North Africa in his mind. Madrid was where he had stayed at his first youth hostel. He paused at this location in his memory and reflected.

The roadway was a mosaic of broken stone smoothed over by the countless feet of both man and beast that must have tread on its surface, over the past three hundred years. A rusty brown kind of crud was binding the stone together like concrete. It was a very narrow road, that in earlier times would have managed an ox cart but nothing wider. On that day only pedestrians, cyclists and scooters traversed the street. No form of automobile could safely navigate the meandering roadway without leaving a significant amount of paint on the walls of the buildings. The gutters running along either side of the roadway were still moist from the rain that had fallen the night before. Garbage was not limited to lying in the gutters but was bunched up in every corner and crevice along the route. The buildings stretching along the stone hardened street were not as run down as one might have thought in this old part of Madrid. They appeared as they might be of original design and the fresh coat of whitewash covered up as best it could the ragged texture of the walls that were emphasized by years of scaling through natural forces or by human intervention. The buildings were small but seemed to serve the needs of the shopkeepers who at this time of day were closing their businesses in order to take their afternoon siesta. A strange custom to a westerner perhaps, but in a sun soaked country like Spain, it was a way in which countrymen could take sanctuary from the scorching heat of the day.

Adam had been strolling down this particular street for what seemed like an hour since he had received directions from the ticket agent at the train station. Even though the street was constantly in shadow due to the narrow lane and three story buildings and situated in what he understood to be the older and poorer part of the city, he did not feel at risk. The street was filled with people including families with children.

He thought to himself that this section of the long street was far different than where it had begun. Not ten minutes from the train station, Adam was approached by some women who were not shy about listing the various services they would perform for him. In a very loose mixture of Spanish and English it was still quite clear what these services were about and Adam wanted to have nothing to do with the prostitutes. It became clear thereafter, that he had, been slowly moving through the red light district. In many cities these famous areas tended to spring up close to railroad stations.

While searching his backpack for a map and his water bottle, a male voice asked him in English "Are you looking for the youth hostel?" The question was posed by a twenty-something man sporting a New York Yankees ball cap, who himself carried a backpack.

"I am," stated Adam, "can you give me directions?" The young man in the cap looked and spoke more like he had come off of the farm in Indiana than a New Yorker. He was a broad shouldered, clean cut, calf throwing country boy in appearance with a real country drawl.

"From Canada I see," said the Hoosier, as he pointed to the Canadian flag that Adam's mother had sewn on to his backpack. "There are a few of you up at the hostel. It's only another hundred yards up this street on the right. Look for a big green triangle. My name is Charlie, maybe I will see you tonight." The American started walking off in the opposite direction from the hostel.

Adam had never experienced drugs first hand back in Canada and so that night at the hostel he was overwhelmed and feeling quite out-of-place, even leery about what was happening when he witnessed so many of the men-only hostel clients partaking in an assortment of soft and hard drugs, mixed with wine. As it happened the night passed without incident. Two French Canadians and two Americans were by far the most wasted, but on the other hand they seemed to be having the greatest of times laughing and telling jokes that somehow they were all able to understand. The two Americans, Fred and Jed, were about Adam's age and had just left the Navy after six years. Adam bought Fred's poncho which turned out to be a Godsend in days following when he had been stranded in the middle of nowhere in the pouring rain. That was about two weeks later and Adam had taken a ride from a fellow just outside of a small town called Puertollano, heading south.

The weather had turned cold in Madrid and Adam was anxious to reach warmer temperatures. The man was driving a small Fiat. There were a number of posters in the back seat where he had placed his backpack. The posters were of Hollywood movie scenes, possibly publicity posters for various movies, he thought at the time. Adam couldn't converse in Spanish and the man could not speak English, but after about a half hour and before a turn-off on the country road, Adam made his feelings well known about the man placing his hand in Adam's lap and gently stroking it. Shocked as he was, Adam showed his balled fists and told the man in no uncertain terms "to get his fucking hands off of him and to stop the car and let him out." The man tried to imply that he meant nothing but Adam wasn't buying it and further demanded in an angrier voice and with animation that he stop the car. And that was it; Adam was left smack in the geographic centre of Spain.

He walked what he believed to be about three or four miles, always ready to stick his thumb out when a car approached. But none of the few vehicles that passed by would stop for him. Not long after, it began to rain and then rain harder. He said a silent thank you to Fred and slung the old poncho over himself. Eventually after another three vehicles passed him by and with the rain pouring down on him, Adam was so forlorn that he simply sat down in the middle of the road thinking the next vehicle that came along would have to stop. He didn't particularly care at that point which direction the vehicle would be heading. When it began to get dark and no vehicles were to be seen, he decided to take refuge among some old ruins he spotted in the distant field. Finding some shelter under a collapsed building, he climbed into his sleeping bag and covered himself with Fred's poncho. Adam was exhausted and disheartened. He was also hungry, not having eaten since the morning. He sat up against the wall with the poncho tented over his head and lit a candle. The light produced by the flame was faint but it was enough for him to see what he was doing. While he was consuming a can of sardines and drinking from his wine skin, he started to jot down some words he was trying to convince himself was poetry. Soon after he found he was simply too tired to continue writing and fell asleep.

Now standing in rain again, Richard recalled the poem from memory. "It's getting colder now, the sun is beginning to set. I've been here almost eight hours and all I have gotten are laughs and thumbs at the nose. I'll stay here though, and keep waiting and hoping and praying. Maybe I'll make my bed here. It's not so bad having the hard ground for a bed and a … I don't know what kind of tree overhead. And maybe in the morning, a brand new day, I'll leave this place, five thousand miles away."

Farther south, Adam was fortunate enough to visit one of the most spectacular and most memorable monuments he had ever seen - the Mezquita in Cordoba. On par with the Alhambra in Granada and the Alcazar in Seville, the Mezquita is a mosque of immense size with a cathedral inside it. The Mezquita dates back to the 10th century when Cordoba was one of the largest and most prosperous cities in Europe, outshining Byzantine and Bagdad in science, culture and the arts. In part, the Great Mosque could be described as a forest of pillars due to the vast number of supports. There are more than 850 coloured granite jasper and marble pillars in total.

Richard left the image behind, still feeling in awe over the enormity and history of the Great Mosque.

Following his thumb Adam headed to the southern coast of Spain where it was both warm and inexpensive, with the idea of eventually hopping a ferry over to Morocco.

A smile came to Richard's lips when he thought about the time he had met up with the two Bens.

They were Canadians from Alberta and they had the same names. Fortunately one was tall and one was short which aided in remembering who was whom. Adam had just emerged from the highway leading away from Matril at about 10:30 in the morning when Ben and Ben were driving along in their Volkswagen Beetle and stopped to offer him a ride. While appreciative of the ride, at first he doubted very much that there would be sufficient room for him. Three good sized men with their backpacks was certainly a challenge for the pint-sized Beetle.

Richard recalled that, at the time, he had a strong sense short Ben was not very keen on picking him up. The more he thought about it, he remembered that short Ben never seemed very pleased with how their journey evolved as the three new companions travelled together over the next few weeks.

These were two regular guys with no particular or outstanding characteristics that would make them memorable other than both sharing the same name. But they seemed nice enough and they were headed in the same direction as Adam with the same purpose in mind. That was enough for Adam, so he struggled his way into the back seat of the Beetle and they were off.

On December 8, the three young men took the ferry from Algeciers to Ceuta. The ferry ride took over an hour. At Ceuta they decided to take a bus to Teteun and progressed as far as the border between Spanish Morocco and Morocco proper. Ben and Ben weren't accepted to cross at the border because their hair was considered too long. Supposedly long hair meant hippie and trouble so they were turned back. The three amigos walked back to Ceuta, which was about three miles, bought a pair of scissors and arranged for a room for the night. While Adam cut tall Ben's hair, short Ben decided to go to a barber. The next day the trio had no difficulty gaining access over the border. Arriving in Teteun at about 2:30 in the afternoon gained them a foothold in the country. They decided that they would continue on to Fez the next day rather than to Casa Blanca for no other reason than Fez was closer and the bus left earlier – the next morning rather than waiting until the next evening. No one had a planned itinerary at this point so there was no concern as to where they would go first.

The two Bens had deliberately chosen to enter Morocco at Teteun rather than the better known Tangiers, primarily because they had heard that they would avoid the normal hassling from beggars and pedlars of all kinds generally trying to sell anything and everything to tourists. As it turned out, Teteun was bad enough. As soon as the passengers had emerged from the bus, throngs of young kids in particular had swarmed them trying to sell everything from trinkets to hash, or willing to take the tourists to do some sightseeing. It really turned out to be a bother. When the men thought they had lost the kids, the rascals would show up again at the next corner and the process would start all over again. Adam tried to be polite and tall Ben took to swearing at them, but the result was just the same - they simply did not go away. Finally after what seemed like hours trying to get away from the mob, the three men, now completely frustrated, agreed to let two young boys, each about twelve years old, to act as their guides. These boys were dressed neater and cleaner than most of the other young hustlers and their English was much easier to understand. The men were in agreement that good communication was essential. After a financial arrangement had been made, the kids led them off to the Médina.

The Médina was an old walled city within the larger city. More than anything else it was a huge marketplace but arranged in the most complicated maze one could imagine. Adam noted that the long winding streets were very narrow – more like alleys really, lined with grubby little cubicles where people sold their merchandise. It looked like a very poor area and he was certain that it was. Adam buttoned his jacket all the way to his neck and held his hands in his pockets constantly keeping track of his pass port and his money and for fear he would accidently touch someone or knock over something which may then cause harsh words or maybe more. Being the only white guys in sight, it was not difficult to become paranoid concerning what could befall you. Thank God they were being escorted by the two local kids who clearly knew their way around. On the other hand, what kept going through Adam's mind at the time was that he and the two Bens were essentially at the mercy of the two kids. The kids could easily lose them in the maze, have them killed and rob them. No one would ever know. As it turned out, that evening was a very interesting experience which they were able to talk about for a long time. Tall Ben and Adam decided they both wanted a djellaba, a monk-like robe worn by men in Morocco. Adam had bargained rather well he thought. He had kept walking away from the gentleman who was selling the djellabas, saying "too much, too much". The vendor would come after Adam enticing him to come back and pay a reduced price. "For you, student price," he claimed. Walking away with his djellaba, Adam was happy with his purchase at 30 durms (which equated to $6. 00 US), down from 60, knowing full well that the vendor was still the big winner. After these purchases, the three Canadians decided they were worn out and convinced the kids that it was time to take them back to their hotel. They would be heading to Fez early in the morning.

CHAPTER THREE

As Richard's driver wheeled the long black limousine up the meandering roadway and approached Lancaster Manor, he noticed that several cars had already found parking places in the generous driveway in the courtyard. Many more were lined up like well-disciplined military troops on the grassy area along the edge of the driveway but closer to the stables. Of course there would be this many cars here already, Richard thought. He had taken a great deal of time at the grave site before Lady Monica Ashton finally convinced him that he had to go back to the Manor and oversee the reception. Lady Monica Ashton was the daughter of Lord and Lady Ashton, very good friends of the Lancasters and now possibly the only person with enough influence to convince Richard to do anything at this time. She was also the one to suggest to Richard that the word "wake" not be used because it sounded so morbid and the purpose of the gathering after the funeral was to celebrate the lives of the Lancasters. Richard had agreed and requested staff to substitute the term "reception" when inviting the guests.

Of Tudor design, Lancaster Manor was originally built in the early 1500's by Charles Lancaster. Always in the Lancaster family, the Manor had been passed down from one generation to another with various additions and renovations occurring during this time. Up until 1932, the original stables were positioned where the current garages are located as part of the east wing of the Manor. A new barn and stables were erected for a second time only fifteen years ago behind the garages toward the East Meadow. In addition to their own horses, the Lancaster's stable staff boarded a number of other horses for people living in the city of Bracknell, just a half hour away. Lady Lancaster was an accomplished equestrian in her youth and pursued the sport after her marriage to Lord Lancaster. However, an unfortunate fall over a water jump while competing in a national championship not only cost her the trophy, but it ended her competitive riding. Even in their 70's and up until the week before last, both Lord and Lady Lancaster enjoyed taking early morning or evening rides across the meadow and through the vast forested areas of the Lancaster Estate. This thought also brought back images of when Richard took rides with Lord Lancaster. While Richard had not had much of an opportunity to ride horses while growing up, he was eager to learn and a good student under Lord Lancaster.

The façade of the Manor had largely remained as originally constructed, with the exception of upgraded windows to better hold the heat within the stone walls. The Manor was built in a horseshoe design having three full stories. Both ends of the east and west wings were fashioned as round turrets, giving even more of a castle-like look to the building. No less than six chimneys emerged from the roof line more or less equally spaced around the entire complex, including the two wings of the

Manor. The front doors were located due centre of the main part of the Manor – the centre block. Made of solid oak and brass, they emerged from the walls of the Manor standing eight feet high and each four feet wide. With these massive barriers one could easily have imagined the Manor resembling a medieval fortress, and yet, as Richard well knew, beyond those formidable looking doors once lived a most gracious, kind and generous old couple.

Reston, Lord Lancaster's incredibly loyal and efficient manservant greeted Richard, Jason and Lady Monica Ashton as they crossed the threshold into the vast entrance lobby of the Manor. As he relieved them of their wet outerwear, Reston whispered into Richard's ear, "Master Richard, I think you ought to know that Mr. Edward Bolden seems to think he is in charge here now. He has begun to order all the staff to essentially undertake the very jobs that they have proficiently conducted themselves in doing since they have been in the employ of Lord Lancaster. Quite frankly I think he is making a complete ass of himself, if you will pardon my language young sir."

Reston was a man in his early sixties and had been with Lord Lancaster for over thirty-five years. He was as tall as Richard but slightly built, giving an impression that he could topple over in a strong wind and break like a twig. This impression would be dead wrong of course. Under the formal suit of clothes that were at all times hanging on his body during his working hours, one would find a well-exercised, well-muscled frame that an Olympic swimmer would be proud to own. Religiously, each morning at 6:00 Reston would be found in the fitness room sweating it out on the various weight and fitness machines, ending with a half mile swim in the indoor lap pool. All this before he would shower, dress, eat his customary cream of wheat and be ready to ensure Lord and Lady Lancaster's day began as always at 7:30 AM.

When Richard had first come to Lancaster Manor, Reston was somewhat suspicious of the young man and his intentions, but over time Reston came to better know and like young Richard and they soon became quite close friends, notwithstanding their respective stations in the house. Often, Richard would even work out with Reston and enjoy playful swimming competitions, which Reston most always won. Clearly, Reston's loyalties were now with Richard.

Richard replied "Well, after all, Edward is Lord Lancaster's nephew and I suppose he feels that he is the obvious one to take over the responsibilities of Lancaster Manor, or at least with respect to this reception and until the Wills reveal otherwise." Despite what he said to Reston, Richard had never grown to like Edward or trust him and he was suspicious now of Edward's motives and intentions in needlessly commandeering the staff of the Manor. Richard turned to Monica and Jason and after a deep breath and a sigh, quietly said to them, "I suppose we should join the guests and see what Edward is up to."

Once the guests had noticed Richard enter the grand room where the reception was being held, two things happened: heads turned and voices lowered into whispers. It was Lord and Lady Ashton, Monica's parents and dear friends of the Lancasters who first approached Richard. "That was a very nice service this afternoon," offered Lady Ashton. "James and Muriel would have been very proud to know of the very thoughtful and sensitive service that you helped to arrange with Reverend Jameson."

"Yes you did a fine job son," added Lord Ashton. "I'm certainly glad you had the mind to organize things before Edward had thought of doing something. I appreciate that it wasn't easy for you when he confronted you and wanted to change the service and this reception. I fully support you in how you handled his outbursts and threats. I fear, however, that Edward will not forget the embarrassing position he put himself into and will seek some sort of revenge. Maybe he has started already."

"Yes," Richard confirmed, "I have already heard about his ranting at the staff."

In a kind and motherly way, Lady Ashton suggested to Richard, "Perhaps you should start to mingle and greet the guests now. I should think that many people here will want to speak to you."

With that encouragement Richard began to visit with the many friends, business associates and public figures who knew and respected Lord Lancaster and his wife. Many had the same things to say. "Wasn't it a terrible tragedy to die in such an awful automobile accident?" "I understand that at least they died instantly and did not suffer!" "Are the police considering if this was more than an accident?"

Just before another well-meaning guest who Richard did not recognize started to approach him, Richard was tapped on the shoulder and at the same instant heard a familiar voice thoughtfully ask, "So how are you holding up?" The caring voice was from Lord Lancaster's friend and business partner who was now steering him away from the other guests. Richard thanked him for the discreet intervention. Sir John Loxley was actually the CEO and President of the multi-national corporation headed by Lord Lancaster and was a significant but still a minority shareholder in the corporation. Lord Lancaster was the majority shareholder and had been the Chairman of the Board for many years. Richard knew Sir Loxley quite well not only through Lord Lancaster, but also through his work with the company. He was an honest and respectable person and businessman and a very good friend of Lord Lancaster.

"Thanks for rescuing me Sir Loxley. I know all these people legitimately cared for the Lancasters but with the funeral and this reception, it's really been is a bit overwhelming. I am sure in a few days the activity will all calm down. Right now however, I am terribly saddened – almost in shock that this could have happened. They were such terrific people with still so much to live for."

"You are right about that, they were both vibrant people and had a keen interest in the future," said Sir Loxley, "and it is in large part due to you coming into their lives. It was like James and Muriel had been given a new lease on life. James often talked about your accomplishments, how hard you worked to recover and how quickly you were able to learn certain aspects of the business. They both bragged about what a nice young man you were. They were very proud of you and they loved you like a son."

"I miss them like a son," Richard replied.

Before he could say anything further to Sir Loxley, Edward Bolden approached Richard and in an extremely aggressive fashion asked him if he had indeed told the staff that after the reception they could have the rest of the day and tomorrow off work and by what authority he thought he had to do it. Richard's fists turned into balls and his body became tense. He wasn't in the proper frame of mind to handle Edward graciously and was about to say something he would have no doubt regretted later when Sir Loxley intervened once again to try and calm Edward down and avoid an embarrassing scene. The Ashtons, joined by the Williscrofts and the Mentors, some other good friends of Lord and Lady Lancaster had overheard Edward's criticism of Richard, and stepped up to lend their support to Sir Loxley by congratulating Richard on his proactive position taken with the staff in respect for the loss of the Lancasters. The cold villain that he was, Edward could still appreciate that he was outnumbered and decided to drop his objections. He left the gathering with a stern look on his face that was directed straight at Richard and which could have been interpreted to say "just wait, I'm not finished with you."

"I feel so sorry for Muriel's sister having to put up with that son of hers," Mrs. Williscroft announced. "Do you know that Judith has had to sell off some of her jewellery in order to bail that ungrateful man out from under a loan shark?"

"He has certainly become less and less popular over the past few years," Lord Ashton commented, "especially after the investigation into alleged fraud and mis-management of the family's funds after his father passed away."

Mr. Mentor removed his pipe from his mouth and cautioned, "I agree, but he was never formally charged. The investigators could not provide sufficient evidence involving him."

"Evidence or not," injected Mr. Williscroft, "I wouldn't trust him farther than I could throw him. I often wondered why James felt compelled to compromise his principles to assist Edward. I suppose it was more for Judith's sake." The small gathering all nodded in agreement.

Edward Bolden was the only child of Judith and David Bolden. David had passed away a few years ago from cancer. He was seventy-two. Judith was Lady Lancaster's younger sister by two years. Muriel and Judith were not from nobility and while Muriel had married into it with her marriage to James, Earl of Lancaster, Judith had, three years later, married David who was an accountant and Financial Director at Lloyds of London. Edward was forty-three years of age and he too worked in the financial and insurance business like his father. However, unlike his father, Edward did not hold an executive position, nor was he thought of or held in such high esteem as his late father had been. Simply put, Edward was a spoiled young man who did the least amount of work he could to satisfy his employer while spending more money than he made. He was not married but seemed to be in the company of a new fresh looking twenty-something woman every weekend. His extravagant spending often left him in debt, and as much as he regretted it, David felt he had to bail Edward out. When his father took sick, the debt relief suddenly halted and it was rumoured that Edward had found himself not only in a difficult financial position, but his personal health situation was also in jeopardy due to the fact that he was unable to pay back certain underground money lenders to whom he owed funds. Then suddenly not long after David's death, it appeared that Edward's financial problems had disappeared. The turn of events wasn't because Edward had inherited a great deal from his father; most of David's assets went to Judith.

Richard spotted Lady Monica Ashton speaking to Judith as they were descending the grand staircase from the second floor gallery. He excused himself from the Lancaster's friends and began to make his way over to the two ladies in the hope of having a quiet word with Judith.

Working his way through the guests, Richard found himself peering up and around the marvellous great hall. It was his favourite room in the Manor. The ceiling reached the full three stories. The room was as wide as it was long. Three stretch limousines could fit end-on-end across it. The grand staircase climbed up to the second and third floor galleries that looked down on the great hall from three sides. Ornate black iron railings skirted the galleries, interrupted by a series of huge sculptured columns precisely set at thirteen foot intervals. Hanging from the great height were two gigantic chandeliers, both comprised of sixteen antique brass arms that curved up from their bases to form an open flower of adorning lights. Situated around the perimeter of the great hall were six matching lamp stands, two of which stood on guard at either side of the grand staircase. The walls of the great room were, like the columns, sculptured to form archways over the staircase and passage ways into adjoining rooms. While primarily a sandstone colour, at various points around the wall and at random heights, delicate engravings were highlighted on coral coloured backgrounds some enhanced with inlaid jade stones as large as one's outstretched hand. While a bright and comparatively new burgundy carpet ran down the centre of the grand staircase, a rather worn but still rich looking Persian rug highlighted the floor of the great hall. It was thirty feet by twenty feet in size. Richard had been informed that the Persian rug was over a hundred years old and had been a gift to Lord Lancaster's grandfather from the then King of England. Centred upon the rug stood a large oak table, which was currently heaped with a variety of finger foods. The stair case and the great hall's floor were made of Italian marble both polished to a fine lustre where, standing at over six feet, Richard could still see his reflection.

Monica saw Richard approach and was relieved for his company as she felt she was talking to an empty body in Judith. Judith's mind was clearly not focused on what Monica was saying. She had a glaze over her eyes and they appeared as though they were searching for something far off in the distance, possibly not of this world. She had lost her dear husband only a few years ago, and now her sister and brother-in-law had left her so suddenly. All she had left of family was her son Edward and this thought did not lend her much comfort. As if Richard's approach had broken a spell, Judith turned to Monica and said, "I am sorry Monica, I haven't been able to pay attention to anything you have been saying; please forgive me." Monica put her hand on Judith's arm to comfort her and replied that she understood how she must feel and not to be concerned.

"I feel badly that I have not spent more time with you these past few days Aunt Judith," said Richard. Judith had asked Richard to call her Aunt Judith rather than Mrs. Bolden, when it was clear that Richard was becoming one of the family. This was encouraged by Lady Lancaster as well.

"Don't you worry about fussing over me," replied Judith, "I know you have been busy here taking care of James and Muriel's immediate affairs and in arranging the funeral. I don't know what I would have done without you making all these arrangements. I am afraid I have been quite a mess since their deaths. My doctor has even insisted prescribing something for depression. I haven't started taking it yet but I am considering it."

"Is there anything I can do for you before you return to Coventry?" asked Richard. "You could of course stay here at Lancaster Manor. It is only a few days before the reading of the Wills and you wouldn't need to trouble yourself with driving there and back again so soon. I'll let Reston know that you will be staying on and ..."

Before Richard could finish the sentence, Judith interjected saying, "No Richard, that won't be necessary. I would rather be in my own home for a few days, by myself. But thank you for thinking of me. I very much appreciate your concern."

In the next moment, the grandfather clock standing in the corner adjacent to them chimed four times, as if signalling to the guests that it was time to take their leave. And almost on cue, the guests began the process of filing out. Due to their position by the main entrance to the great hall, each of the guests had to pass by Richard, Judith and Monica and the trio had to graciously say their good byes and accept yet again all the guests' condolences. Richard had regretted placing himself at that precise location at that precise time.

The procession ended thirty minutes later, but for Richard, most of that time was split in both a conscious and subconscious state. Somehow he was able to appear as if he were paying attention, mechanically acknowledging all those who passed by him, while at the same time continuing the uncontrollable urge to recall earlier events leading up to this point.

CHAPTER FOUR

The two Bens and Adam boarded the bus to Fez at 6:00 in the morning. They arrived in Fez at 3:30 in the afternoon, having experienced an extraordinary ride. Adam's first observation when climbing up into the old bus was the condition of it. He knew from the inexpensive ticket that the bus was going to be economy class. He imagined it would be similar to the bus he and his family took in Mexico when his Dad had suggested using the local transportation for some sightseeing. At that time he had thought he had experienced the lowest economy class there could be. He was wrong. This bus had no class. The interior was barren of any comfort. It looked like the bus had been rescued from a junk yard. The bench seats may have had padded cushioning in some earlier life, but on this day they were bare metal, dented and scraped. More windows were missing than in place and most of those held cracks. Towards the back of the bus, several passengers shared their seats with cages of chickens. Loose feathers from the anxious birds floated like snowflakes in a Canadian winter. As more passengers climbed aboard, the scene became even more chaotic with hands waving about in gestures trying to supplement loud voices competing to be heard.

After accepting the state of the bus, Adam then took notice of the size of the driver. The man reminded Adam of the round bellied Friar Tuck as he was depicted in the Robin Hood movies. He doubted that few men could put their arms around this man's girth and claim they could link opposing fingers. As it turned out, the driver's size and strength were to come in handy in settling down the boisterous and argumentative crowd, as well as dealing with a situation later in the day. Adam further noticed how many of the older women were dressed, essentially in layers upon layers of cloths wrapped around their bodies. Part of the cloths served as shawls that covered their heads and much of their faces. Some of their belongings were half hidden within the folds of the cloths around them. And strangest of all, they were forcing pieces of mint leaves up their noses. Adam had been told later that the mint's aromatic properties acted like gravol, to assist against motion sickness. He didn't put much belief into this remedy since a number of the passengers had gotten sick on the trip and their vomit flowed in the grooves in the floor back and forth as the bus made its way up and down the hilly terrain.

Ben and Ben were fortunate to have found two open seats next to each other in the middle of the bus. Adam, however, was forced to sit next to two male passengers on one of the longer side seats facing the aisle and close to the front of the bus. Like many of the passengers, the clothes these men wore were dirty and foul smelling. Their breaths spoiled the heavy air with garlic; their teeth were badly stained and deformed; and their hair was greasy and tangled. Sitting beside them was not pleasant.

An hour or so out of Fez the two men started arguing. Voices became louder and angrier and poking gave way to shoving. At this point Adam was not feeling comfortable at all and tried to lean away from the ruckus. The bus driver casually yelled to them, likely telling them to settle down. Whatever he had said didn't seem to do any good as the shoving turned into a full-fledged fight. First they began wrestling with each other and then fists and feet started connecting to various parts of the body and face on each fellow. Being so close to the action Adam was repeatedly jostled and absorbed several wayward punches that hadn't hit their intended marks. At one point Adam was inadvertently shoved to the floor of the bus. He gagged at the smell and sight, only six inches below his eyes, of the raw vomit drooling its way to the front of the bus as it suddenly came to a halt. The bus driver was no longer casual in what he was yelling at the two men. In spite of his sizeable mass, he scrambled out of his seat, grabbed both of them by the collars of their robes with his massive hands and without much effort, literally threw them off the bus on to the sand at the side of the road. He spared few words on them before entering the bus again, closing the door and engaging the gear shift to motivate the bus to start moving its way down the highway. The two former passengers had been left in the middle of nowhere and no one seemed to care. Adam gathered that this type of incident could be a common occurrence, but with this bus driver, he surmised it would only happen once. And with confidence in that thought, Adam took a sigh of relief and began to relax.

There were no further incidents on the bus ride that day, but there had been one more interesting occurrence not long after the fighting had abruptly ended. While there didn't appear to be any reason to stop, nonetheless, it became quite clear that the bus was slowing down and eventually the driver pulled it over to the side of the road. There were no buildings in sight. As a matter of fact nothing was in sight other than a sea of sand and scrub brush and a small hill on Adam's side of the bus perhaps a hundred yards away. What initially came to mind was that there was a mechanical problem or a flat tire, but the driver didn't venture outside to investigate. After what he thought had been about fifteen minutes, Adam turned his head to look behind him and was surprised to see eight horsemen appear from over the hill waving what turned out to be old musket rifles. The riders were pulling two horses wearing empty saddles. When two men emerged from the rear of the bus, having to pass by Adam on the way to the door, they began to hail the horsemen with cries of joy and jubilation. It then became evident that the band of horsemen was on schedule to meet the bus and pick up two of the passengers. Moments later the bus was on its way again.

Having been seated closer to the front of the bus, Adam was the second person off and had to wait for Ben and Ben to disembark. They had made it to Fez and Adam was grateful to still be in one piece.

"That was one eventful trip!" tall Ben exclaimed to the other two. "At one point it looked like you were part of the fight. You got knocked down a couple of times."

"I'm just glad it's over. At the time I was afraid that the driver was going to think I was part of the commotion and haul my ass off the bus too."

Short Ben entered the conversation having one of his more enthusiastic moments, "Did you see those horsemen and their rifles? God, when I saw them riding up my first thought was that we were being attacked."

"Welcome to Morocco. I told you it would be worth coming here." As Adam looked up and around at the City of Fez he continued, saying, "I wonder what other little gifts this place has waiting for us."

She was sitting on a brick wall dangling her short legs and in conversation with her friends when the two Bens and Adam approached. Her hair was a soft amber and hung straight and just below her shoulders. She was wearing blue jean overalls with a red jersey underneath and a red and white bandana tied around her neck. Even from the distance between them Adam had at once become infatuated with her. She was attractive in the normal sense but it was the sincerity of her smile and the hearty and confident laugh that, in that brief minute of observation, radiated a friendly, caring and perhaps an adventurous spirit that so captivated him.

"Hi there," Adam called to the group in general, "where are you from?"

"Martin replied for all of his friends saying, "We're from the UK, England actually; how about you?"

Adam responded with, "We're from Canada. I'm Adam, this is Ben and this is Ben." In unison slight smirks met the faces on each member of the new group before tall Ben suggested they call him Bengi.

Martin reciprocated by introducing his friends. Martin and Susan were a couple. Whitney, Sam and Baily were nurses. A fourth nurse was back in Almunecar Spain, house sitting the villa the four women had rented for two months. Baily was wearing the overalls.

"Have you been in Fez long," asked Bengi. "We just arrived by bus from Teteun."

During the next hour and a half the two groups spent the time talking about where each other had come from and where they were going next. It was Susan who mentioned that the five Brits had only arrived in Fez yesterday from Casa Blanca. She further indicated that she, Martin and Whitney would be leaving the next day to travel farther east through North Africa and that Sam and Baily planned to head back to their villa in a few days. At some point in their discussions, the directions to the hostel were offered to the Canadians and Baily invited them to go out to dinner with her and her friends after they were settled. "Listen," she said, "we're going out to celebrate tonight, why don't you guys join us for dinner?

Bengi and Adam looked at each other and nodded then both glanced over at Ben who shrugged his shoulders to say "whatever". "That sounds great, we'd love to join you." Adam accepted the invitation for the three of them and it was agreed that they would meet back at the same spot at 6:00 PM.

They were standing inside the door of the eating establishment waiting for the staff to arrange two tables together so that all eight could sit together. Adam looked at Baily, who was standing beside him, and commented, "That's an unusual looking pendant you're wearing." He paused for a moment then continued, "Is that a mouse?" Adam had noticed that Baily had taken off her bandana since he had seen her earlier in the day which made the pendant clearly visible. It was sterling silver and hung nestled in the little hollow at the base of her throat.

Baily's face expressed surprise before saying, "Do you know that you are the first person who has ever guessed that this is a mouse."

"Is there some significance to it being a mouse?" Adam asked.

"My father started calling me Mouse when I was little. It stuck and when I was sixteen he gave it to me for my birthday. He said he had found it in an old antique shop in London. I'm never without it"

"That's cute. It sounds as if you and your father may have a strong bond."

"We do. We always have."

When the tables were ready, Adam made a point of placing himself in the middle of the long table and across from Baily. In this way he was strategically seated to see and more easily communicate with a larger number of the group, and especially with Baily. Being in close proximity with her now, Adam was able to confirm his initial feelings about her. Sitting directly across from her, he was in a position to notice and be impressed by her poise, her outgoing personality and her willingness to really listen to people.

The evening was fast becoming a great success in that it seemed like all the new friends were getting along well. The conversation, while perhaps a little slow to begin, soon became very casual and free flowing. Part of the reason could have been the amount of wine that was being consumed. Everyone had different stories to share about their respective journeys so far.

At a convenient pause in the general conversation within the immediate grouping around Baily and Adam, he took the opportunity to look across at Baily to ask her how it was that she came to be travelling in Europe and North Africa.

"Sam and I graduated from nursing in June and have been accepted to work in a hospital back home, but we decided that we wanted to travel for a while first. Whitney and Dana, the one back at the villa, were a year ahead of us but we had become good friends with them. When Sam and I had learned that they were planning on going to southern Spain, they asked us if we would like to join them and split the cost of a villa. We jumped at the chance. Dana rented the villa for two months but we are thinking that we might stay longer. We have been using it as a base camp, travelling east and west along the coast and just recently here to Morocco." Without wanting to go on for too long in answering his question, Baily asked, "And what about you, what's your story?"

Adam told Baily how he too had recently graduated and wanted to travel before settling into a job and career. He told her about Jeff changing his mind about the trip and generally the route he had taken before meeting up with the two Bens and coming to Morocco. At this point he left out any details about his adventures so far.

"What kind of engineer are you?" asked Baily.

"Electrical, I have been specializing in the design and development of a new era of hydro electric generators and transformers for major generating stations. Canada has a great deal of water power with all its lakes and rivers. But there is a lot of potential to do consultative work all over the world. That's my goal, to become expert enough in this new technology that, in time, I can pick my projects overseas."

"It sounds like you have a plan."

"More like a dream maybe. I don't actually have a job nailed down, but I do have a few offers waiting for me when I return home."

Sam was stationed on Baily's right and was part of the immediate group. She posed a related question across to Bengi, who was sitting on Adam's right. "So Bengi, what do you do? Have you finished school?"

Bengi waited until he had swallowed and replied, "I'm a pilot. I fly bush planes up into the northern part of the country, usually taking supplies or hunters into remote camps."

"That sounds exciting," commented Baily. "I've never been in a small plane like that before, but I hear it can be thrilling. How long have you had your pilot's licence?"

"I've been flying since I was first able to obtain a licence, at sixteen. My uncle owns a hunting lodge in northern Alberta and flies his own plane. I worked for him during the summers, had a real interest in flying so he encouraged me to take lessons. He convinced me that if I could fly I could make some good money to help with university costs. I did what he suggested, went to UBC, that's University of British Columbia. I studied forestry for two years then dropped out. I decided that I wanted to fly. When I get back I am going to start studying for my commercial license and work towards being a national or international airline pilot."

"That really sounds great," said Sam. "I know you will do it."

The next day, Martin, Susan and Whitney left Fez by train for Nigeria. The Canadian men went with Baily and Sam to wander the local Médina. Just as Adam was very fond of Baily and took every opportunity to be close to her, Bengi also seemed to have an attraction for Sam. That of course meant that Ben was the odd man out and he wasn't too happy about it. Both Adam and Bengi realizing this, tried to ensure he wasn't being purposely left out of activities. The men also both tried to temper their feelings toward the girls when Ben was around.

As in Teteun, a young boy guided the five foreigners through the Médina, down the dark alleyways to various shops that sold the kinds of merchandise they were interested in looking at or purchasing. Even though it was mid-afternoon, the alleys were covered for the most part or shaded by the close buildings so it still appeared quite dark. Having experienced the Médina in Teteun, Adam had fewer misgivings about visiting the Médina in Fez. Besides, he felt he had a duty to protect the girls as well, which made him feel less concerned about his own safety.

Baily had seen Adam's djellaba the previous night and declared that she wanted one for herself. The young guide had taken them to two stands before Baily found a djellaba that she liked. Adam had a huge smile on his face as he stood back and watched as Baily bargained with the vendor.

Being as direct as she could, Baily exclaimed to the vendor, "You want 60 durms for this thing? I can get it for much less down the street."

As she began to walk away the vendor rushed up to her and with an abundant smile said, "For you lady, a special price – only 50 durms."

Baily looked down at the robe again turning it over in her hands and said "That is way too much. My friend bought one recently for only 20 durms." She lied. "I'm not interested anymore, thanks anyway," and she began to walk away again.

She almost made it to Adam before the vendor called out to her to say, "Alright lady, you nice lady, for you I give my very special price but do not tell anyone. 30 durms."

"I'll give you 25. Take it or I'm out of here," replied Baily.

The vendor must have feared that Baily would never pay his prices, since he relented with, "OK lady, you give me 25 durms." As she was withdrawing her money from her bag, Baily noticed that the vendor had switched the djellaba. He actually had the nerve to try to give Baily a different djellaba! That's when she tore into him saying that he was a bloody dishonest shyster just wasting her time and she wouldn't buy a djellaba from him now, no matter what the cost.

As they were walking away, Adam put his arm around Baily in a casual manner and said "You little faker, you actually got the djellaba you wanted for only 20 durms. You have a real knack for this don't you? Remind me not to start bargaining with you about anything important."

At the end of a tiring day, the men said good night to the girls after escorting them to their hotel. The men carried on to the men-only hostel. Apparently Fez did not have a women's hostel and this was the reason for the girls staying at the hotel. The hotel wasn't much to look at but the girls didn't pay much for their room either. They said it was reasonably clean and they felt safe. Before leaving them, the men agreed to meet the girls at the bus station at 7:00 in the morning to head back to Teteun. Ben claimed that he had had enough of Morocco and reminded Bengi about their plans and timetable to continue touring Spain. Bengi and Adam agreed it was time to go back to Spain, but not for the same reasons Ben had. They wanted to go where the girls were going, at least for as long as they could. The four of them kibitzed and flirted all through the day and it seemed evident that the girls were accepting Bengi and Adam's affections.

It was five minutes to 7:00 the next morning. The men had arrived at the bus station twenty minutes earlier and purchased their tickets. The girls had not yet arrived.

"Where the hell are they?" asked Bengi, as he paced the sidewalk in search of them. "Their hotel is about a fifteen minute walk from the station. If they haven't left by now, they won't make the bus."

Adam looked in the direction of the station and said, "I'm going to talk to the station attendant and see if they will hold the bus for a little longer. Damn, I wish there was a way to contact the girls." Adam ran over to the attendant to plead his case, but the language barrier was not helping his cause. He ran back to where the two Bens were standing and advised, "It's no use, the agent insists that the bus must leave on time."

The bus driver was giving a last call to those paid passengers not yet on the bus. The clock on the adjacent building showed that it was 6:58. "What are we going to do if they don't show," asked Bengi. He was addressing his question more to Adam than to Ben.

"I don't want to leave without them. I also want to know that they are alright." Adam moved over to the ticket agent to try again to have the bus held for just a little longer saying that the two girls were on their way but have been delayed. He assured the agent that they would appear shortly. He was unsuccessful.

It was now one minute after 7:00 and the bus driver was adamant that if the three men did not get on the bus immediately, they would be left behind. While the men were drawing out the time as much as they could, Adam saw a taxi turn the corner on the far side of the bus station and recognized the girls. He immediately raced to the ticket agent to tell him that the girls had just arrived and to buy two tickets for them. The ticket agent rolled his eyes, yelled to the driver to wait, and within the next two minutes all five of them were in their seats on the bus as it pulled out of the parking lot. Sitting beside Adam, Baily hugged his arm tightly and between gasps of breath blurted out, "Oh Adam, thank you, thank you, thank you. I am really sorry that we were late, but it wasn't our fault. We were awake and dressed early enough but the desk clerk messed up our billing and then got called away, and by the time we had finished with him it was already five minutes to 7:00. We ran out of the hotel intending to sprint to the station hoping you could hold the bus from leaving when we hit some luck and saw the taxi driving by. Sam jumped out in front of him forcing him to stop. The taxi driver wasn't too happy about having to slam on his breaks but when we hopped in his taxi and waved a handful of US dollars in front of his face he immediately calmed down. We really overpaid the guy but he got us here in time, or at least before the bus had left, thanks to you guys. I really appreciate what you did. Oh, I almost forgot. How much do I owe you for the tickets?"

CHAPTER FIVE

The view was spectacular! The sapphire blue water of the Mediterranean glistened from the sun's rays as it stretched to the horizon. Gentle swells were moving along the surface of the water mimicking a giant centipede and rocking a lone fishing boat like a baby's cradle. Two separate islands could be seen in the distance, each appearing like green humps on a camel's back. The shoreline directly below, where the pathway emptied on to the fine white sand, seemed to go on forever. While the view was outstanding, there was a downside to the villa being located on the hill above the sea. No less than four hundred and eight steps were carved out of the sandstone, making it a major undertaking to descend and then return again up the hill. One quickly learned not to forget essential items when going to the beach.

Adam was standing on the patio. He had stopped for a moment to take in the sight before continuing to carry his and Baily's back packs into the villa. Baily was a step ahead of him with an armful of groceries she and Sam had purchased at a tiny grocery store along the roadway leading from town to the villa. Baily and Sam had invited the men to crash at the villa for a few days until they decided whether they would stay in Almunecar in their own apartment or move on as they had originally planned.

They had overnighted in Ceuta before taking the ferry back to Algeciers. The ferry ride was on calm seas and seemed to take less time than Adam and Baily had hoped it would. For most of the ride the two of them were cuddled together in a corner of the boat speaking softly to each other and thoroughly enjoying their time together. Baily had expressed once again her gratitude to Adam for waiting at the bus station and planted a gentle kiss on his cheek. Adam responded by pulling Baily closer to him in a comforting hug, assuring her that he would never have left her and Sam behind. The emotions grew slowly but progressively during the afternoon voyage with more quiet words, more flirting, and more hugging. At times they found themselves in each other's arms speaking with only their eyes and communicating words they would dare not say out loud. Lips gently touching were enough to confirm that the unspoken messages had been heard and understood.

They arrived back in Almunecar on December 17th. During the next couple of days the two Bens had had some serious discussions about their priorities. In the end Ben had convinced Bengi that they should move on and not wait until after Christmas. They would leave on December 20th. The question that remained was whether Adam would go with them. He didn't have the same ties to the two Bens as they had to each other and therefore was not bound by their decision. On the other hand, after being among friends for the past couple of weeks he didn't really relish the idea of striking out on his own again, when the time came. And the time would come. While he wanted to be able to spend more time with Baily they had both concluded that the timing of their little romance was not ideal. Baily was very clear that although she liked Adam very much, she was committed to herself and her friends to carry on with her plans to travel as much as she could before returning to England in October of next year. Sheer fate had provided Adam with a win-win situation in the name of TJ Wilson. TJ was a fraternity brother of Adam's. He and his friend Tom had been living in Almunecar for the past month and were planning to head to Italy right after Christmas. Adam was welcome to go along with them if he was prepared to share gas costs. Adam now had more time to spend with Baily and he had someone to travel with, at least for a while longer.

The next several days were pleasantly busy for Baily and the girls who volunteered to organize Christmas dinner. What Adam had soon come to realize during his first days in Almunecar was that a whole colony of young people, travellers like him from all over the world had collected here in the past few months and that over twenty of them would be coming together to enjoy the holiday festivities. Everyone was pitching in by donating food, wine or decorations. The celebrations were to be at the girls' villa. He had learned that the four girls always seemed to be at the centre of activity largely because they were so outwardly friendly and inviting, but also for practical reasons - their villa was very large and could accommodate everyone.

There may not have been any snow and it certainly wasn't cold, two ingredients for a Christmas Day in Canada, but the day had everything else one would wish for. Adam and the two Bens went into the hills and cut a fir tree. A pair of French Canadians were able to scrounge up some coloured lights, while two girls from Germany created tree ornaments out of aluminum foil and ribbons. Instead of a turkey the girls cooked three large chickens. Everyone contributed something toward the festive day. Baily insisted that all twenty-three guests must sit around the same table. In order to accomplish this feat, a number of people were asked to bring their own dining tables so that they could be joined together to make one large square table in the main room. Since the patchwork table was so large, much of the normal living room furniture had to be moved out to the patio. The girls used bed sheets as table cloths and as a centrepiece, extra boughs from the fir tree were assembled into a wreath wrapped around several large red candles. The dinner was a huge success, measured by fine food, lively discussion, entertainment and above all else, camaraderie.

By 3:00 in the morning everyone had gone home and Dana and Sam had fallen asleep upstairs. After Baily and Adam had cleaned up some of the remaining mess they settled in front of the fireplace. They were both exhausted but neither of them wanted to sleep. Adam sat on the floor against the sofa with Baily cradled in his lap leaning her head on his chest. They sat for a long moment just gazing into the crackling fire.

Adam gently drew his fingers through Baily's hair massaging her scalp in a manner meant to sooth the mind. A few moments later she handed her brush back to him saying softly, "here, use this." For a good part of an hour Adam carefully pulled the brush through her amber hair, the colour being enhanced by the light of the fire. After each stroke there was less and less of a tug and the brush soon eased downward from the crown of her head to the end tails hanging beneath her shoulders. "That feels so nice; I could sit here all night like this."

"I'm sure you could and I would love to continue, but my arm is getting numb and my back is stiff from leaning on the wooden arm of the sofa."

"Oh you poor boy," Baily said with a sarcastic and mischievous smile, "Roll over and let me massage those sore muscles. It's the least I can do".

With his back toward her, Adam glanced over his shoulder to say, "Baily there is something I should …"

Before Adam could finish with his warning, Baily shrieked in a whispered and concerned tone, "Adam, what happened to your back?" She had removed Adam's jersey to see lines of ragged scar tissue running the entire length of his back. While several smaller lesions were randomly scattered, two almost symmetrical sets of vertical lines stretched from his shoulders to his waist. The four lines on each side reminded Baily of a remote African tribe she had seen on a National Geographic documentary and the different ways in which tribesmen purposely scarred their bodies to demonstrate their courage or to symbolize their rank in the tribe.

"I'm sorry I didn't warn you sooner. I guess they can look pretty ugly," Adam said as he tried to pull his jersey back over his shoulders.

"No don't put your jersey on; I don't mind. I am a nurse remember. I was just startled. How did this happen?" She gently began to move her hands over his back being particularly cautious not to rub too hard against the scars.

"Remember when I told you that I had planted seedlings a few summers back."

"Yes, I remember."

"Well, a friend and I came across a Grizzly Bear one afternoon who wasn't too happy to see us. We both got tossed around and sliced up pretty badly. We were just fortunate that our supervisor happened to be in the area and had a rifle to scare the bear away." Baily cringed as Adam replayed more of the graphic details about the mauling, explaining how it had taken weeks for him to recover both physically and psychologically. He confessed that he still had the odd nightmare about that day, but that his therapy had been very effective in dealing with them and reducing the frequency.

"Adam, do you realize how lucky you are to still be alive? I can't imagine how horrible it must have been."

"Let's not discuss it anymore OK? Here give me my jersey."

Nurse or not, Adam thought. Baily had not responded like other girls had when they saw his marked body. Many times he would consciously not take off his shirt while at a beach, just so he could avoid the reactions he had received so many times. No, Baily surprised him. She proved once again that she was special.

Once he had slipped on his jersey, Adam brought Baily close, encasing her with his arms. He said, "I don't think we need to brush your hair any more. You look beautiful enough." With that he raised her chin and dropped his head so that their lips met to enjoy a long full kiss.

With tears forming in her eyes, Baily eventually broke the seal of their lips and looked up into Adam's eyes to say "I'm going to miss you Adam. I know we agreed that it was best for you to leave tomorrow but that doesn't make it any easier to accept. I'm afraid I'm never going to see you again."

Adam rested his chin against Baily's damp cheek. "I'm going to miss you too. These past few weeks with you have been fantastic. We have each other's email addresses, so we'll find each other at some point when we are finished wandering around the planet. I plan to leave for home from London and I promise I will try to contact you by then."

They sat in front of the fire all night, just talking and cuddling, until it seemed that in mid-sentence all was silent. Sam found them in the morning with Baily wrapped in Adam's arms both covered with a blanket. She tiptoed around them on her way to the kitchen to start a pot of coffee. It was 8:25.

There were more tears later that afternoon when Adam left Almunecar with TJ and Tom. On their way out of town, Adam made one more desperate attempt to call his parents to wish them a Merry Christmas. He had been trying for the past three days to get through to them but the international telephone lines were always busy and he wasn't able to reach them. On the one occasion he did make it through, no one was at home.

Encouraged by the ring tone in his earpiece, he waited five rings before he heard, "This is a long distance call, will you accept the charges?" and the response from his mother who said, " I will."

"Mom", he shouted, a little stronger than he had intended. "It's me, Adam, Merry Christmas."

"Oh Adam, it's so wonderful to hear your voice." Adam overheard his Mom yelling in the background, "Ed get on the other phone, it's Adam." She continued, "We were hoping to hear from you yesterday, did you try to call?"

"I have tried to call for three days but the phone lines are so busy at this time of year."

"Hi son, how are you doing?" Ed had retrieved the other phone. "Where are you calling from?"

"I'm doing fine. I'm in southern Spain right now but leaving today for Italy. I met up with a couple of guys from Alberta a few weeks ago and we went to Morocco together. We ran into some girls from England and came back to their villa in southern Spain. Well, the villa they are renting. I don't know if you remember him from the fraternity, TJ Wilson? Anyway I met him here and I am leaving after this call with him and his friend."

"You sound excited; you must be having a good time," his mother said. "Did you get my last letter? I sent it to Seville, where you had suggested."

They spoke for about twenty minutes before Adam said, "This is costing you a fortune, I had better go. I'll write you soon, OK?"

Both his mother and father bid him good bye with a Merry Christmas. Adam couldn't see them of course, but he knew there were tears in his Mom's eyes.

That was the last time Adam would speak to his parents.

CHAPTER SIX

Richard suddenly jerked himself awake and cried out "I don't know, I don't know." It was 3:00 in the morning following the funeral reception. He was now in a sitting position in his bed. The sheets and blankets had been thrown askew from his turbulent tossing and turning during the night. His hair was damp with perspiration and beads of sweat dotted his face. From the minute his head had hit the pillow, Richard's mind began racing in all directions trying to answer all the why, what if, and what now questions that were swirling around inside his head. First it was as if an angry and boisterous crowd was assembled behind his eyes demanding to be heard. There were too many of them; there were too many questions; he felt trapped as the mob grew closer and surrounded him, their fists in the air, their voices screaming at him. Then he saw the giant bear from the corner of his eye. The great furry beast was charging at him, fuelled by some demonic rage. Strings of saliva were drooling through razor sharp teeth and three inch claws were fully extended at the end of its outstretched arms demanding to slash him, demanding answers.

Richard hastily gulped water from the glass he had earlier set on the night table, remnants of which dripped down his chin and chest. He pulled himself up and crept to the washroom where he splashed water on his face. After towelling off he returned to his bed, flipped his wet pillow over and fell back upon it. After a few more minutes his heart beat recovered to near normal and he began to relax with some deep breaths. Richard desperately wanted to solve the many questions before him, but he suspected that many of the answers lay hidden in that part of his past life that had brought him to Lancaster Manor. Feeling much calmer, Richard closed his eyes and attempted to focus on positive images, of better times. He held dearly the thoughts of those few weeks with the two Bens, Baily and Sam and later with the gang at Almunecar. It wasn't easy to say good bye to Bengi and Ben on the day they left Almunecar and especially to Baily when he, TJ and Tom headed for Italy a week later.

As it turned out, Adam had parted ways with TJ and Tom two weeks later, after they had toured Barcelona, Nice, and Marseille and had entered northern Italy. TJ and Tom were headed north and Adam wanted to see more of the Italian country side. They wished each other well saying they would catch up once they were back in Winnipeg.

Adam travelled by himself in Italy for the rest of the month of January. While he thoroughly enjoyed the ancient sites, the fabulous food and abundant wine the country had to offer, he was beginning to admit to himself that he was feeling lonely. An idea came into his head and without too much further thought he made the decision to head up to England to visit his Big Brother from the fraternity. Ron Williams was attending the University of Oxford on a Rhodes Scholarship. Adam had always intended to visit with Ron, but just not so soon. He rationalized that seeing his friend would give him an extra spark he had been lacking since Almunecar and that he could easily head back south again using his Eurail pass.

The train from London to Oxford swayed from side to side as it was running full steam down the tracks. It seemed similar to a ship on the ocean rocking with the waves, he said to himself as he thought back to a family cruise in the Caribbean one winter. Adam thought it was strange as he hadn't remembered experiencing that same motion with other trains on which he had been riding.

Seeing the green rolling hills pass by his window gave Adam a sense of calm, which was much different than the scurry of activity in the train station in London over an hour ago. Sirens were screaming and blue and red lights were flashing as police and emergency vehicles surrounded and entered the train platform. He was peering out of the window of the dining car when the commotion erupted. At that same instant the train's engineer must have opened the throttle because the train gave a jolt and began grinding its wheels, steel on steel, to advance forward. Adam surmised that the engineer was likely hoping to exit the station in a hurry and not be held back due to the events unfolding before him. Several gun shots had been fired and Adam had witnessed two policemen falling to the ground. He did not know if they were dead. The last he heard before the train had escaped the station was a voice over a loud speaker or a mega phone, demanding someone to drop their weapons and come forward.

The University of Oxford is the oldest university in the English-speaking world, where the earliest record of teaching dates back to 1096. In the 13th century riots broke out between the townspeople and the students and as a result a number of residence halls were established to better contain student activity. These halls were later succeeded by the development of the many colleges that make up the University of Oxford. All students at Oxford must be a member of a department or faculty as well as a college or hall. Seven of Oxford's thirty-eight colleges are dedicated to graduate students only. Linacre, where Adam's friend was resident, is one such college. Linacre is a relatively new college at the university, founded in 1962. Being relatively new, it was located closer to the river and the university parks, but still only a ten minute walk to the centre of Oxford.

Adam made his way from the train station to the university and was now walking along St. Cross Road towards Linacre College. He had not contacted Ron ahead of time to say he was coming. He thought he would just show up and surprise him. As he was approaching the college, Adam was now concerned that he probably should have tried to reach Ron. Actually it was really stupid on his part, he thought, not to have contacted him. There was a good chance that he might not be around or that he would have plans of his own and wouldn't be available to visit with Adam. "Too late now", he said to himself. "If I miss him, I miss him. No big deal, I'll just hang out here for a while and then decide what I do next." Adam had only expected to stay a night or two with Ron in any event, assuming he could crash with him, before he moved on. The short stay would be worth it.

After asking different people if they knew a Ron Williams and where he was living, the third person he spoke to was very gracious in not only telling Adam where Ron lived but leading him there as well. Ron's room had been on her way to class. Adam knocked on the door, but there was no answer. He knocked again – still nothing. Figuring that Ron too was at a class, Adam decided to drop his backpack and himself onto the floor in front of the door and wait. His watch said 1:00 PM.

It was nearly 3:00 when two men in their flowing robes appeared around the corner of the hallway, both carrying large bundles of notebooks under their arms. The two students were in an intense conversation before they suddenly came to a stop in front of Adam, who was lying on the floor with his neck propped up on the backpack. With great surprise and some concern one of the students asked, "Are you waiting for Ron?"

Adam raised himself up saying, "I am. Would you happen to know when he might be back?"

"Sorry but he's not here. Actually he won't be in for the rest of the week. He and a few others went on a ski trip." He turned to his fellow student and asked, "They all left yesterday, didn't they David?" David confirmed this with a slight nod of his head.

"I knew I should have called ahead," Adam muttered to himself. "My name is Adam Ramsey. I'm a friend of Ron's from Winnipeg, Canada. I've been travelling in Europe and changed my original plans in order to visit Ron a little earlier than first intended. He didn't know I was coming. I took a chance."

"That's too bad," said the student. "I'll let Ron know that you were here though."

"I would appreciate that." To be certain the student didn't forget his name, Adam said to him again, "It's Adam Ramsey." Adam wished them a good day and turned to leave. Before his fourth step he stopped, looked over his shoulder and asked the students, "Say, could you recommend a youth hostel or a bed and breakfast somewhere within walking distance – something inexpensive?"

Adam spent the night at a nearby bed and breakfast called the Corkscrew Inn. It was so named for the hundreds of corkscrews that adorned the old building as quaint knick knacks, as the main feature within the many stained glass windows, and in the collection displayed in the corkscrew museum located in the lower level. There were corkscrews of every size, shape and material and they represented many different countries. There was even a special collection set upon a shelf in the WC. Functional corkscrews were carved out of wood in the form of a man or a beast, with the screws acting as a large erect penis. Some were especially gross looking. Adam commented to himself that he would have to remember to tell the guys at home about this particular collection and show them his photos.

At breakfast the next morning he shared the table with four other residents of the B&B. All were friendly; all were fellow travelers like himself; and all but one were actually much older than him. He guessed that the three were perhaps seventy to seventy-five years old. They all had grey hair and their faces appeared tanned and leathery, likely from spending a great deal of time outdoors and in the sun. The man and one of the women were a married couple and the second lady was a sister of the married woman. They seemed to share similar facial features. Adam learned, while eating his way through a sumptuous smoked salmon and cream cheese quiche, that the three were from Belgium and that they had been travelling for the better part of a year. They entered the UK a week ago and were on their way back home. Interestingly, the trio was comprised of both professional and amateur botanists and had spent the past summer crossing the northern parts of Canada in search of local fauna. His fourth breakfast companion was a young American woman from New York. She had recently come over to England to meet up with her American friend who had moved to London two years ago with IBM. The two had planned a holiday touring the UK.

Somewhere during the conversation Adam gave a short summary of his travels and how he had missed seeing his Rhodes Scholar friend by a day. He told them that after breakfast he was going to start heading back to London. Saying he wasn't in any rush, he indicated that he thought he would hitchhike, maybe along some back roads, rather than take a train. He further shared that he planned to head to southern France soon after he made London.

It didn't take Adam long to reach the outskirts of Oxford. The inn-keeper had instructed him on which bus to take to get him closest to the point at which the A40 entered the city. Adam walked a few hundred yards along the road then set down his backpack and stuck out his thumb. Within fifteen minutes an old man and his dog in a half ton truck pulled off the road beside him and through an open window the old man said that he was headed as far as Stokenchurch and if that would help, Adam could ride in the back of the truck. There were some bales of straw on the bed of the truck as well as a paint stained canvass sheet. After determining that it wouldn't be too cold sitting on straw covered with his sleeping bag and the canvas sheet, Adam thanked the old man and hopped in the back of the truck. He got himself settled, slapped his hand twice on the top of the cab in order to say it was alright to go, and the truck slowly moved from the side of the road onto the highway. The truck began to pick up speed and Adam was on his way in the general direction of London. It was Wednesday.

CHAPTER SEVEN

Three days earlier, just a half hour drive away from Oxford at the Castle Inn in Tetsworth, an important meeting had taken place that would put into force, events that would forever alter the life of Adam Ramsey. Two of the three men had arrived earlier than the pre-arranged 8:00 PM meeting time in order to enjoy a few pints before the boss came. They knew that he would demand their full attention and limit their drinking while going over the plans for what was to happen in three days. The boss was like that. Sure he liked to party as much as the other guy, maybe more. But when a job had to be done, especially a job like this one, he was totally focused and expected his men to be the same. He would not tolerate anything less. Some former colleagues of these two gents had once worked for the boss and paid the price for not heeding his demands. Both were lucky to survive the beating laid on them. To this day their noses remained bent at angles and neither of them had full use of their right arms.

The two men sat drinking their beers at the bar. The shorter of the two was called Spike because he had an unusual knob protruding out the side of his bald head. Spike was boasting about his latest female conquest saying that while her face wasn't much to look at, her huge chest more than made up for her lack of beauty and she would do anything he wanted to please him. He emphasized the word anything. He was further describing some of the x-rated images when the taller man, Maxim, interrupted and nodded over Spike's shoulder. The third member of the party, the boss, was coming through the door and heading straight to them.

While Maxim was tall, the boss was big – both tall and wide weighing in at over 245 pounds. He actually had a gentle looking face, but those features only fooled a man once, before they witnessed the attitude and physical force the boss could wheel. His hair was a light grey, almost white but his moustache was still mostly dark. He customarily dressed in army green clothes, as he did this evening - not that he was currently in the army, but he had been for several years. He was pushing fifty-five but looked as fit as a man half his age. Perhaps more than his physical appearance, or perhaps because of it, his most memorable characteristic was his leadership presence. Sarge looked straight at his two men and without a word communicated that he wanted them to follow him over to the corner booth in the back of the pub. Spike and Maxim leapt to their feet leaving their unfinished beers behind.

It was Sunday. The pub had very few patrons at this time of the evening but then Sarge had known it would be so. He had selected this place and this time so he could carry on the business meeting without anyone overhearing them. The booth against the back wall gave him full view of the whole room so he could guarantee no surprise visitors. The serving maid had come with their drink orders – black coffee.

Sarge told her to leave the pot and not return unless he called for her. With a sizeable tip in her hand, she smiled and nodded her head acknowledging his demands.

"I see that you two low lifes have had your refreshments," Sarge said in his most sarcastic tone. "Now listen to me and listen good. We have a major job going down in just three days and I don't want any fuck ups. It is important that you pay attention and commit the plans to memory. You are being paid big bucks for this job and our benefactor will not tolerate mistakes." The big bucks that Sarge had told his men about were only a pittance of the amount Sarge was actually receiving from the man who hired his services. "On Wednesday at about 1:00 PM, an old man and a woman will be eating lunch at the Country Squire in Stokenchurch. About an hour later they will leave in their car and travel down Marlow Road to meet up with the M40 to continue their way south. The road is not well used at this time of year but it is a short cut to the M40. The road also happens to run through a forested area for about four miles. That's where we'll hit them."

"How do you know these people will be doing all this at these times?" questioned Spike.

"I know because I've been doing my homework you shit head. I found out that they have this same routine every other month. This job should be easy if you two follow instructions. Now here's what I want you to do."

CHAPTER EIGHT

The ride from Oxford to Stokenchurch only took forty-five minutes and while it wasn't the most comfortable, Adam wasn't about to complain. He was warm and he had a great view of the countryside from the back of the truck. When the old man pulled up at the cross roads, about three hundred yards within the town limits, Adam threw his backpack onto the ground and jumped out of the truck. He dusted the straw off of him as best he could and approached the open passenger window. He patted the dog and rubbed her throat while saying to the old man, "Thanks very much for the ride sir, I really appreciate it. Can you tell me where I might go for an inexpensive lunch?"

In answer to Adam's question, the old man said to him, "Do you see that red roof sticking up over the car garage, that's the Ugly Duckling Inn. Find your way over there. Old Mary serves up the best steak pie you will ever taste. Tell her Anthony sent you." With that testimonial the old man turned the steering wheel and before Adam could thank him again for the ride, the truck proceeded on its way down a gravel road.

After checking himself again for any stray pieces of straw and confirming that he was as tidy as he was going to get, he started across the street in search of the inn with the red roof. It didn't take long and the inn was not difficult to recognize from the street. Over the door of the inn hung a sign with the ugliest looking duck boldly painted upon it. Whoever drew this duck must have been high on something, Adam thought. He then said to himself, "I hope the old man is right about the food. If it's anything like the quality of the sign, I'm in trouble."

The inn's pub was not fancy by any means, but his first impression was actually quite positive. The room felt warm and comfortable and inviting. The aesthetics drew upon the dark panelled walls, the dark maroon carpet, and the heavy false beams that created a grid on the high plastered ceiling. The lights were turned low, but the fireplace in the far corner was stoked and blazing, even though it was midday. Adam sat himself down in a booth built for four. Even the chairs and booth seats, while old and worn, were still well cushioned and much easier on his backside than the bed of the truck had been. He only needed two hands to count the number of patrons in the pub. All were seated except for a pair of old gentlemen throwing darts. As he turned his head to look in the direction of the bar, a very short and round woman with curly grey hair was coming from behind it, her eyes cast upon Adam. She was wearing a blue and white stripped apron over a pale blue cotton dress with little red and yellow flowers upon it. Adam guessed that the lady was over seventy years old and possibly closer to eighty. Her face was well aged, but her good looks were not completely hidden. He believed that she had at one time likely been a very beautiful young woman. As she approached him, her face transformed and the friendliest of smiles greeted him.

"Good day there young man, what can I get for you?" she inquired with a hearty voice to match her pleasing smile. "Our specials are written up on the board behind the bar if you haven't yet seen them. I can tell you that the fish and chips are always a favourite."

Adam countered with, "An old gentleman I met recommended your steak pie. His name was Anthony. If you are Mary, he claimed that your steak pie was the best he ever tasted."

"Anthony", repeated the woman, obviously surprised to hear his name. "Why he's sure no gentleman, but he's still a good and decent fellow and he's right about the pie. It's the specialty of the house and I make it myself. I'll rustle you up some straight away and because you are a friend of Anthony's, I'll bring you a half pint on the house."

Adam ate and paid for his steak pie. He told Mary that Anthony had been correct about the pie and that it was delicious. After she had given him directions to the road running east out of town, Adam said good bye and wished Mary a good day.

At the same time that Adam had reached the far side of town, a lady and a gentleman had pulled their black town car into the parking lot at the Country Squire. It was 1:05 in the afternoon. The pair exited the vehicle in full conversation and with generous grins upon their faces. They seemed in a playful mood, possibly sharing a joke of sorts. Both were seniors in their early 70's. Both had styled white hair and the gentleman wore an equally groomed moustache. Both were expensively dressed, yet casual. They were respectively elegant and distinguished in their appearances, but there was no sign of pomp in how they looked or acted. The gentleman took the lady's hand as he escorted her toward the door and into the inn. The Country Squire was a level or two above the Ugly Duckling in terms of modern décor. Opposed to a plain wooden plank booth table adorned with salt and pepper shakers and pocket knife marks scribed into its surface found in the Duckling, the lady and gentleman were seated at a round clothed table with a vase of orchids spotted in the centre and sparkling glassware sprouting matching cloth napkins waiting to receive a chilled bubbly liquid.

When the waitress approached the couple, it was the gentleman who greeted her with, "Good afternoon Audrey, you look very nice today. You'll have to tell us about your Christmas holiday with your parents. It doesn't look like you broke any bones on the ski slopes."

The young waitress was a bright and friendly eighteen year old who had been working at the Country Squire for almost a year to save money for college and was well known to the lady and gentleman who frequented the inn for lunches.

The young waitress smiled and responded in a pleasant voice saying, "It's nice to see you again Lord and Lady Lancaster. The holidays were smashing thank you! And no I didn't break anything, but my brother managed to break his finger falling off the chair lift. Serves him right though; he's such a show off. Shall I fetch your usual orders?"

"Yes please Audrey dear," answered Lady Lancaster.

Before Audrey could turn in the direction of the kitchen, Lord Lancaster said, "For some unknown reason, I feel like having something different today. I'm going to try the quail please Audrey, and light on the berry sauce." With the final orders recorded, Audrey hurried away after promising to return shortly with the champagne.

"James, I'm worried about Judith. There has been a measured change in her since we saw her on our last visit, and I mean both physically and emotionally. Surely you must have noticed?"

Lord Lancaster looked up at his wife and replied, "Yes I did notice, Muriel. I was waiting for you to mention it before I said anything. I'm certain she must be in despair about the allegations concerning Edward. It's not so much the loss of money but the fact that he might have acted behind her back and for all intents and purposes, stolen from his mother. If I had a shred of evidence that he was involved in such a swindle, I would have nothing more to do with him, despite your sister's pleas. David was a good man. He built a solid reputation and a respectable living for his family. I was very proud to have him as a brother-in-law. To see all that shattered by an ungrateful son just makes me furious."

"Please don't get upset James, remember your blood pressure. We don't know that Edward was involved in this. He claims to have no knowledge of how the funds could have gone missing." After a short pause, Muriel carried on, "Will Judith still have enough income from David's estate to continue living in her house in Coventry. It would be a shame if she had to move. She and David loved that house so much. I remember when they purchased it. David had just received his big promotion at Lloyd's."

"There is no reason why Judith should need to keep supplementing Edward's income. It is time the boy started to make his own way in life. He's a grown man for heaven's sake. If Judith concentrates on her own needs, she will be quite fine I'm sure." James was giving some thought to his next words and then said, "Perhaps I should have another word with Edward. I've already hinted to him that I am prepared to cut him out of my Will if I ever find out he is stealing from his mother."

As Audrey was returning with champagne James said, "On a different subject, I don't believe that I told you yet that Loxley and I have to fly to Geneva next Thursday. The Swiss government has some reservations about the standards the company has put into place with regard to the new generators that are supposed to be installed and operating by October. It will be a short visit, but if you would like to come along, you'd be welcome."

"I would come if I wasn't busy with the church's charity auction. The committee is still short on donations so we have to start making some calls. Mrs. Jacobs was very pleased that you donated the art pieces from the old offices that had been renovated recently."

Soon after a half glass of the champagne was consumed, Audrey brought the Lancasters their lunches. When they finished, they thanked Audrey, gave her a healthy tip towards her college savings and left the building. The time was 2:15 PM.

That same afternoon Sarge found the truck he wanted. He and Spike had been combing the streets of Stokenchurch all morning in search of possible trucks that would serve his purpose. It didn't have to look good but it did need to be in good mechanical condition and heavy- like a three quarter ton. They followed this particular truck at a safe distance so as not to appear suspicious to the driver. Both doors had the name Nelson Construction painted on them. As luck would have it, the driver and his partner were beginning their lunch break. They pulled into a parking lot behind a pub Sarge was not familiar with and marched around to the front of the building, presumably to go in. Sarge instructed Spike to follow them. Upon Spike's return confirming the two men were in the pub, Sarge said, "Alright Spike, get to work, and be quick about it."

While Sarge was well aware of how to hotwire a vehicle himself, he knew that Spike was better and quicker. This particular talent was one of the main reasons Sarge had employed Spike in the first place. As Spike was doing his job, Sarge was keeping watch for any passers-by. He said to Spike, "So far so good. There's no one around and there are no windows on the back side of the building. Those gents will be at least an hour scoffing down their meals. By the time they finish and notice their truck is missing, the job will be done and we'll be long gone." Moments later, Sarge heard the engine come to life. Sarge gave a thumbs up to his companion and yelled over the motor's noise, "Alright, head over to find Maxim. He should have our targets under surveillance by now. I'll follow you in the van." It was exactly 1:45 in the afternoon.

Adam waited by the side of the road for about thirty minutes without seeing any vehicles. He looked at his watch. It read 1:35 PM. He said to himself, "In the worst case scenario, if no one stops to pick me up, I'm going to have to hike the whole length of Marlow Road to reach the main highway. And if I want to reach the highway before it gets dark, I better start now." He slung his pack over his shoulders and plodded down the road.

Maxim waved Sarge and Spike over to where he was standing in watch of the man and woman. They were well hidden behind a dumpster in the alley but had full view of the door to the inn. Maxim whispered to Sarge, "They've been in the place for almost an hour."

"Perfect, they should be coming out at any time," Sarge said, relieved he hadn't missed the couple. "Now, do we all remember what we do when they come out? Maxim, you'll be driving the van with the traffic sign in the back. You'll follow immediately behind the targets. I'll drive the truck with Spike and follow you." Looking at Maxim, he continued, "As soon as you are two kilometers out on Marlow Road, turn off the road and set up the "no through traffic" sign. "We'll continue to follow the targets until they are in the forest area, then we'll make our move. You come along and pick us up and we will be home free. Is everyone clear?" As an afterthought, Sarge added, "You've already put the first sign at the other end of the road, right?" Maxim acknowledged that he had.

Both Spike and Maxim new the plan well. It had been drummed into their heads several times before. In unison, they said, "Got it Sarge!"

The plan was set. The targets were heading to their car. The car drove out of the parking lot and to Sarge's relief, it was pointed in the right direction – to Marlow Road.

Adam was used to walking and he appreciated the chance to be out in the fresh county air again. London and even Oxford, were too large for him, with too many cars and too many gasoline fumes. In Portugal and Spain he spent most of his time in the country and in small villages rather than in large cities. He preferred it that way. Besides his problems with the traffic and the air, the people were always much more friendly in the country.

The sun was bright and warm with few clouds in the sky. Adam had walked far enough and long enough to have built up a sweat. He took off his jacket and weaved it through his shoulder straps. He took a drink from his water bottle and looked over at the thick wall of trees. The forest was all around him, mostly evergreens but with a spattering of oak and birch. After the water he decided that it was an appropriate time to relieve himself. Before he headed to the trees he considered the chances of a potential ride coming along while he was hiding in the forest taking a leak. Conceding the chances were next to none and he didn't have anything to lose, he proceeded into and over the ditch, across the grass and scrub until he came to the edge of the forest. "I wouldn't want to get lost in there", he said to himself. Adam advanced beyond the tree line only far enough so that he wouldn't be seen from the road.

They were on the move. A white van followed by a blue truck belonging to the Nelson Construction Company, were driving cautiously less than a hundred yards behind the car. Sarge was keeping an eye on the truck's odometer and at two point one kilometers he saw Maxim signalling to turn off the road. The truck was now the only vehicle behind the car. The truck and the car were the only vehicles on the road. Sarge applied more pressure to the accelerator.

CHAPTER NINE

The gentleman driving the car noticed in his rear view mirror that a van and truck were following them. He also noticed that the van had turned off the road and that the truck decided to pick up speed. None of this seemed unusual to him and he anticipated the truck would pass momentarily. When the full force of the truck viciously attacked his car, he was absolutely stunned and had no idea what could have caused the sudden jolt and crushing sounds. Concurrent with the screeching metallic sounds came an equally loud shriek from the passenger seat. The gentleman had no time to react and any actions would have been futile in any event, as the mass of the truck easily redirected the car on a sharp angle over the side of the road. The much lighter vehicle literally dove into the ditch, its undercarriage scraping up gravel and clay as it continued moving forward. The car's forward thrust then propelled the car up and over the lip of the ditch on such an angle that required the car to slowly spin over eventually landing on its roof and skidding a few more yards before coming into contact with a rock outcrop. There it came to an abrupt stop.

There were no human sounds. Only the hissing of steam from the spent engine, the vibration of tires that had continued to spin upon final impact, and a gurgling of some liquid could be heard. Dust filled the air all around the wreckage, as to hide the true images of the collision.

Adam picked up his pack and started racing toward the scene. He hadn't actually witnessed the crash as he had his back toward the road when it happened. He was not even aware that vehicles were anywhere near his position. He pulled up short of the wreckage, taking a moment to get a better look through the dust and assess his next move. Even though partially obscured, he could see twisted iron everywhere. The sudden sparks and erupting flames at the front of the car immediately prompted him to take action. Calling out in the hope that whoever was in the car could respond, he dashed to the overturned vehicle and skidded to his knees. There were two passengers. There was blood on both foreheads and the woman's arm seemed to be twisted in an abnormal position. Neither seemed to be conscious but they did not seem to be dead, at least that is what Adam told himself. He knew that extracting the people from the wreckage could be risky; neck or back injuries could be severely compromised. But he also knew that time was running out, the flames had grown higher, and he was afraid of an explosion that could kill them all. He took a moment to wonder why the passengers in the other vehicle hadn't come to assist him. But then it occurred to him that perhaps they were in the same desperate way after the crash. With all the dust blocking his sight and his focus on the car before him, he hadn't even noticed the damage done to the other vehicle. He couldn't think of them now, these people needed immediate attention.

Adam managed to free the gentleman who had been driving the car by dragging him directly over top of the woman he assumed was the man's wife. It was the only way he could remove the tall and heavy man without eating up precious time. Unfortunately, in so doing, the man's left boot clawed at his wife's forehead opening further a wound that was already dripping blood. Adam swore to himself for causing more damage to the woman, but then quickly rationalised that it was a minor piece of collateral damage, all things considered. Once he set the man up against a rock at a safe distance from the burning car, Adam went after the woman. He would worry about tending to the wounds later.

The flames were expanding in height and towards the passenger compartment. The heat was becoming quite noticeable and a constant reminder that time was running out. The smoke was now thicker and mingling with the dust. Adam's eyes were burning as he twice heaved with all his might in attempts to extract the woman from her position in the car. The woman's seat belt just would not unfasten. Rather than making more useless attempts with the buckle and wasting precious time, Adam ripped open his backpack in search of his pocket knife. His Dad had always emphasized the importance of a sharp blade and that lesson proved itself as he easily sliced the canvass belt apart. Grabbing hold of the woman from under her shoulders was difficult for Adam due to her position. But he thought it was the only grip he could use that wouldn't contribute more harm to her already deformed arm. He lifted and pulled at the same time with all the strength he could gather. He thought he heard a gasp from the woman, but the sound could just as well have come from the fire, now raging before him and eager to explode. The combination of adrenaline and physical and emotional exertion was having its effect on Adam. He was becoming exhausted. His shirt was soaked with perspiration and sweat was dripping from the tip of his nose. It was all he could do to pull the woman's body up close to her husband's. He placed a sweater from his pack under her head. Just as Adam had reached the man, he heard the man speak softly and with great pain, "Thank God you got her out." The man said nothing more.

Now that his first priority of moving the couple safely away from the burning car was achieved, he immediately began to assess their injuries. The woman had been unconscious the whole time. The bleeding from her forehead did not look serious. He ripped a piece of material from a clean shirt he found in his pack and wrapped it around her head to stem the flow. What Adam was more concerned about was the deformed arm and the large bump on the side of her head. Since she wasn't moving about, perhaps he could leave the arm alone for now. But sooner than later it would have to be reset. Adam recalled overhearing the doctors at the hospital discussing his broken and dislocated ankle several years ago following a slip on some ice. They had insisted that irreversible damage could result if the dislocation wasn't attended to straight away. Before attending to the gentleman, Adam unrolled his sleeping bag and placed it gently over the woman to keep her warm.

The gentleman was still unconscious. While he did not appear to have anything broken or out of place, Adam now had the time to discover that the man's surface wounds were more apparent and more serious than the woman's. Taken together, his body was losing a fair amount of blood. As best he could he arrested the flow oozing from his stomach by stuffing underwear into the deep wound, covering it with more of his shirt and keeping pressure on the makeshift bandage by tying the man's belt tightly over it. Thank goodness he had just washed his clothes yesterday, he thought. Adam then turned his attention to the man's head. The bleeding was coming from his forehead and he very quickly used yet another strip of his shirt to cease the flow. He was shredding his last shirt to bandage some minor cuts of the man's arm, when the car erupted.

Sarge was surprised at the amount of back lash his truck had taken immediately after smashing into the car and was not prepared for the necessary reaction. In a panic he over turned the steering wheel losing control of the truck. In a matter of seconds he found himself on the opposite side of the road staring down into the ditch. Compared to the terror and destruction involving the car, the after effect with the truck was like a joy ride at the fair.

Maxim pulled up with the van as the other two men were climbing up to the road. "Holy shit, you guys did a number on that car. How did you land up in the ditch?"

Sarge considered Maxim's question to be purely rhetorical and did not bother to respond. Instead he was all business and asked, "Did you remember to gather up the sign?"

"It's in the back of the van. What do we do now?"

Sarge looked at Spike and said, "Back the truck out of the ditch. It's not that steep, you should be able to get it out if you use the low gear in four wheel drive. Just take it easy, so you don't get yourself stuck."

Not knowing Sarge's plan, Spike challenged him saying, "What do you need the truck for? That's just wasting time. We need to take the van and get out of here."

"Back up the truck and place it across the road. It won't entirely stop any one from coming after us but it will slow them down. Now get to it. Maxim and I will check to see that the old man and lady are dead."

They were crossing the bottom of the ditch when the explosion threw them back against the slope, bits of fire scattered all around them. The sound couldn't have been more deafening if lightning had struck the ground at their feet. In fact the men would describe it later as being next to a mega bomb. The flames from the blast bellowed upward deep into the sky, much higher than any of the surrounding trees, holding their height for several seconds before receding back to the ground.

Maxim was shaking with fear. He couldn't hear and shouted to Sarge, "There won't be anything left of them now but ashes. Let's get out of here before someone comes along. The whole town must have heard or seen that blast."

Sarge wasn't feeling much better than his partner, but yelled back, "We've got to make sure they're dead."

"You gotta be kidding," Spike chimed in as he had approached the two men. Spike had been in the far ditch and had not suffered nearly the same shock waves as his friends. He was walking up to them when he heard Sarge say they needed to check the bodies. "That wreck could go off again. You're crazy if you think you'll find anyone alive in there. I'm with Maxim, let's get our asses out of here."

"It won't explode again. It will only take us two minutes. Let's not waste more time arguing." The way Sarge screamed his last words left a clear message that Spike and Maxim could understand. The three of them moved cautiously around the smoldering mass of metal, ready to dive for the ground at the slightest hint of a spark.

The light and sound occurred in unison, one as bright as the other was loud. While protected from the direct shock of the blast, due to his position behind the rock outcrop, the forces together still completely overwhelmed Adam. He sat cradling himself against the solid wall of rock shivering from anxiety with signs of shock spread across his face. After the crushing sound and blinding light, the heat generated from the fusion enveloped him like a hot, dry desert sun. It was only the movement and groaning from his patients that snapped Adam from his state of fear. The catastrophic blast had appeared to have woken those almost dead. Shock was clearly visible in the gentleman's expression as he called out to his wife attempting to comfort her. The woman had regained consciousness, at least for a few moments only to display sheer terror in her eyes accompanied by ear piercing cries that could have been mistaken for an ancient wild beast no human had ever heard before. Her head fell back on to the sweater. She was silent once again.

"Are you alright sir?" asked Adam in a hushed voice.

"My wife, is she alive?" His concern was massive in his question.

"Yes, she's breathing. The shock has caused her to go unconscious again. What about you? Have your wounds opened again, are you still bleeding?

"No", the man replied, clearly in pain. "I believe the bleeding has stopped. My head and body hurt like hell, but I can live with that. We must get my wife some help."

"Her right arm is dislocated and possibly broken, Adam said. "We will have to be careful if we try to move her. I don't think we have to be concerned about another explosion. There's nothing left to ignite. Someone must have heard or seen the explosion. We should make you and your wife as comfortable as possible and wait for help. I wonder if the other people from the accident survived?"

"That was no accident," the gentleman said sternly to Adam's face. "We were run off the road on purpose by two men in a truck. They are likely miles away by now. If you hadn't pulled us away from the car as you did, we would be nothing but soot." The gentleman's expression turned suspicious when he asked, "Where did you come from anyway?"

Just as Adam was going to explain how he had been close by in the forest, two images emerged from the smoke on his left side, a third became visible a moment later. Adam did not have a good feeling in his gut. Very slowly so as not to be noticed, he brought the end of his sleeping bag over the woman's head, completely covering her. He was aware of the obvious signs of surprise in the expressions of two of the men, the short one and the tall one. He wasn't certain that their look of surprise included a concern for their safety and health, however. The third man held a more telling expression, not of surprise but of disgust. Adam had this sense confirmed when the man spoke.

"Where the hell did you come from?" The large man's tone was mean, his eyes were pure evil and they were targeted directly at Adam's.

Playing dumb, but hoping for the best, Adam began to rise from his knees to address the man. Before he could stand, the man yelled, "Stay down!"

The gentleman was about to challenge the large man, but Adam cautioned him by holding his arm. Adam was still playing dumb to what was really happening when he said, "I was in the woods when I heard the crash. I came out to help these people. They were pretty banged up. The lady didn't make it."

The man looked down at the sleeping bag, acknowledging that a still body lay underneath. He didn't question Adam's claim. If the gentleman was concerned with Adam's words, he didn't show it. Suddenly realizing that time was slipping by, time they could not afford, the man simply said to his men, "Kill them!"

CHAPTER TEN

It was a massacre and it didn't take long. Spike immediately went for the gentleman, whose old and weak body already yielded cuts and bruises, as well as dangerous gashes on his torso and head. Spike began the assault with his boots, escalating to more vicious kicks focusing on the ribs. In a rush to end the old gentlemen, he picked up a large branch nearby and swinging it like a club, thrashed him again and again until a blow to the back of the skull knocked him down for good. His head struck the rock he had been leaning against when Adam had first pulled him to safety. The red liquid of life was leaving him, trickling down his cheek and neck as it was down the rock. He lay motionless beside the covered body of his wife. Content with the outcome, Spike then turned his attention to Adam, who was fending off the two larger men.

In the few seconds before the attack, time seemed to transform into slow motion allowing Adam to survey his environment, to strategize and develop a battle plan, and to gather resources that were close at hand. Slowly not to draw attention he reached into his pocket. He took what he had found and behind his back opened the blade. It was small but it was sturdy and razor sharp. He rested it behind his shoe out of sight. Just as slowly he reached under his light blue sweatshirt and released his belt buckle. Strategically if he was to have any chance at all he could only fight one at a time. He had to go for the weakest first, get rid of him and then take the next weakest. He would have to move fast, be clever and lethal. Fighting fair would not be part of the rules of this game, on either side.

When Spike made his move toward the old gentleman, rather than try to defend the old man, Adam hoped his first move might draw Spike away as well as take down the weaker of the two larger men. Both Maxim and Sarge started toward him. Adam took a handful of sand in his left hand and without warning cast it broadly to reach both the faces in front of him. The grit found its marks, halting the two men and forcing them to hold up their arms in defense while struggling to clear their vision. In that brief window of time Adam grasped his pocket knife in his right hand, leapt to his feet and surged upon Maxim thrusting his pocketknife as hard as he could into his stomach. As they were falling together Adam took aim at the Maxim's throat, but the man's spontaneous body movements caused Adam to miss, instead slicing his earlobe almost clean through. Maxim held the wound in his stomach with one hand and with the other reached for his ear. He rolled in pain screaming like a wild man. Adam didn't accomplish his goal to permanently down Maxim, but he believed he had done sufficient damage to keep him out of commission long enough to move on to his next adversary.

Because his actions took but an instant, Adam still had time to free himself from Maxim, spring to his feet, and with his belt, whip thirty-six inches of leather toward Sarge's face. The belt lashed out fully extended then snapped back as the silver tip ripped into his left cheek an inch under his eye. Sarge hollered in pain and cursed Adam to hell, and then he began to charge. Adam was prepared for Sarge's attack, but he wasn't prepared for Spike lashing out at Adam's right knee with the club that he had just finished using on the old gentleman. The heavy stroke to Adam's knee brought him down hard and momentarily disoriented him. In that moment Sarge was upon Adam, using his size thirteen work boots to their full potential. While Sarge was kicking Adam in the stomach and the ribs and whipping him with his own belt, Spike was hammering him with the club focusing on Adam's upper body and head. Adam tried valiantly to get off the ground but he was being besieged by the two strong men and their respective weapons. All he could do was draw himself into a ball with his legs together to protect his groin and with his hands over his head.

The beating continued with greater force. They were two wild men nearly out of their minds with rage. Adam's soiled sweatshirt was more red than blue. The ground around him was becoming soaked in his blood. His hands were broken and bleeding. His eyes were swollen shut and weeping. There was so much blood covering his face, it was impossible to see the gashes beneath. At some point, Maxim found he was able to stand on his feet and with great pleasure started his own vengeance upon Adam's body. Adam was beyond any capacity to protect his body or head. He was barely conscious but still enough to feel each and every severe blow. His pain was tortuous. He wanted to die.

The men were totally out of control, losing all sense of what they were doing and the time they were taking to do it. The brutal attack ended soon after Maxim had to back away and rest. While he had severe wounds, he hadn't let them stop him from assisting in the attack. But he was exhausted and hurting. As he stood watching the others he held his head at an angle elevating his ear in order to catch more of a sound he thought he had detected. "I hear something", he said out loud. He looked around and in the distance he saw a small parade of three different vehicles. "Sirens", he yelled, this time so Sarge could hear. As if soaked in the face with a bucket of ice water, the two men stopped their assault and listened and looked.

"They're long past dead", said Sarge. With urgency in his voice, he commanded, "Get moving. Run. Run like hell to the van."

The three vehicles represented three local authorities: the police, the fire department, and the medics. With the local authorities arriving at the scene more or less at the same time, they immediately launched into their respective jobs. The firemen set about hosing down the remains of the smoldering vehicle, as well as surrounding grass and brush that had caught fire thrown by the explosion. The chief was certain his men could easily suppress what remained of the fire without calling upon any additional resources. The two medics separated. The first medic went straight to Adam. Looking down on what he would later describe to his friends back at the station as a pile of raw meat, he made only a superficial assessment attempting to hear or feel a heartbeat. With no response, he rushed over to aid his partner who was administering to the gentleman and the lady. Passing the two policemen, he remarked, "That one's gone. No one could have lived through that kind of beating."

The lady and gentleman had both become conscious by the time help had arrived, but the lady was clearly disoriented and unaware of what had occurred over the past forty minutes. She was given a sedative after her crazed reaction upon seeing the remains of the stranger who had tried to help her. Once she had calmed down, the medics conducted a thorough assessment of the lady and debated whether they should try to set her arm on site or wait another thirty or forty minutes for a doctor to do it in the hospital. They decided to rush her to the hospital, explaining to the lady that the procedure would be extremely painful without certain medication, which they did not carry and were not licensed to administer. As one of the medics was readying the lady for transport, the second medic attended to the gentleman acknowledging that whoever had applied the makeshift bandages, especially to his stomach, had prevented a major loss of blood and probably saved his life. He also told the gentleman that it was his initial assessment that both he and the lady had suffered concussions but that with proper rest, they should be alright. More tests would still be required once they were transferred to hospital.

While the medic was treating the lady and gentleman, the first policeman began his inquiries. "Sir, my name is Henderson and I'm with the county sheriff's office. I need to ask you and your wife a few questions. First, sir, can you tell me your names?"

The gentleman answered for both he and his wife. "My name is James Lancaster and this is my wife Muriel."

The policeman looked up from his notes in surprise and taking a closer look at the couple responded, "Lord and Lady Lancaster from Maidens Green?" Lord Lancaster nodded that they were.

"I'm sorry sir, I didn't recognize you." After the policeman collected himself he continued with his questions. "Can you tell me what happened here sir?"

By the time the medic had finished treating Lord and Lady Lancaster, the policeman had a pretty good picture of what had occurred, as well as descriptions of the attackers. He noted that Lord Lancaster was at times unconscious and therefore not party to all that had taken place, especially the beating of the stranger. He knew nothing about the smaller patches of blood in the sand more than three yards from where the stranger's body was found. Nor was he aware of who the stranger was or where he had come from. Lord Lancaster admitted that the description he gave to the policeman of the stranger was the best he could do under the circumstances. He was a young man between twenty and thirty, Caucasian, perhaps six feet tall, maybe more, with brown hair. He carried a backpack. The policeman made a note that after a search of the scene, no backpack was found.

At the same time the policeman was interviewing Lord Lancaster, the second policeman was on his hands and knees next to Adam searching for any shred of evidence to the crime that could possibly be found when he turned with a start. He looked closely at Adam then cried out to one of the medics, "He's still alive!"

The medic that had first examined Adam was buckling the final strap across the lady in her stretcher and casually said, "What you hear is just air being released from the body. That's normal."

"I tell you he's alive, I can hear him trying to breath," argued the policeman, with high anxiety in his voice.

"Go take a look," Lord Lancaster insisted to the medic that was attending him.

The second medic got to his knees and leaned over Adam, placing his ear over a mouth that was torn, bloody and swollen. He then quickly placed his stethoscope on Adam's chest and yelled to his partner, "George, get over hear. He is alive, barely, but alive." For the next fifteen minutes the two medics focused their complete attention on Adam in the hope they could make him stable enough for transport. The second medic finally declared, "We've done all we can for him. His life is hanging by a thread and chances are he won't survive the trip to the hospital. Sir we only have room for two stretchers in the ambulance, you will have to ride with the policeman. You will be fine. Alright let's get moving here. Chief, can I get your men to help us down to the truck please?"

The gentleman kissed his wife and told her she would be fine and he would meet her at the hospital. He then turned to the medic in charge and said, "Where will you be taking them?

"Mount Royal hospital sir."

Lord Lancaster said to the medic, "You tell the doctors at Mount Royal that I want absolutely everything possible done for this young man. They are not to give up on him. If they need to bring in specialists, then they do it. I'll be responsible for any costs. Do you have that son?"

The medic replied, "Yes sir, I'll pass that message on."

While Lord Lancaster was giving further assurances to his wife that he would see her shortly, Mr. Henderson of the county police was making a phone call to London.

"Scotland Yard," answered a female voice.

"Please connect me to Inspector Giles. Tell him it is Neil Henderson calling and that it is urgent."

Henderson did not have to wait long before he heard a familiar voice, "Neil my old friend, how are you?"

With urgency in his voice, Henderson said, "I'm fine John, but there is something you need to know. Someone tried to kill Lord and Lady Lancaster this afternoon, along Marlow Road east of Stokenchurch. We are just now headed to Mount Royal. They are pretty banged up and probably have concussions, but I think they will be fine. Here he comes, I have to go. I'll give you more details when I see you at the hospital. You may want to send a crime scene team here. I have asked one of my men to wait until they arrive." Putting his phone away Henderson greeted Lord Lancaster and helped him into the back seat of the police car.

At Scotland Yard, Detective Inspector Giles made two calls directly after ringing off with Henderson. He first called one of his top men, Detective Tony Read and instructed him to leave with a crime scene unit as soon as possible for the site of the attack. He also said that he wanted a preliminary report on his desk first thing the next morning. His second call went to the Chief Inspector, Mark Sanders. He knew his superior would want to be kept in the loop as the investigation progressed. People would want answers and soon.

CHAPTER ELEVEN

The doors of the emergency department at Mount Royal hospital in London burst open as the two medics quickly wheeled Adam's body down a short hallway and into a corner room used for only the most severe cases. Doctors and nurses had been waiting for the arrival of the ambulance and immediately took over responsibility for Adam. Not only had the medic called ahead to advise them of the serious nature of the situation, but Lord Lancaster had also made a call to the President of the hospital. The President assured his friend that the best care possible would be arranged.

Lord and Lady Lancaster were taken to a separate emergency area for examination. Lady Lancaster urged the doctors to keep them apprised on the status of the stranger in the corner room and to let them know the minute there was any change. Now having a better sense of what all had occurred while she remained unconscious, she was grief stricken for the young man who had saved them from a burning car crash and was close to death after trying to save them again – from being murdered.

A team of doctors and nurses swarmed around Adam attaching him to various machines to monitor his breathing, his heart, and his oxygen levels. An IV was placed in his wrist to immediately provide needed liquids due to dehydration and to administer morphine for his pain. Simultaneously nurses were cleaning his body and face in order to allow the doctors to see what they were working with. Their first priority was to ensure the young man would live, that is, they would have to stabilize his heart and his breathing. Second they would begin to treat the most dangerous wounds and address any internal bleeding issues. Exterior and cosmetic work would have to wait.

Four hours had gone by since the Lancaster's last saw Adam rushed to the emergency room. A doctor now entered their private room wearing operating greens and a clean white gown. As he approached, he greeted them. "Hello Lord and Lady Lancaster, my name is Dr. Rogers. I am the senior emergency physician heading the team working on the young man downstairs. I understand you are recovering quite well, but we will still want you to stay at least overnight for further observation. As for the young man, he managed to survive the ambulance ride under the watchful eyes of the medics. Being at the hospital now under special care can only increase his chances for survival, but I warn you he is far from being out of danger. He has endured a great deal of trauma to his entire body. It will take a few days at least before we will know if our treatment has helped. We have stabilized him to a degree. He is still on a ventilator but his heart beat has gotten stronger. He is not conscious. We have given him a moderate pain killer. There was some internal bleeding in the stomach area and we believe we have arrested that. He has several broken and bruised ribs. Parts of both hands had been broken and they have been casted to the extent possible. The various gashes and cuts to his body and arms will heal in time with some scarring. He has a concussion and his jaw is broken as are several teeth. If he responds well to treatment over the next few days, we can start reconstructive surgery. We may face a cross road at that time. If he is still in a coma, the surgery becomes a greater risk. On the other hand, the longer we wait to undertake the surgery, the worse our chances of being successful in the reconstruction. We'll wait a few days before we decide our next steps. Do you have any questions?"

The Lancasters waited patiently and listened carefully until the doctor had completed his report. Lady Lancaster first thanked Dr. Rogers for coming to see them and for providing his very thorough report. She then asked, "What do you think his chances are Dr. Rogers?"

"I really can't say at this time, Lady Lancaster. It is still too early. I am surprised he has made it this far and so I am taking that as a hopeful sign. We should know more in a few days. In the meantime we will be monitoring him around the clock."

"Thank you for your time doctor," said Lord Lancaster. "Please keep us informed."

"I will. If that is all, I had better get back downstairs." The doctor turned and headed out the door. Stepping back into the room he said, "Oh, I almost forget, there is a policeman from Scotland Yard here to see you. If you feel up to it, I will send him up to your room."

"That would be fine, thank you again doctor," replied Lord Lancaster.

"The poor young man," Lady Lancaster exclaimed out loud. "He's all alone. We don't even know who he is or how old he is. We don't know where he lives or if he has a family."

Lord Lancaster said in an unconvincing voice, "Perhaps the police have some answers about the young man."

After several minutes a man in his early forties appeared in the door way. He was a shade under six feet tall, had dark hair, and was neatly dressed in a grey suit with a lighter grey shirt and a red and black tie. He found the Lancasters each propped up in their respective beds appearing like they had been expecting him. He greeted the Lancasters, apologized for the intrusion and introduced himself as Detective Inspector John Giles of Scotland Yard.

"Mr. Henderson of the county police department contacted me about the incident, knowing that the Yard would want to be involved in the investigation. I have one of my senior detectives and a crime scene unit at the site right now. I expect a preliminary report in the morning. I know you have had a very difficult time of it and you have already answered questions from Mr. Henderson, but I am hoping you will indulge me for a few minutes so that I may get my own sense of things."

The Lancasters agreed to the interview and Inspector Giles began his questions. After more than a half hour, the Inspector indicated that he only had a few more questions. "You say that that the larger of the men that attacked you appeared to be the leader. Were any names mentioned?

"I didn't hear any names," said Lord Lancaster.

Facing Lord Lancaster the Inspector asked, "You gave descriptions of the men to Mr. Henderson. Is there anything further you may wish to add, now that you have had more time to think about it?"

"I don't believe so, Inspector. The one I saw the clearest was the short fellow who beat me. As soon as he was on me, I never really noticed anything else. Like I said to the policeman, he was bald. He wore a dark blue sweater and dark pants. He had some kind of a tattoo on his left wrist, but I can't describe it to you. It wasn't very large though. His face was round and he likely had not shaven for a few days."

Turning to Lady Lancaster the Inspector said, "I know you didn't see anyone because you were covered with a sleeping bag, but was there anything you heard that you could tell me about?

"As I told the officer at the time, I heard three different voices, but they didn't say very much." With a quiver in her voice she continued, "The last words I heard anyone say was kill them. I was so terrified, I couldn't move. I knew I couldn't help anyone so I continued to play dead."

"Lord Lancaster had passed out and then all three continued to beat upon the young man, is that right?" asked the Inspector.

"Yes, that is what it seemed like. But wait." She paused to think for a moment. "Before or at about the same time one of the men was attacking James, I heard one of the other men cry out. I don't think it was the young man though. He swore and said something about his stomach. Most of the rest I heard was grunting and swearing and cries from the young man."

The Inspector thanked the Lancasters for their time, wished them well and said that he would likely have follow up questions as the investigation proceeded. He exited the room as a nurse was entering. It was time to change the dressing on some wounds again.

In the basement of an old house many miles north of London, two other men were being treated for their wounds. There wasn't a team of physicians and nurses, the operating room was not bright and sterile and the equipment wasn't state of the art. A handful of cash was passed between the injured men and the doctor, who knew better than to inquire about the circumstances surrounding the injuries. The doctor was doing his best to repair a small knife wound to one man's stomach and stitch together a wide gash in the other man's cheek. There was no conversation.

On his way out of the hospital, Inspector Giles was met by a mob of reporters and television cameramen. Word had reached the media that Lord and Lady Lancaster had been involved in a terrible car crash. They had also found out that one of Scotland Yard's finest detectives had been summoned to the hospital to see the Lancasters. As the Inspector passed through the main doors, the mob surrounded him with a fury of questions:"Is it true that Lord and Lady Lancaster were run off the road?" "What is the state of their condition?" "Was this a case of attempted murder?" "What can you tell us about a third individual brought to the hospital?" "Was he the one who caused the crash?"

The questions flew at the Inspector like pellets from a shotgun blast. After a few seconds of being bombarded with questions he had no opportunity to answer even if he had wanted to, he simply put his head down and pushed his way to an awaiting car at the side of the road. A driver had the door open for him. Just before lowering himself into the car, he raised his hands in an attempt to subdue the media mob. The crowd finally hushed and he spoke. "I do not have a great deal I can tell you at this time. Lord and Lady Lancaster were involved in a collision on Marlow Road at approximately 3:00 this afternoon. Their vehicle crashed and burned. I cannot comment on their status at this time. The medical staff are doing everything they can for them. It is not uncommon for the Yard to be called in under these circumstances. We are looking into all possibilities as to the nature of the incident. That is all, thank you." And with that purposely ambiguous address, the Inspector jumped into the passenger seat, closed the door and said to his driver, "Move it."

The media crowd was not very pleased with the little information Inspector Giles had given them. They would have to embellish his words and be suggestive in their reporting the story during the evening newscast. They would use words like "suspected of being dead following a horrific crash."

Prior to leaving the hospital, it had been agreed between the Lancasters, the hospital staff, and the police that for the time being, there would be no mention of the Lancaster's state of health or the nature of the incident. No mention would be made of the stranger either. There would be no visitors, not even Lady Lancaster's sister. Clearly this looked like an attempted murder plot, but the Inspector wanted to have further evidence to substantiate the claim. He also wanted time on his side to run down any leads on any suspects that may surface in the investigation. The plan was to allow those who attempted the murder to think they had been successful and perhaps drop their guards enough to make a mistake the police could capitalize on and make an arrest. The challenge would be how long they could keep up this ruse. The local police and medics had been sworn to secrecy, as had the hospital staff, but soon word would get out. It always does. They may have two days tops.

At 9:00 the next morning Inspector Giles and Detective Tony Read met Mark Sanders in the Chief Inspector's office. For the past two hours Read and Giles had been discussing the findings of yesterday's crime scene investigation and were now about to brief the Chief Inspector. The Chief Inspector welcomed the police officers saying, "Come in gentlemen, I am eager to hear what you have to say. I am afraid I do not have more than a half hour before I must meet with the Mayor, so be as succinct as possible."

Inspector Giles took the lead. "First off sir, we not only have the Lancaster's statement that they were deliberately run off the road, we now have physical evidence indicating that the truck was driven into the Lancaster's car intentionally for that purpose. Moreover, the beatings alleged by Lord Lancaster and inflicted on the stranger have been corroborated through the medical assessment of the nature of the wounds. Finally the blood patches on the site further substantiate post-crash beatings. We have concluded this is a matter of attempted murder. With the cooperation of the Lancasters and hospital staff we have taken measures to suggest that the Lancasters are near death. We'll hope that the thugs may feel they can relax and possibly make some mistakes."

"Any suspects at this point?" asked the Chief Inspector, knowing that it was unlikely they would.

Inspector Giles answered, "We've begun to make a list of those who would benefit from the deaths of Lord and Lady Lancaster. The obvious ones are family members and business partners. In any event, at this point we do not consider them suspects in the direct attempt on their lives. We've even considered that terrorists could be involved. Lord Lancaster does have a high profile."

"What about the stranger?"

Inspector Giles glanced over at Detective Read before responding. "According to Lord Lancaster, the young man came out of nowhere and pulled them to safety before the car exploded. While he may have had some initial concerns that the young man had something to do with the collision, he ruled those out when the young man had been beaten by the three men who showed up right after the explosion. Lord Lancaster said that one of the three men, likely the leader, was genuinely surprised to see that the Lancasters had been pulled away from the burning wreckage. Lord Lancaster indicated that the man then went into a hysterical rage and ordered the other two men to kill them all. We believe that the young man was simply a good samaritan who was trying to assist."

Detective Read added, "There was nothing found at the site that appears to have belonged to the stranger. He didn't have any identification on him at all. Actually the only thing we found that was out of place was a small pocket knife. It was found in the patch of blood eight feet away from where we found the stranger in a pool of his own blood. The smaller patch of blood did not come from the stranger, nor did it come from the Lancasters. We believe that the stranger may have stuck the knife into one of the assailants before he himself was beaten."

"What about finger prints?" asked the Chief Inspector.

"There were some smudged finger prints on the knife, sir. We tried to match them with the stranger's, but his hands were so ripped apart, probably trying to protect his head from the beating, that the comparison was in-conclusive."

The Chief Inspector then asked, "And how is the young man doing?"

"Still on life support," replied Inspector Giles. "The doctor doesn't hold much hope for him."

The Chief Inspector shook his head slowly and turned toward his desk. He started to assemble some papers and as he was placing them into his brief case, he said without looking at his officers, "I know you will do everything you can as soon as you can John. I won't keep you any longer. I just thank God the Lancasters survived or there would be real hell to pay."

In the two days following the incident the combined forces of Scotland Yard and the local county police asked thousands of questions to hundreds of people living in and around Stokenchurch inquiring about three men who may have looked suspicious. Without any descriptions other than one was short and bald, one was tall, one was big, and one might have a stomach wound, there was very little to offer potential witnesses in helping to identify the thugs. Interviews with local hospital and medical practitioners yielded only nil reports of stomach wounds. Two individuals had advised the local police that they had come upon a road barrier on Marlow Road and having accepted the road to be closed, went off in an alternate route. The owners of the Nelson Construction company truck were questioned, but the pub staff confirmed that the two men had been in the pub eating lunch at the time of the incident. The construction men had discovered their truck missing and reported it stolen at 3:45 in the afternoon. A thorough examination of the truck revealed no further clues as to who had stolen it. Further interviews with the Lancasters did not yield any names of people who might wish harm to come to them. There were of course various competitors who had lost major business deals to Lord Lancaster's company; some had lost millions of dollars and had become bankrupt. But Lord Lancaster was insistent that these few did not pose this kind of threat to them. The Lancasters concurred with the Inspector's list of people who would likely benefit from their deaths, but assured the Inspector that none of them could ever be involved in something so terrible. Inspector Giles indicated that he still hadn't dismissed the possibility of terrorists.

At the end of the two days the police had no real leads. The media, however, was much more successful in learning that the Lancasters had actually survived the crash and had been released from the hospital with bruises and some significant cuts. An arm of Lady Lancaster's had been dislocated but not broken and it had been reset. The Lancasters would suffer aches and pains for a while, but they would be fine. The evening newscast on the third day following the incident showed an interview with an official spokesperson of Scotland Yard who revealed that the police were now considering the incident to be one of attempted murder and the whole ordeal was described, what they knew about the crash, about the attackers, about the stranger and the beatings. No information was known about the identity of the stranger, but he was expected to undergo the beginnings of reconstructive surgery in the next day or two.

CHAPTER TWELVE

Lord and Lady Lancaster had been released from hospital as discretely as possible Friday evening, two days after the incident. Before leaving they had a meeting with Dr. Rogers and the President of the hospital insisting again that everything possible be done to help the young man. Lord Lancaster would cover all costs. If specialists had to be brought in, he wanted the very best. His message was clear and again the President assured Lord Lancaster that the young man would be treated to the very best care.

When the Lancasters arrived home Reston and all the staff were present, even those who were to have had the weekend off. They all lined up neatly in the lobby in order to greet and offer well wishes to the Lord and Lady of the Manor. Lady Lancaster spoke, "Thank you, thank you everyone for your kind words. Now please don't fuss over us. We are fine, just a few bumps and bruises as it turned out." She continued, "I am so very sorry we could not tell you sooner that we were fine, but I think you now know the reason for the deception."

"We are just happy to have you safe at home," volunteered Reston on behalf of all the staff. "Now, what can I do for you to make you comfortable?"

"I think a warm bath and a cup of tea, then to bed for a good night sleep would be in order," said Lord Lancaster.

The weekend did not provide the Lancasters with the rest they had hoped for. Rather, they were occupied much of the time with well-intentioned visitors. The Ashtons, Williscrofts and Mentors all arrived at the same time on Saturday just before lunch, after having called earlier in the morning to ensure it was alright to pay a visit. They all stayed for a light lunch and queried the Lancasters about every detail of their terrible adventure. Lady Ashton asked, "When will the doctors perform the surgery on the young man?"

"They said it could be as early as Monday or Tuesday," replied Lady Lancaster. "They will let us know. I made it quite clear that James and I wanted to be available at the hospital following the operation. The poor boy is all alone. He is still in a coma you know. He hasn't regained consciousness at all since …" Lady Lancaster had difficulty ending her sentence. ". . since that day."

Later that afternoon, Sir Loxley drove out to the Manor for a short visit primarily to speak with Lord Lancaster about certain business matters. Sir Loxley also indicated to Lord Lancaster that this incident served as a good reminder to them both that they were going to have a serious discussion about succession responsibilities should either of them become unable to carry out their duties with the company. They initially made this vow five months earlier after Sir Loxley had suffered a minor heart attack following a squash match but had not got around to discussing it further. Lord Lancaster agreed and pledged to discuss it with Sir Loxley within the next three weeks or so. By then he hoped the young man would be well on his way to recovery from his ordeal.

On Sunday afternoon, Judith arrived at the Manor from her home in Coventry. Edward drove up only a few minutes later. Judith had not been very happy with her sister after she had been advised that the Lancasters had hidden the truth about their health situation even from her. If truth were known, it had actually been Edward who had bated Judith into expressing these feelings of betrayal. After a lengthy discussion, souls were soothed and Judith was once again genuinely happy that her sister and brother-in-law were well after such a horrible incident.

Edward and Lord Lancaster were by themselves in the library sharing a cocktail when Edward asked, "So it seems from what you say that the police really do not have any leads in finding the bloody bastards who harmed you? I find that difficult to believe."

"Well, it appears these men knew what they were doing. They had probably done this sort of thing before. There were no finger prints or any other evidence left at the scene. As far as describing the men, the young stranger likely had the best look at them, but he may not even survive. For the life of me, I just can't figure out why anyone would want to do this."

"To be on the safe side, perhaps you should use your chauffer from now on and not go driving on your own."

"Perhaps you are right, Edward. Thank you for suggesting it. At least I will insist Muriel not drive on her own."

Lord Lancaster stared into the fire for more than a minute sipping his drink. Reston had only recently added some new logs and now the flames were dancing wildly to full height, filling the voluminous cavity under the fireplace mantle and casting great warmth into the room. He was debating with himself inside his mind, considering whether he ought to introduce a sensitive topic. "Edward," he said as he turned away from the fire and looked directly at his nephew. "Since I have you here alone, I would like to discuss something rather important with you. Your mother and you are the only family that we have and we care for you because you are family."

With those few words "the only family we have", Edward inwardly smiled to himself reasoning that this recent clash with death had caused the old man to think about what he would be passing on to Judith and him when the day came. He was eager to hear more.

Lord Lancaster continued, "I am not happy with the way in which you seem to be managing your mother's financial resources from your father's estate. I am well aware of the value the estate had originally held just as I know the current value of Judith's resources now. While a great deal of funds have been lost or at least unable to be accounted for, her current resources, if managed properly should yield a comfortable life style for her. I will be recommending to your mother that she allow one of my financial advisors to manage her financial matters from here on in. She will agree because I will guarantee her a rate of investment you could never equal."

Edward's internal smile wilted and he stood before his uncle in shock because he had completely misread what he thought his uncle was going to say.

"Edward, you have a good job and you are making a decent wage. You need to start living within your means. You squandered away your own inheritance from your father. You can no longer supplement your own income using your mother's resources. I will not stand for it. As long as you do as I am telling you, I will keep you in my Will. You will not become wealthy from any inheritance from me, but you will be very comfortable. Quite frankly I think I am being more generous to you than you deserve." Lord Lancaster straightened himself to look as large as his body would allow and as directly as he could he challenged Edward saying, "Do you understand what I am saying to you?"

Edward by this time was seething inside but dared not divulge his real emotions. He did his best to remain calm and responded to the question thrown at him, "Yes sir, I understand."

"And will you do as I said?"

"Yes sir."

"I'm glad to hear that. Now, let's go join the ladies and have another drink."

The two men met the ladies in the parlour. Edward did a fine job keeping his emotions in check, acting as if he had not just received the most severe dressing down of his life. He would follow his uncle's orders, for now. But he wouldn't forget the humiliation.

CHAPTER THIRTEEN

Eleven hours and twenty minutes after the orderly wheeled Adam's bed into the operating room, a new orderly on a different shift wheeled him into the post-op observation room. It was 7:30 Monday evening. Adam had had a peaceful weekend and the surgeons determined that he was strong enough to undergo the surgery that had been tentatively scheduled for 8:00 in the morning. The Lancasters had been called to the hospital at 6:00 PM and had been anxiously waiting in the operating room lounge.

Lord and Lady Lancaster were both reading magazines when Dr. Rogers appeared at the entrance of the lounge. Another doctor who they had not met before accompanied him. They noticed that Dr. Rogers had a smile upon his face. "Lord and Lady Lancaster, this is Dr. Harold Stronger. Dr. Stronger performed most of the reconstructive and plastic surgery on Richard today. I'll let him tell you how it went." Dr. Stronger of the London Medical Centre had an international reputation as a leading facial reconstruction specialist. He had agreed to undertake the surgery, rescheduling a presentation he was to give in Sydney, Australia the next day.

"You referred to the young man as Richard," Lord Lancaster said with a note of confusion.

Dr. Rogers explained, "Oh yes. The doctors and nurses, in fact all hospital staff who have had anything to do with him have become very attached to the young man. Not knowing his real name but not wanting to refer to him as John Doe, they, out of affection, named him Richard, after Richard the Lionheart."

Dr. Stronger said, "I am very pleased to say that virtually all aspects of the procedure appear to have been successful. The total operation time had to be altered because of some complications with the skin grafting, but there were suitable work-arounds that allowed the team to complete the grafts as we like them to be. Richard is stable right now and resting in the observation room. He is being closely monitored. The next seventy-two hours are very critical though. The worst thing possible of course is for infection to set in that cannot be controlled. There will be some infection of course, but the antibiotics should take care of that which is normal. If all goes well, his bandages won't have to be disturbed for a fourteen day period. The young man is still in a coma and quite frankly I hope he stays that way until the bandages are off. Waking up from a coma will be frightful enough. If he has to deal with a face wrapped in bandages at the same time, it could be too traumatic for him."

"You know, I never thought about that," declared Lady Lancaster. "I can't imagine how it will be for Richard when he first gains consciousness and he sees that everything and everyone around him are complete strangers."

"The staff have already given some thought to that very dilemma," said Dr. Rogers. "A team has been created just for that specific eventuality. The team is comprised of two of Richard's nurses, an occupational therapist and a psychologist. They are on call 24/7 in anticipation of him awakening. Special protocols have been developed, including contacting you as soon as possible."

"When might we see Richard?" asked Lord Lancaster.

Dr. Rogers answered, "I'd say you could visit for a short while in about another half hour. I'll have a nurse come and fetch you then. Even though he may still be in a coma, I would encourage you to speak to him. He may be able to hear you. I know the nurses speak to him all the time."

The next seventy-two hours of post-op recovery passed without any significant concerns.

On one of the evenings during that seventy-two hour period a phone call was made from a phone booth in London to the Old Squire Inn, an ancient and seedy looking drinking establishment located in a dark alley in the town of Kingsash. The Old Squire was an unofficial club for rough men, most of whom had had their share of troubles with the law. The short bearded bartender went to the ringing phone that hung on the wall at the end of the bar and took the call. "Sarge, it's for you," the barman yelled. Sarge emptied his glass and yelled to the barman for another before he rose and made his way over to the phone. Sarge didn't have a phone where he lived and even if he did, he was rarely there to answer a call anyway. The best place to track Sarge down was here, his home away from home.

Sarge took the phone and answered, not having any idea who had called him and not caring. "Yeah, what do you want?"

"Is it safe to talk?" a familiar voice asked.

The voice had gotten his attention. Sarge stood straighter and said, "Sure, what do you want?"

The voice was direct, "You didn't finish the job. I hope you don't think I'm going to pay you for bungling it."

"I can explain." Sarge turned his back to the bar room and spoke in softer tones. "This kid came out of nowhere and pulled the old man and lady out of the wreck. If it hadn't been for him, they would have blown sky high."

"So why didn't you take care of all of them then, you idiot?"

"We thought they were dead. We beat the shit out of them then heard the cops, so we got the hell out of there. But we were sure they were dead."

"Well they weren't. You really fucked up. I handed them to you on a silver plate and you screwed it up royally."

"OK, we messed up, but we can still take them out for you. Same price."

"Not just now," the voice responded. "At least the cops don't have any suspects or evidence. You and your incompetent friends stay low. I'll call you again when things settle down. Just keep low." The voice broke the call.

For the next two weeks, Lady Lancaster visited with Richard every day. She sat by his bed for an hour or two talking to him. She explained who she and her husband were, where they lived. She spoke of her hobbies, how she used to ride horses in competitions and her work with the church. She even started telling Richard about her childhood. Lord Lancaster also visited as much as he could, at least every second day. He began to read a book to Richard - the Tales of Ivanhoe.

Every day, the nurses or a therapist would exercise Richard's arms and legs, sometimes they would do this in a special pool utilizing a hoist and cradle. They would massage his whole body and ensure that he was turned onto various positions to avoid bed sores as much as possible. Awake or not, it was imperative that he continue to have physical stimulation in his muscles and joints.

Inspector Giles had met with the Lancasters on two occasions but the investigation was not very fruitful. The Inspector indicated that while they would keep the case active, the Yard would have to cut back its resources dedicated to this case alone. The Lancasters understood.

On March 8th, fourteen days after his surgery, Dr. Stronger removed the bandages from around Richard's face and head. Both Lord and Lady Lancaster were present in the room along with Dr. Rogers and the two nurses who provided ongoing care to Richard. Slowly and carefully, Dr. Stronger made a vertical cut of the bandage along the right side of Richard's head. He then made a similar cut along the left side. The bandages were lifted from the face one layer at a time. Finally the pads around the eyes were removed as gently as possible. "Ladies and gentlemen, may I present the new Richard," a proud Dr. Stronger announced. "He will still have some swelling for a few more days, but on the whole I believe everything has healed just fine.

"I think he looks rather handsome," remarked nurse Kelly, one of the nurses assigned to care for Richard.

Lady Lancaster asked from behind the nurse, "Doctor, how much different does he look compared to his real face? I really never knew what the poor boy looked like."

Dr. Stronger replied, "It is difficult to tell really since when any of us saw him, his face was so broken and battered. When undertaking a facial reconstruction, one of the first steps is to try to create an image of what the original facial structure was like. For this occasion, I brought in a physical anthropologist to look at Richard's broken face. He first used a computer model to draw a three dimensional image of Richard's face as he saw it. Then, using an extrapolation program, he developed the image to what he believed the original facial structure looked like. By that I mean the jaw and cheek lines. Finally a clay model was sculpted and that model was basically what we tried to replicate. I have no doubt Richard will notice a difference in himself, but we believe he will certainly come to realize he is the same person. By the way, all mirrors and reflective materials have been removed from his room. We will have to introduce him gradually to his new image."

"Everything has been going along well so far," interjected one of the nurses. "Now we just need him to wake up."

"That will present its own challenges," said the other nurse.

Dr. Stronger turned to the nurses and said, "Now that the bandages are off, please see to it that his massages include his facial skin and mouth. Until he wakes up we must stimulate those areas for him." The nurses acknowledged the doctor's directions, assuring him that they would see to it.

CHAPTER FOURTEEN

I t was 7:15 Tuesday morning, the sixteenth day of March. The day began pretty much as it usually had for many years at Lancaster Manor. Reston completed his workout, dressed himself and finished his cream of wheat anticipating Lord Lancaster's arrival downstairs at any time in search of his paper and his own breakfast. Lady Lancaster emerged from the second story a half hour later in time to kiss her husband good bye and see him off to work. She then enjoyed a casual breakfast herself of fruit, yogurt, a poached egg and coffee before readying herself to attend the first of two meetings involving charitable organizations, of which she was a board member. One was for a local organization and one was international.

Both Lord and Lady Lancaster had made a conscious commitment many years ago to devote a significant amount of time and financial resources to creating better living conditions for impoverished communities in third world nations. While Lady Lancaster sat on boards of organizations administering the programs in select communities, Lord Lancaster was the impetus behind leveraging financial resources beyond those considerable resources his own company contributed toward these projects. Lord Lancaster had a great many connections with industry leaders and government heads and he could be very persuasive when he met with them. In addition, Lord Lancaster's company provided much of the technical management resources for many of the projects, especially where infrastructure development for new water sources and power were involved.

Lady Lancaster would recall at a later time that the morning sunshine was particularly bright and that the sun's rays flowing through the window of the family dining room were warm on her skin. She would recall for all time the moments leading up to hearing the nurse's voice on the telephone – the phone ringing; Reston hurrying into the dining room with the mobile phone, his eyes revealing that the call was extremely urgent; her own anxiety that had suddenly erupted as she spoke into the receiver, "Hello this is Lady Lancaster." The three words she heard spoke volumes. "He is awake!"

"When?" asked Lady Lancaster.

"Just five minutes ago," the nurse replied. "He seems a little groggy, which would be normal. I wanted you to know as soon as possible."

Lady Lancaster thanked the nurse for calling and indicated that she would be leaving for the hospital as soon as she could. She asked Reston to have the car ready for her and to make some calls on her behalf to explain her regrets for not being able to attend the scheduled meetings. She would call her husband herself with the news.

Just moments before in a private room on the third floor of the Mount Royal hospital, nurse Kelly was ringing out a wet face cloth she was using to wash and refresh Richard's face. She was telling him that it was a bright and sunny day and how wonderful it would be if he could go out this afternoon to sit in the garden and enjoy the warm air. When she returned to face him again she stood for a few seconds in silence and disbelief as she witnessed for the very first time, a pair of brown eyes looking up at the ceiling. "Richard!" she exclaimed, "You're awake!" Then without any panic in her voice nurse Kelly called over to an orderly who was standing outside the door with a tray in his hand. "Harry, he's awake. Call the team."

When she looked down at Richard again, she noticed that there had been no further change in his facial expression or in his eyes. They were still pointed straight up and as if focused on a particular mark on a tile. They were glazed and they were blinking lazily and intermittently. His head had not moved on the pillow. She then thought she noticed a movement in his fingers on his left hand. Perhaps not, as no further movement occurred. Yes, there it was again. His fingers had stretched only a little but she was certain they had moved. She bent over the bed and spoke in a casual tone to him as she had only a few moments ago. "Well good morning. We have been wondering when you were going to wake up. Can you hear me Richard? Can you understand me?"

In what seemed to be an effort for him, Richard turned his head just enough so that his eyes could face the voice he had heard. At the same time nurse Kelly saw within her peripheral vision that he was also attempting to move his fingers again, this time on both hands. She reached for his left hand and gently placed it in her own. She hoped he would be comforted by the soft touch. When she turned back to his face, rather than fear she recognized what she believed was more a sense of confusion in his eyes. She said, "It is alright Richard, you are safe. You are in a hospital and we are taking good care of you."

His first words were awkward but clear, "Thirsty. Water please."

"Yes you can have a little water, but not too much right now." She tilted a cup of water ever so carefully such that only a few drops settled between his lips. She repeated this action twice before saying, "That's all for now. I'll give you some more later."

"Thank you," he said in a faint voice. "Why am I in a hospital? Where is the hospital?"

By this time much of the team had entered the room. They were considerate enough to stand back and not crowd the young man. The second nurse, the psychologist and Dr. Rogers all showed delight and wonderment in their expressions as they looked on from behind nurse Kelly.

The doctor stepped forward and said, "Hello Richard, my name is Dr. Rogers. You are in the Mount Royal hospital in London … England." The doctor chose his next words carefully. "Apparently you had been involved in an altercation with some men that beat you up quite badly. We have patched you up and you should be fine after some rest. You have actually been in a coma for several days."

"I don't remember any fight," said Richard, a little more volume to his voice and just as much confusion in his eyes.

"How are you feeling? asked the doctor. "Do you feel pain anywhere?"

"I feel stiff all over. I can't seem to move."

"That's normal," explained the doctor. "As I said you have been in a coma for several days and have not moved other than from the physical therapy you have been given. In time we will get you moving and walking again. What about pain?"

"I'm sore all over too, but the worst is my cheek and my side."

"We'll give you something to help you with that pain." The doctor nodded to the second nurse.

Trying to arch his body and reset himself in the bed, the young man asked, "You have been calling me Richard. Is that my name?"

Nurse Kelly spoke up, "We didn't know what your name was. You didn't have any identification on you when you arrived at the hospital. We just gave you that name so that we could talk to you while you were in the coma. What is your real name?"

Looking even more confused, Richard scanned the faces of the people near his bed hoping for some clue as to what to say. Finally he said, "I don't remember what my name is. In fact, I don't remember anything." Confusion changed to fear. He started to become agitated raising his voice and shouting, "Where am I? What am I doing here? Who are you?" Richard tried to force his way up to a sitting position, his legs wanting to reach for the floor and to run away.

"Nurse, sedative now!" The doctor and nurse Kelly struggled to keep Richard from moving off of the bed. An orderly was called into the room to assist in restraining Richard from doing physical harm to himself. Several seconds later the sedative took affect and Richard relaxed back onto the bed.

"We're going to have to take this slowly," the psychologist said. We'll have to manage the process with light sedation, at least for a while."

Lord Lancaster was able to leave for the hospital right after his wife had informed him that Richard was awake. They arrived at the hospital at virtually the same time but in two different vehicles. Lord Lancaster was driving his own car.

It had taken only thirty-five minutes to reach the hospital and only a few more to the door of Richard's room. Nurse Kelly was coming out of the room at the very same time. "How is Richard doing Kelly?" asked an anxious Lady Lancaster. "Can he talk yet? May we see him?"

Nurse Kelly guided the Lancasters over to the chairs just a few feet away from the door. Lady Lancaster did not like the expression on her face and asked, "What is wrong?"

"Richard has recovered well from his surgery," she began. "And he is fully awake now. The problem is that he has amnesia. He doesn't remember who he is or anything about what happened to him or anything at all about himself. He became quite frightened as you may imagine and began to react to his fear by trying to get up and flee. We had to sedate him."

"Oh my goodness!" responded Lady Lancaster. Her concern was clearly marked on her face.

Lord Lancaster asked nurse Kelly, "Would it be alright for us to see him, Kelly?"

"Yes you can go in. I just wanted you to be forewarned. I will go in with you and introduce you to Richard. Since he has not yet met you, at least not as Richard, a familiar face will aid in your first meeting."

"Yes, of course," said Lord Lancaster. "We understand perfectly."

They entered the room and saw that Richard was lying in his bed. His head was turned to face the window, presumably looking out into the bright sky and watching as the wind shuffled the leaves in the trees. His hands were in his lap and he was nervously massaging his fingers. He did not hear the three enter the room or if he did, he didn't acknowledge them.

Nurse Kelly led the Lancasters further into the room and spoke to Richard in her usual and casual manner. "Richard, you have some visitors. This is Lord and Lady Lancaster. These are the people that helped you come to the hospital and have been very concerned about you. They would like to visit with you for a little while. Will that be alright?"

Richard slowly turned his head so that he could face directly at nurse Kelly and the Lancasters. He was still heavily sedated. Nurse Kelly had advised the Lancasters that Richard likely wouldn't remember this visit and the next time they would have to repeat the introductions. She indicated that they all would have to be patient during this difficult transitional period.

"Hello Richard, it is nice to see you. You look very well," said Lady Lancaster. And she meant it. Physically the doctors were extremely happy with the results of the surgery. Only faint scars appeared and most of those would fade away over time. The young man sitting before her was a very good looking young man. She often wondered, while visiting him and speaking to him before he had woken, how different he must have looked before the incident.

The Lancasters and nurse Kelly spent the next fifteen minutes trying to make small talk with Richard in the hope he might respond, but he was just too sedated at this point to be able to understand, never mind respond. The three of them left the room as silently as they had entered it. Nurse Kelly said, "I expect that the sedative will wear off enough that he will be alert in a few hours. If you would like, you may come back at that time."

"I have actually cancelled all my appointments for today," said Lord Lancaster. "Could we just stay here with him?"

"Of course," said nurse Kelly. "If you need me just ask one of the other nurses to find me, otherwise I'll check back a little later."

The Lancasters settled themselves into the two cushioned chairs that sat beside Richard's bed. These were the same chairs they had occupied for several days while Richard had been in a coma. Lord Lancaster had purchased two coffees from the cafeteria. For the first half hour the Lancasters discussed the latest international project that Lady Lancaster was promoting with her charitable organization. Three impoverished communities in a remote area of South Africa that were located in close proximity to each other had requested assistance to establish a clean water supply that could be shared. The initial research into the request noted that the communities were strategically located near a waterfall that could provide drinkable water without too much treatment or infrastructure development in each community. The project had a great deal of merit and the efficiencies created by the strategic locations of the three communities allowed for a better than average cost per community compared to previous projects Lady Lancaster's organization had sponsored. Lord

Lancaster was very much in support of the project and had committed his company to manage the project and provide the engineers and technical support to design, develop and oversee the construction of the infrastructure. He had already had preliminary discussions with a few material suppliers and government officials in South Africa. There was still a long way to go before any direct work could be started. This was simply the way it was. Not only did they have to secure the financial resources or materials in kind, but they had to have the senior and local politicians on board and of course the labour side of the equation was always an important step along the way. In more recent years, it became necessary also to undertake an environmental impact assessment of the proposed project. This alone could take months, even for a relatively small project such as this.

Lady Lancaster excused herself from the room in order to freshen up. When she returned she found that Lord Lancaster had resumed reading Ivanhoe to Richard. It wasn't clear whether Richard was asleep or simply still sedated, it was all the same to Lord Lancaster. He paused from reading and commented to his wife. "Do you know that this book was one of my favourites when I was a boy? I read it again when I was a young man and now this is the third time. I still rather enjoy it." He carried on reading, demonstrating great expression with the words as if he could bring the adventurous scenes to life.

Over an hour had passed and Lord Lancaster was still emerged in plots and characters. Richard had begun to stir somewhat which only encouraged Lord Lancaster to read more vigorously. After a few more pages and in mid-sentence, Lord Lancaster abruptly stopped reading and said, "Excuse me." He was responding to what he thought was a question coming from Richard's direction.

Richard repeated his words. "Who are you?" He seemed alert and was facing directly at Lord Lancaster. Lady Lancaster heard the words as well and lifted herself off of the chair so to be in Richard's line of vision.

Lord Lancaster replied, "Hello there young man. Well, in answer to your question, my name is James Lancaster and this is my wife Muriel.

Richard moved his eyes back and forth from Lord Lancaster to Lady Lancaster. He then said to Lord Lancaster, "Are you the one who has been reading me the story of Ivanhoe?"

"Yes I have," said Lord Lancaster. He was bursting with pride and held himself tense so as not to shed a tear that was so close to forming behind his eye. The boy had actually heard me all this time, he thought to himself.

"I think I have heard the story before," managed Richard.

He then turned to Lady Lancaster. "And are you the lady who was an equestrian?"

Lady Lancaster could hardly speak in response, but after a moment she collected herself and said, "I am, although it was many years ago."

Richard added, "I'm sorry you had the accident and couldn't compete anymore."

The Lancasters were beside themselves with joy. Their emotions were overflowing knowing that all the time they had spent by Richard's bedside had been worth it. He had been unconscious but still able to hear them and remember them.

"Who are you people? Why did you stay with me?" Then with more excitement in his voice he asked, "Are you my parents?"

During the next twenty minutes Lord and Lady Lancaster summarized what had happened nearly four weeks ago. They sensed that Richard was strong enough to hear what had happened but still they softened the story as much as possible concerning the depth of the beating that had been given to him. They said that they were very grateful to him for saving their lives, not once but twice. Richard countered by expressing his thanks for what they had done for him.

From out of the blue, Richard asked, "Where is nurse Kelly?"

"You remember nurse Kelly too?" asked Lady Lancaster, expressing even more surprise to the morning's events.

"Oh yes, very much. I have seen her as well. She's a red head right? And very cute?"

"Yes she is very pretty," said Lady Lancaster. "She has been taking very special care of you ever since you were admitted to the hospital." With excitement in her voice, she said, "James, go find her."

"Would you mind helping me sit up please, Mrs. Lancaster?" requested Richard.

"Well I can try. Now which button do I push? Oops, not that one! Ah, that's better. Tell me when it's enough."

"That's fine, thank you. Could I ask you for one more favour please?"

"Certainly," replied Lady Lancaster.

"Would you pass me that glass of water on the table? I am really thirsty."

Before Lady Lancaster could warn him not to take too much water at one time, Richard had almost emptied the glass. The reaction was immediate; he choked and sprayed much of what he had taken into his mouth in Lady Lancaster's direction, effectively leaving some very damp marks on her blouse. In order to help Richard to stop the convulsive coughing, Lady Lancaster instructed him to raise his arms straight into the air. She offered him encouragement that the coughing would end soon. It did and Richard was visibly shaken. He was also extremely embarrassed about the deluge that had come forth from his mouth on to the kind lady.

Gasping for breath he managed to say, "I am so sorry Mrs. Lancaster. I didn't mean to do that." He tried to keep apologizing but Lady Lancaster cut him off and assured him that it was nothing to be concerned about. It was just a little water. She was more concerned about Richard and the effect of gulping the water and the coughing might have on him.

"What happened?" asked nurse Kelly as she, Dr. Rogers and Lord Lancaster walked into the room. She had noticed Richard sitting up and that the front of Lady Lancaster's blouse was wet.

Before Richard could respond, Lady Lancaster remarked, "Oh we had a wee bit of an accident. I was giving Richard some water and spilled it down my front. How clumsy of me!" She looked at Richard and winked. "It was just a little. It will dry in no time." Switching the subject, she then said, "So look who's bright eyed and bushy tailed today, pointing to Richard. We've been having quite a conversation."

Dr. Rogers moved forward and asked Richard a few basic questions as to how he was feeling, what pain he still had and how bad it was. He explained that since he was alert now, staff would begin some physical therapy to help him walk, move and have control of his hands, as well as assisting with jaw movements that were at this point hampering his speech somewhat, but not as much as the doctor had anticipated. Dr. Rogers took a moment to contemplate Richard and thought to himself that the young man had come through this ordeal really quite well, much better than anyone could have hoped.

"We'll start you off with some physical therapy here in the hospital. If you progress the way you have been, you may be able to be released in about a week. You can then return as a day patient for more physical therapy as needed. As for your memory, it should return gradually. We have therapists here who can help with that process as well. Any questions?"

"Dr. Rogers, what happens to me if my memory doesn't come back before I am released from the hospital? I mean, what happens if I still don't remember who I am or if no one can identify me? I won't be able to contact my family. What will I do?" Richard was very calm in his question, unlike his first time out of the coma, but still obviously concerned about his future. And he had a good right to be concerned.

Lord Lancaster sprang forward and eagerly stated, "Don't you worry about that Richard. Until you can manage by yourself, you are welcome to stay with Muriel and me. We have already discussed the possibility and I have made arrangements with the hospital." He added, "If that is alright with you of course?"

It was all decided.

CHAPTER FIFTEEN

Over the next seven days Richard learned four things: he needed more physiotherapy than he thought; there was still no sign of his memory returning; Mr. and Mrs. Lancaster were actually Lord and Lady Lancaster; and he was having nightmares. Dr. Rogers had disclosed to the Lancasters that on two occasions during the week, Richard was found in the middle of the night calling for something to stop and while he was not very coherent, it sounded like a bear was beating him. Knowing what had happened to Richard the psychiatrist suggested that the man doing the beating probably was a very big man and reminded Richard of a bear. This would make sense as Lord Lancaster had testified that one of the attackers was a very big man.

The hospital staff, as well as the Lancasters also learned something about Richard. He was a strong willed and determined young man. He displayed great effort and endurance in keeping up with his therapists, pushing himself to do more each day in order to reach his goals. Lady Lancaster also commented to her husband that Richard possessed other important characteristics as well. She saw that he was a level headed and considerate person and he had obviously been brought up to be polite and to demonstrate good manners.

On the eighth day after coming out of his coma, Dr. Rogers signed Richard's release papers. Lord Lancaster had made arrangements with the local authorities that Richard would be released into his care and supervision. Until such time as Richard could be identified, Richard would be known for the records as Richard Lion and he would be a ward of Lord Lancaster.

The Lancasters had purchased three sizes of clothes and shoes for Richard to be certain something would fit him when he left the hospital. Fortunately he found a combination of khaki pants, a light blue shirt, loafers and a light jacket that fit him well. They were about to leave the hospital room when he said to them, "I have to tell you, I'm a little nervous. All I've known is this hospital."

"That's understandable," said Lady Lancaster. "But don't you worry, we are here to help you."

Looking more in Lord Lancaster's direction Richard then said, "By the way, I've been told who you really are, I mean you being the Earl of Lancaster. I apologize for not addressing you by your titles. Should I be calling you Lord and Lady Lancaster now?"

The Lancasters glanced at each other for a moment, each with a questionable look on their face. Lady Lancaster spoke up in a sincere voice, "Richard, you don't have to apologize. Besides, Lord and Lady are so formal and I think we have a special enough relationship that you should continue to call me Mrs. Lancaster. I would like that. James?"

Lord Lancaster simply said, "Mr. Lancaster works for me. Now, let's get out of here"

Saying goodbye to the good folks at Mount Royal hospital was a trial for Richard. He would miss them all, especially nurse Kelly and Dr. Rogers. Kiddingly he told Kelly that if she ever broke up with her boyfriend, she knew where to find him. At the hospital entrance, Lord Lancaster, Lady Lancaster and Richard piled into the black limousine that was waiting for them. Lord Lancaster looked at his driver and said, "Alright Stewart, let's go home."

On their way from the hospital to the outskirts of London, Lord Lancaster pointed out many different sites including the sixteen story building where his office was located. He didn't mention that he owned the building. Lord Lancaster indicated that he preferred the rural drive much more than the busy streets of London. He revealed that he had been raised in the country and liked nothing more than spending time outdoors trout fishing or roaming the hills on horseback.

The drive to Lancaster Manor took forty-five minutes at a leisurely pace. When they were within a mile of the Estate, Lord Lancaster mentioned that they were almost home. Soon after his announcement they turned off the main road on to a stone drive bordered by a thick forest. They drove on for a hundred yards before coming to an iron gate that opened as they approached. Stewart had activated the remote opener. Another two hundred yards along a meandering stone drive and suddenly Lancaster Manor appeared around a corner. Richard was in awe! It looked like a castle to him.

Reston had been alerted by Stewart that they were approaching the Manor, which explained why he was already perched upon the steps leading up to the huge entrance way. The car stopped. Lord Lancaster said to Stewart that he did not think they would require the car again today and further indicated that he could manage the few bags they had brought along containing different sizes of clothing. Richard did not have any personal belongings.

"Reston, this is Richard." Lord Lancaster continued the introductions. "Richard, please meet Reston. He runs this house and looks after us. And by God, don't get on his bad side or we'll all be sorry." Lord Lancaster gave Richard a wink that Reston could easily see as well.

Richard noted the formal attire worn by Reston as soon as he had seen the manservant on the steps of the Manor. He thought to himself that this seemed quite natural given the surroundings. Richard extended his hand and said, "I'm pleased to meet you Reston."

Reston in turn gave Richard a hearty shake of the hand and replied saying, "It is nice to finally meet you. Lord and Lady Lancaster have spoken of you often. Welcome to Lancaster Manor Master Richard."

While Richard had thought he was awestruck outside the Manor, he caught himself gazing like a tourist when he entered the main lobby and looked around to see the great hall with the chandeliers, the tapestries and the winding grand staircase leading to a second and third balcony. The Manor staff were lined up in the great hall as if ready for inspection. Lady Lancaster introduced Richard to the kitchen staff and the maids, all of whom had genuine smiles on their faces. All extended welcoming wishes to him.

Since it was almost noon, Lady Lancaster said to Mrs. Roberts, the lady in charge of the kitchen, "We should be ready for lunch anytime you are Mrs. Roberts. I am certain that Richard will appreciate your fine cooking, especially after having to eat that dreadful hospital food."

As the staff were about to return to their duties Richard casually asked, "Excuse me Mrs. Lancaster, could you tell me where I can find the washroom?" The staff suddenly halted and with open mouths turned toward Lady Lancaster. Lady Lancaster could immediately see that the term Mrs. Lancaster had definitely not gone unnoticed. She quickly and without hesitation addressed the staff. "Oh, I should mention to you, we have asked Richard to call us Mr. and Mrs. Lancaster, so don't be concerned. Reston, perhaps you could show Richard where the bathrooms are on this floor and as well, could you show him his room?"

"Yes Madam," said Reston. "Please follow me Master Richard and we will get you settled."

At that point the entire group disbanded to different corners of the Manor.

To a great extent the next two weeks were quite regimented for Richard, as Lord Lancaster had arranged daily rehabilitation sessions for him utilizing both the gym and the lap pool. The speech therapist came to the Manor twice a week as well. Richard was not adverse to all the therapy. In fact he regularly pushed himself beyond the goals the physiotherapist had set for him. It was tiring and he was exhausted after the work outs, but he also noticed measurable improvements and that only inspired him to work harder.

When he wasn't in rehabilitation sessions and if the Lancasters were not at the Manor, which was most often the case during the week, Richard busied himself reading or exploring the Manor and grounds. He quickly became known to not only the inside staff but also to the gardener and stable staff. He would often pick up a pitch fork and help the stable hands clean out stalls, while talking with them. This was often awkward for the stable staff. Richard relieved their concerns by telling them that he had mentioned to Lord Lancaster that he would like to help with chores when he could, and Lord Lancaster had no problem with it. Richard did not seem to know how to ride a horse very well but wanted to learn. The staff offered to teach him. Within days he started to get the hang of it and pleasantly surprised Lord and Lady Lancaster when they suggested he ride with them one Saturday morning. Again inspired to become better, Richard made his unofficial riding lessons part of his regular routine.

Spending time in the vast library was also a thrill for Richard. The room seemed to overflow with books. The shelves rose fifteen feet on each wall. Ladders moved along the walls on rails in order to reach the higher shelves. Richard had observed that old books outnumbered new volumes by far. And many of the books were very old. Some were precious as well and enclosed in special glass cabinets. After a time, Richard discovered a few historical books that mentioned former Earls of Lancaster. This reminded Richard that he had wanted to ask Lord Lancaster to tell him about his ancestors and the history of the Manor. He made another mental note to speak to the Earl. It also occurred to him that Lord and Lady Lancaster did not seem to act like he thought nobles would act. They seemed from the start like really down to earth people. They certainly treated their staff with respect. They did not seem snooty in any way. He wondered why they didn't have children. At least children were never mentioned.

On Saturday, Lord and Lady Ashton arrived for a visit and lunch. Their son Jason accompanied them. Jason was about the same age as Richard, give or take a year, since no one really knew how old Richard was. He was an inch or two shorter than Richard and looked fit. His hair was blond and cut over his ears. Jason was home from university where he was studying law. He appeared to be friendly in his greetings with the Lancasters and in meeting Richard. Actually it was apparent that the two of them seemed to get along quite well given the circumstances. Both young men were outgoing and interested in being involved in conversations with their elders. They were not afraid to state their opinions or debate them for that matter – but in a non-confrontational manner.

During lunch the Lancasters shared the humour in their quest to find the right sized clothes for Richard to come home in. They indicated that now that they knew his sizes he would have to shop for some more clothes very soon. It was Jason who volunteered to take Richard shopping for clothes. He indicated that they could go that very afternoon. Richard did not want to be a burden to Jason but he eagerly and genuinely seemed to want to help, so it was settled. Lord Lancaster thanked Jason for this gesture and asked him where he thought would be the best place to look for suitable clothes. Lord Lancaster indicated that he wanted Richard to have sufficient clothing for all occasions: casual, business, semi-formal dress. And of course all the basics as well.

Richard was becoming quite embarrassed by all this discussion concerning him and the fact that he had no money to pay for anything. He was quite aware that he was totally dependent on the Lancasters. He interrupted and said, "Excuse me Mr. Lancaster, please don't go overboard here. I don't require much." After a brief pause it was evident that he was having difficulty expressing himself, but he continued. "What I mean to say is that I feel badly that I am so dependent on you and Mrs. Lancaster. I don't feel right about it. I wish I could do something to earn my keep while I am here."

Sensitive to how Richard was feeling, Lord Lancaster responded saying, "I'm sorry Richard for carrying on the way I have. I'm just excited to be able to do this for you. Of course I understand how you may be feeling, but please know that Muriel and I owe you much more than a few clothes and a place to sleep. We owe you our lives. But I tell you what, let's consider this a loan. When we figure out what skills you have we can see what kind of work you could do. I know very well that you are not afraid of work. How does that sound?"

Richard appreciated what Lord Lancaster said and they quickly came to an understanding. The Ashton's were gracious people and applauded Richard for stating his concerns and his position. Lord Ashton indicated he would be prepared to help find Richard a job as well, once he knew more about his interests and experience.

By 1:30 Jason and Richard were on their way in Jason's car. It was after 8:00 in the evening when Jason dropped Richard off at Lancaster Manor. They had finished shopping by around 5:30 but decided to stop for a beer and then dinner before driving back to Maidens Green. Reston had to help Richard in with all the bags and parcels. It was easy spending someone else's money and apparently Jason had as much fun as Richard. After Jason told Lord Lancaster where he would be taking Richard for clothes and shoes, Lord Lancaster called ahead to the managers of the stores advising them to bill all costs to him. The store managers were quite excited about the prospects of outfitting a young man with a completely new wardrobe.

Richard was becoming stronger every day and formal rehabilitation sessions were less frequent. In three weeks they would end. Jason had introduced Richard to some of his friends who were also back from university. Richard seemed to fit in with the young men and women, all curious about what he could and couldn't remember. For a time Richard was very self-conscious about not having a memory and not being able to contribute to conversations that required describing past experiences, but soon he, as well as his new friends, accepted this for what it was.

On one afternoon Lady Lancaster had persuaded Richard to accompany her on a visit to one of her charitable organization's homes for special needs children. It was evident to Lady Lancaster as well as to the house mother that Richard was very familiar with the needs of these children and how to work with them. The house mother said to Lady Lancaster that Richard must have had some past training or experience because not many people had the skills that he was demonstrating while on their visit. Part of the skills involved a type of music therapy. Here too Lady Lancaster found out that Richard could play the guitar and was obviously very accomplished. He was very surprised himself when he reached for the guitar standing in the corner and just started playing and singing a children's song. The guitar had not been played since the former owner of it died three years ago. Richard happily accepted the opportunity to volunteer twice a week to lead some recreational activities at the home.

It was his second time exploring the depths of the barn out behind the new stables when Richard discovered a jewel in the form of an abandoned 1975 Pontiac Firebird. The bold red car with white interior and a 350 under its hood was a toy Lord Lancaster had purchased for himself following a business trip to Montreal many years ago. Apparently he had his thrill for a few years and then hid it away in the barn, covered with a tarp. Over the years the car had been camouflaged as more castoffs began to accumulate on top of the tarp. The sports car was virtually hidden and forgotten until now. Richard was nervous with excitement as he carefully removed all the debris from on top of and around the fabulous car. It took him an hour to clear a path to the door of the barn wide enough to drive the car outside. But where are the keys, he said to himself; they weren't in the ignition. He looked under the floor mats and found them. Not expecting the car to start, he turned the ignition anyway secretly hoping. Nothing! No sound at all. He went to the front of the vehicle and lifted the hood. Ah ha, no battery he observed. Richard then began to make a mental note of several things he would check with the engine. He would check and probably have to buy new spark plugs. The gasoline would have to be replaced, if there was any at all. The oil would have to be drained and replaced. He would also check the radiator and the fuel and water pumps. It suddenly occurred to him that he appeared to know something about cars. He felt quite confident that he could get this car into running order, but just to be on the safe side he would consult with Stewart. Stewart not only drove for Lord Lancaster, he maintained the three vehicles in the garage. Richard couldn't wait to tell Lord Lancaster of his discovery, hoping that he would receive permission to fix it up and drive it. What he really wanted was a paying job so he could purchase the parts he needed himself.

Lord Lancaster was delighted about Richard's find and admitted that he had forgotten all about the old Firebird. He said that if Richard felt he could do the work himself, saving the labour costs would more than pay for the parts required and it would be his to drive. The car was indeed precious. It was not only one of the earliest Firebirds ever built, but even though it was over twenty-five years old, it had less than ten thousand miles on it. It was in mint condition and just needed cleaning and polishing. What a find! Richard's focus for the next two weeks was on the Firebird. All his spare time was spent in the barn assessing what work was required, finding parts and installing them. The last few days of his mission were spent on cleaning and polishing and fine tuning the engine. Lord Lancaster helped arrange for a driver's licence which was no small feat, given that Richard had no real identity. Finally everything was ready. He called Jason to go with him on his first road trip. The Firebird performed superbly on the winding roads and on the straightaways. Jason took the wheel for part of the time and said that he had never experienced such a car. It was an American built muscle car.

They had been touring for about an hour along country roads when Jason said, "There's a small town coming up just around the next bend. Let's stop for a coffee. I know a nice café." They drove into the town with Jason giving Richard directions to the café. The closest parking space was in front of a pub, which was next door to the café. As Richard and Jason were getting out of their car, three men exited the pub. One of them was Edward Bolden.

"Well look who's here!" Edward declared as he saw Richard. Looking at the bright red and gleaming vehicle, Edward added, with sarcasm dripping from his mouth, "Nice car. Did the old man buy that for you too?"

Richard had only met Edward once before at the Manor on his fourth day out of the hospital. He had arrived with Judith for a visit with the Lancasters. Of course the real reason for the visit was to see the new kid. He recalled that Judith was nice enough. She seemed to get along quite well with both her sister and Lord Lancaster. On the other hand, Richard did not like Edward from the first time he laid eyes on him. They only spent about an hour in each other's company but it was long enough to assess the fellow. He appeared to have a chip on his shoulder. He had a rather negative attitude with just about anything being discussed. He didn't seem to have any interests in common with Richard or Lord Lancaster. He rarely partook in any conversations unless they were about him. Most answers to questions posed to him were comprised of three words or less. Richard didn't get the impression that the Lancasters saw much of Edward and he was glad of that. He didn't want to have any more do with him than he had to.

Other than a "Hi Edward", Richard ignored him. He was more concerned about one of Edward's friends who clearly had too much to drink and was stumbling his way closer to the Firebird. Richard called to Edward's friend. "Hey, be careful. I wouldn't want you to accidently scratch the car with that big belt buckle." The man ignored Richard or just didn't hear him as he kept moving towards the car. "I said back away from the car you idiot." Richard lunged to grab the inebriated man as he was about to collapse on the hood of the car.

"Hey, get your hands off me. I'll go wherever the hell I want to."

"Edward, will you get this oaf away from here. We don't want any trouble."

Edward quickly figured that he was in enough hot water with his uncle already and if there were any altercations here today the new kid would blame him. He wisely told his friends to back off and steered the buckle man towards their own vehicle, four down from the Firebird.

Richard and Jason stood by the Firebird until Edward and his friends drove off. When they were convinced the three weren't coming back, they proceeded to the café where a small group had gathered to see what the earlier commotion was about. Five minutes later they were sitting down finally drinking the coffee they had come for.

CHAPTER SIXTEEN

On Thursday of the following week, it was agreed that Lady Lancaster would accompany her husband into London so that she could attend an early meeting and do some shopping. Lord Lancaster had only planned to go to his office for a few hours in the morning that day to deal with two business matters. He indicated that he could easily finish his work in time to meet Lady Lancaster for a late lunch. During breakfast, Lord Lancaster suggested that Richard come with him to the office and later they could all have lunch together. Richard had not yet been to Lord Lancaster's office and thought that it would be interesting, so he said that he would go.

Stewart first dropped Lady Lancaster off at the Hyatt Hotel, the location of her meeting. The plan was to meet her again in the hotel restaurant at 1:00 in the afternoon. Stewart then drove Lord Lancaster and Richard a few blocks away and left them in front of Lord Lancaster's office building. Lord Lancaster indicated that he would call Stewart when they were ready to be picked up.

While the sixteen story building's exterior consisted of glass and stainless steel, the interior lobby was constructed primarily of granite. There was a large curved reception area with a receptionist and a security guard stationed behind the counter, both of whom said a cheery good morning to Lord Lancaster when they passed by on the way to the elevators. Lord Lancaster smiled and offered a good morning in return. Several other people in the lobby and in the elevator also said hello or good morning. Lord Lancaster acknowledged them all. They arrived on the fifteenth floor and were immediately greeted by another receptionist, a forty something lady who was very pleasant. She said, "Good morning Lord Lancaster, isn't it a beautiful morning? Sir Loxley and the others are waiting for you in Sir Loxley's conference room."

Knowing exactly where the room was located, Lord Lancaster said to the receptionist, "Thank you Mrs. Waters, we will go there directly. And yes, it is a wonderful morning."

Sir Loxley was the President and CEO of Lord Lancaster's company, Port of Grace Enterprises, and a business partner. He was also a trusted friend. He and three other men and one woman were seated around a large conference table that could accommodate thirty people. There were several piles of papers and note pads resting on the table. The outside wall of the room was all window. The view was outstanding and Hyde Park could be seen in the distance. There were three other tables against the glass wall, two of which held a pile of maps and engineering drawings.

Sir Loxley looked up and as he rose from his chair said, "Good morning James." Only Sir Loxley would call Lord Lancaster, James. "And Richard, it's nice to see you again. I didn't know you were coming down today." Richard had already met Sir Loxley soon after he moved to Lancaster Manor. He liked Sir Loxley as soon as he met him.

Lord Lancaster greeted all the people around the table, knowing all but two of them. He then introduced Richard. Word around the building had circulated about the young man who had saved the Lancaster's lives, but now these few employees actually got to meet the stranger. After all introductions were made, they sat down at the table. Richard was invited to sit with them or wander about. He said that he hoped he would not cause a distraction for them.

"Alright, we have two items to discuss this morning," began Sir Loxley, "the on-going problem with the turbine system on the Switzerland project and Lady Lancaster's South African project." Richard was not really paying a great deal of attention as he was examining various pieces of art and appreciating the sensational view out the window, but his ears did perk up at the mention of the second item.

"John, would you take us through the Switzerland matter please." John was John Maxwell the President of the Engineering section of the company known as Regal Engineering. He oversaw virtually all local and international projects, including design, business development, installations and project management aspects of the business.

"In a nutshell, here's the problem. We received the turbines last November. The installation was completed in February. Testing was completed on the first three turbines by the end of March and we have been testing and retesting the fourth ever since without success. It is now the first week in May and we aren't any further ahead. We have had the manufacturer on site for the past few weeks and no one can come up with a reason for the problem, never mind a solution. We don't know if the problem is with the one turbine or if the problem is in the consolidated system of turbines working as one. The manufacturer insists that nothing is wrong with the turbine and blames the installation. Therefore, they are not prepared to bring us a new one, unless we pay for it. We are behind schedule and even if we were to solve the problem tomorrow we would likely be looking at a loss of two to three million dollars. If it takes another month, we might as well buy a new turbine now and mitigate the loss. The problem is we don't know if it is the turbine or the combined system. We could end up with two turbines that don't function."

Unnoticed by the people around the table, Richard had been flipping through the engineering drawings on one of the tables by the window for the past several minutes, first as a matter of interest, then as if he knew what he was looking at. Concentrating on one of the drawings while holding another up for comparison, he casually asked a question to the gathering at the table, "Are these the engineering drawings for the turbines you are talking about?"

Conversation abruptly ended at the table. In one motion all heads turned toward Richard, somewhat surprised by the interruption. Sir Loxley responded, "I'm sorry, did you say something Richard?"

"Yes, excuse me, but are these the engineering drawings for the turbines you are discussing?"

"Yes they are," replied John Maxwell.

"Well, at least part of the problem is due to a design flaw on the fourth turbine", Richard said as if he knew what he was talking about. "The secondary impeller shown on this drawing is missing an ancillary spoke and the electrical connection for the adjusting membrane is located too close to the adjacent connection. Are you sensing an abnormal build-up of heat and a sluggish response after a period of time during the tests?"

George Casper the department head for project management and David Seemings one of the senior engineers lifted themselves off of their chairs while George asked, "How do you know there is a design flaw and yes we are experiencing the problems you mentioned."

Now everyone at the table was on their feet and crossing over to the table where Richard was standing. George and David were staring down at Richard's finger as he pointed out the flaws, noting how the drawings differed from the other turbines. They took a few minutes before they looked up in amazement and George asked, "Are you an engineer? How did you spot this?"

"Is he right?" asked Lord Lancaster.

David supplied the answer. "Well, he is certainly right about the flaws. Whether the impact is as he is suggesting would have to be confirmed through further testing. I can't believe no one has been able to see this."

John Maxwell said, "If Richard is correct and we can prove it, we'll at least have leverage over the manufacturer to replace the turbine and be liable for the losses we have and could still incur. Are you sure George that what Richard has uncovered has merit?"

George took another look at the drawings then at David before answering the question. "Yes we definitely need to look into this further."

"Alright then. As soon as we finish this meeting you start the process to thoroughly review these drawings again and set up further tests. Also gear up the legal department. And we have got to act on this straight away."

Sir Loxley asked, "George or David, would it help if Richard had a further look at this problem. We don't know if he is some kind of an engineer or not but so far he's the only one who has come up with any kind of reason for the mal-functioning turbine." Sir Loxley didn't wait for a reply, he turned to the young man and said, "Richard, would you be prepared to work with George's team?"

Richard was uncomfortable responding to Sir Loxley before George could give his advice. George took advantage of Richard's hesitation and said, "I think it is a good idea. It certainly won't hurt. We'll know soon enough what kind of knowledge Richard has."

Richard looked at Sir Loxley and said, "I'd like to help if I can. I'm more surprised than you that I was able to see the flaw and suggest a causal effect."

"Good boy!" exclaimed Lord Lancaster, with obvious surprise yet pride in his voice. "I'm glad you are willing to assist. Now I suggest we leave further work on this matter for the moment and move on to the South African project. Unless you have anything further to discuss on this one John?"

"No sir, we can move on," replied John Maxwell.

"Richard, would you like to join us at the table? This next matter deals with the project Lady Lancaster is involved with. You will remember her mentioning it to you." Lord Lancaster pointed in the direction of an empty chair beside one of the engineers.

After John Maxwell had summarized the status of the South African project to bring fresh water to three adjoining communities from a nearby waterfall, he asked the lead engineer, Jennifer Strong, to outline the current issues. Essentially the project was in good shape from a design point of view. A few more decisions were required from Lady Lancaster's organization and certain material commitments were required in order to proceed. There wasn't a major problem with the project in terms of time frame. Changes or enhancements could still be made but after another month or so the situation would begin to be of a concern unless decisions were reached. The window for the company's free involvement of engineers and project managers would start to shrink, as other commitments for which the company would be paid were on the horizon. Everyone agreed that the project was very worthwhile. Lord Lancaster acknowledged that much of the decisions that Jennifer had pointed out required his involvement. He indicated to the group that he would speak to his wife and her board members and that he would turn up the heat on the suppliers he had been meeting with.

Richard had been listening intently to the business being discussed, while flipping through one of the status reports that had been placed on the table before him. He actually knew quite a bit about the nature of the project and had taken an interest in reading the project plan that Lady Lancaster had shown him several days ago. Even at that time he had wanted to say something about the project and make a suggestion, but he did not have enough confidence in himself. He didn't want to appear ignorant. Now that he had further information before him, he was itching to speak up. He hesitated until John asked around the table, "Does anyone have any further questions or something to add?"

No one spoke so Richard did. "I was just wondering if anyone has considered adding the development of some hydroelectricity to the communities as part of the project? It seems to me that it would be a natural thing to do if costs were not an impediment and I don't believe they would be from what I've seen on the descriptions of the waterfall and the terrain around the communities, and the labour costs of course."

Again those around the table all looked at Richard with some confusion on their faces. They were collectively thinking, how does this fellow think he knows enough about the project to ask such a question and to state that what he is suggesting would not be cost prohibitive?

George spoke up. "We were handed the project plan that you see. It didn't consider a second objective for hydro development and we have not questioned it. Our own project plan has been strictly related to fresh water. As for costs, we would have no way of knowing unless we were asked to explore them."

Lord Lancaster then said, "I am not aware that the production of hydroelectricity was ever discussed by the board. I may be wrong and I can inquire, but do we want to go there? Richard, why do you think hydro development should be considered?"

"I actually have a fair knowledge of the project from Mrs. Lancaster. I studied the project plan she had and had a good look at this information while you were providing the status reports." He was holding the project document in his hands. "The strategic location of the waterfall to the communities, the research on the range of flow capacity over the next twenty years, the sloping terrain toward the communities and the recent designs in low cost small system generation make me think that for a relatively few extra dollars, three remote communities currently without any electricity other than a couple of generators could receive enough hydro to power three, let's call them resource centres. The resource centres could be designed to house a small medical clinic and a community kitchen. Fridges and freezers, computers and radios all could be utilized with the power generated. The existing generators could be used as backup power rather than as the main power sources."

"What do you mean by recent designs in low cost small system generation?" asked David. "That's probably one of the key cost factors in such a proposal."

Without hesitation Richard was able to describe what he thought he knew, although he didn't know how he knew, about this new technology and the cost savings compared to earlier technology. He even mentioned two examples where they were being used.

Lord Lancaster did not hide his surprise and astonishment when he said to Richard, "I don't know how you know this stuff or if you really do, but it sounds convincing to me. You must have some engineering background. Judging from your age, my guess is that you only recently graduated from an engineering school."

John added, "I agree. You would have to have some significant engineering training to talk about the things you have this morning. Either that or you are the greatest con artist that ever lived." They all chuckled.

Sir Loxley took back control of the meeting. The time was 1:15. "What you say Richard is very interesting and if you are correct in your assessments, the value of having modest hydro power in these communities would be worth some extra costs. I think we should look into it on our own for now and not mention it to the organization's board, including Lady Lancaster, James. Let's not get hopes up. We need an enhanced project outline and new cost estimates. And James, we need new sources of funding. I am thinking that we could help the three communities to obtain much needed electricity and at the same time, score points with the South African government – something we have been after for a long time. John and George, can I speak with you for a moment?" The three men left the room returning five minutes later. Sir Loxley continued speaking. "Here's what I would like to do and John and George are supportive. Richard, we want to put you on the payroll as a special consultant. We want you to assist with the Switzerland project as loosely described earlier and we want you to head up the investigation into the feasibility and cost of enhancing the South African project. You will work in conjunction with Jennifer. You will be working in George's area. He can provide you with some engineering support as well as research and administrative support. The Switzerland project will take precedence but as you have heard, we don't have a great deal of time to change the South African project either. What do you say?"

Richard couldn't believe what was happening. How did he know what it seems he did know about all these engineering matters? Was he in fact a professional engineer?

"I would really appreciate the opportunity, sir. I can't explain why I know what I do. I just hope this doesn't backfire on you. When do you want me to start?"

George said, "Today's Thursday. We need to get some things in order tomorrow. You start Monday. Make a note to meet with me at 9:00 AM in my office. I'll have all the administrative paperwork for you by then. We'll meet with the team at 10:00. We'll set you up in Roger Blake's office since he's away on sick leave for at least a few months."

Sir Loxley turned to John and the rest of his team and said, "We will need to jump on Switzerland right away. I want our position wrapped up by the end of next week. John you better speak to the legal boys on Monday. Be prepared for some long hours and likely a trip to Bern the week after people. Richard you may need to go to Bern as well, if this all makes the kind of sense you have been talking about. OK, anything further?

Lord Lancaster motioned that he had something to say. "Thank you all for what I believe to be a successful meeting. Congratulations Richard on joining the team." The others agreed with a hearty, here, here!"With respect to going to Switzerland, that might be a problem. I don't know how we are going to get you a passport. Anyway, leave that to me."

"Alright everyone, we are adjourned," declared Sir Loxley.

After everyone left the room, Lord Lancaster shook Richard's hand and said with pride, "You never stop amazing me young man. We are learning more and more about you every week. Now we better get a move on. Muriel will be wondering where we are. And remember, we can't talk about South Africa to her, at least not yet."

CHAPTER SEVENTEEN

The next week was as hectic as Sir Loxley said it would be, but it was also a very profitable one as well. Richard's theories about the faulty turbine were confirmed after he and the company's senior engineers scrutinized the drawings and specifications, while the on-site team performed similar tasks with the actual turbine sitting in Switzerland. The company also contracted with another engineering company to assist with the investigation to give further expertise and credence to the findings. This would help with the anticipated legal dealings down the road with the manufacturer. The next step would be a series of tests scheduled for the following week that would focus on identifying cause and effect scenarios associated with the flaws identified. These tests would be performed on site and Richard had been asked to participate. Lord Lancaster had pulled some strings to arrange for a temporary passport for a two month period, so he was free to go.

Richard was also able to pull a team together to begin the feasibility study for providing small scale hydroelectricity to the three communities named under the South African project. The first thing the team had to research was whether the new small system generators Richard had mentioned actually existed and to learn as much about them as possible. Once they had that information they would insert certain system specifications into a computer model that had already been designed for the project that included information on precise locations, water pressures at various locations along the drop, the terrain and likely paths for running electric cable, and so on. This would be a preliminary examination. An on-site visit would eventually be necessary to confirm some additional data that wasn't collected for the fresh water project alone. The primary objective for the study was to determine the most cost-effective design for the hydro system, while requiring some minimum hydro output. Ideally, the maximum hydro output scenario would be found to be affordable.

By the end of the week, good progress was being made. The small system generators were indeed new technology, only a few years old. The examples Richard had mentioned were legitimate. Representatives of respective project teams who undertook the projects raved about the efficiencies and effectiveness of the systems. Additional data for the computer modeling was being assembled, using some assumptions until real data could be collected. The team would create a range of data, assuming that the real data would fit somewhere within the range. In this way, they would have a sense of the range of costs versus hydro output. If none of the scenarios within the broad range turned out to be feasible, they would not pursue the concept any further. Richard was convinced, however, that the study would prove him right. He anticipated that by the time he returned from Switzerland, all the data would be ready for analysis.

It was past mid-May now with June and summer right around the corner. The air was warmer, the grass and trees were greener. It was a fine day for a Saturday morning ride into the hills on the Lancaster Estate. Lord Lancaster had arranged the early morning ride with Richard the night before. They had agreed that they would head out at sunrise after a light breakfast. Lord Lancaster was interested in hearing more about Richard's first two weeks as an employee of Regal Engineering. The engineering consulting company was one of many subsidiary companies under Lord Lancaster's parent company Port of Grace Enterprises. Since Richard had been putting in so many extra hours at the office or was out of the country for most of the last week, Lord Lancaster had not had much opportunity to chat with him.

They had galloped across the meadow and were starting a gentle climb into the hills. A few minutes later they reached a level area and Lord Lancaster signalled that they should stop and allow the horses to rest. They got down from their saddles and walked the horses toward the sun. The air was fresh and cool on their faces. Steam could be seen rising off of the horses' backs and from their nostrils as they exhaled.

"I understand people at the office are saying good things about you Richard. I am happy that you have made such a positive impression so soon. You have handled yourself extremely well after being thrown into the mix like that. They also say that you have some natural leadership skills to match your technical knowledge. Of course they've only confirmed what I have thought myself. How do you like working for Regal?"

"Sometimes I feel I have to pinch myself to know that it is all not a dream. I am very grateful for the opportunities presented to me and the managers and staff have been very supportive. And in answer to your question, I like it a lot. I feel I am in the right place. I suppose though, my bubble will break sooner or later. Things have been too good to be true."

Lord Lancaster interrupted Richard and said, "Don't sell yourself short Richard. You earned the work you are doing. I had nothing to do with you being hired. John and George recognized the skills you can contribute to this company and they hired you. I am certain that in time we will also come to know just what credentials you possess. And don't worry, not all weeks will be as crazy as the last two, or should I say the first two." He laughed at his little joke.

"I wonder when I will gain my memory back. It's taking longer than Dr. Rogers said it would. Although at times I have to admit I have sensed some recollections that I can't explain."

"You've never mentioned any to me. What recollections?"

"The first time was when I was with Mrs. Lancaster at the children's home. I felt so comfortable playing with the kids and it reminded me more than anything I suppose of another place and time. When I was commenting on the design flaws with the turbine, I was certain that a person's face came to mind giving me encouragement and telling me that I was on the right track. I think this person may have been one of my professors."

"You see, things are starting to happen. The egg is starting to crack, so to speak. It won't be long now, Richard."

After a few moments scanning the valley land in all directions, Lord Lancaster asked, "Richard, I belong to a country club on the other side of Maidens Green. I don't frequent the club very often any more, but I plan to attend a fund raiser next weekend and I was wondering if you would like to attend with me. It will be just for the boys, no women. Lord Ashton and Jason will likely be there, and perhaps one or two of Jason's friends."

"Sure, that would be nice."

"Good. Now perhaps we better make our way back. You probably have your own plans for this weekend."

When Lord Lancaster and Richard appeared in the parlour, after having first cleaned themselves up, Lady Lancaster had some news for them. Lady Monica Ashton, Jason's sister, had returned home early from her travels and the Ashton's were going to hold a party in celebration. Richard's name was on the invitation along with Lord and Lady Lancaster's. "It will be so nice to see Monica again," remarked Lady Lancaster. "She's been away for almost eight months. You'll like her Richard. She's a very pleasant girl, not a precocious bone in her body."

A week later Lord Lancaster and Richard were sharing a drink in the bar at the country club with Jason and his father. Richard was telling them some highlights of the past three weeks, leaving out more confidential information like how Regal Engineering had convinced the turbine manufacturer to produce a new and flawless turbine without a law suit. There was also written agreement to cover the losses Regal had experienced as a result of the faulty turbine. More exciting to Richard, however, was that the preliminary feasibility study for the hydroelectricity enhancement to the South African project proved extremely favourable. Richard would be off to South Africa sometime within the next two weeks to lead in the collection of final data. After that data was collected, placed into the model and analyzed, he hoped that they would be in a position to speak to Lady Lancaster and her board about it.

"Why don't we show you around the club," Lord Ashton suggested. We have tennis, golf, billiards, fencing, and skeet shooting. Plus of course there is a pool, card areas, restaurants and a smoking room."

They moved past the card room and the billiards room before coming to the entrance to the fencing salon. They peered into the room to see two combatants just completing some training. Richard wondered off several feet along a wall to an open cabinet and inspected the various swords on display. The trainer was coming toward him so he asked if it was alright to feel one in his hand. "Certainly," said the trainer. Richard chose a sabre. "Do you fence?" asked the trainer.

Richard had a questioning look upon his face when he replied. "I think I do, but I'm not sure."

The trainer looked at Richard strangely and before he could say something, Jason spoke up. "Let me explain Albert," Jason said to the trainer. "My friend here is suffering from amnesia. He can't remember anything from his past."

"I see," said Albert. "Well there is one way to find out. What is you name young man?"

"Richard," he replied.

"Then Richard, bring that sword and come with me," commanded Albert.

Richard followed Albert into the centre of the salon. "Let's see what you know, if anything. I will take it easy on you just to see if you know any basic fencing moves. Alright?"

Richard said alright, looked over to Lord Lancaster, Lord Ashton and Jason and shrugged his shoulders. "I'll give it a go," he said.

At Albert's command, "en garde," they both assumed a fencer's stance. Albert immediately took the offensive and Richard was forced to defend. And he did so with strength, tact and finesse. Albert abruptly stopped play and said, "Wait! Wait! You have definitely had some fencing training. Before we continue we better protect ourselves." Albert asked one of his associates to bring him and Richard the necessary equipment.

Lord Lancaster called out to Albert, "Are you certain he has had some training?"

"Most definitely," replied Albert. "I can tell because he knew how to take up traditional position and by the defensive moves he displayed. I was going slow but I was using strategic movements. Now we will see just how much training he has had."

After about fifteen minutes of progressively aggressive sword play, Lord Lancaster saw Richard flash a few rapid offensive sword strokes in succession effectively disarming Albert of his sword. The sabre flew off in the air toward a blank wall.

"Well that settles it. You are an experienced swordsman my friend," said an enthusiastic Albert. "I don't know where you learned this but I would welcome another opportunity to fence with you. My guess is that you have trained internationally at some point. You favour a North American style but you integrate a French and British style as well. When you regain your memory, come and see me."

"I'm very impressed Richard," said Lord Ashton. Then looking toward his good friend he said, "James, did you have any idea of this young man's talents?"

"I keep telling him that he never ceases to amaze me," replied Lord Lancaster. "I have said this before that lately we are learning more and more about him. I feel strongly that very soon he will regain his memory. We discussed this last week. There are clues that are pointing to his recovery."

CHAPTER EIGHTEEN

The celebration party in honour of Lady Monica Ashton's return was being held on the second Saturday in June at the Ashton Estate. The Lancasters were a little late in arriving due to the fact that they waited to pick Richard up at the airport where he had arrived from South Africa. They had brought his formal clothes along for him to change into. By the time Stewart pulled the car into the Ashton's large circular driveway, they could see that the court yard was already full of parked cars, all shiny and many with foreign names.

The Williscrofts were the first to see the Lancasters arrive and offered greetings. Of course they were forced to defend their late arrival which then prompted Mrs. Williscroft to ask countless questions of Richard about his work, his recent trip, whether he was regaining any of his memory, even if he had met any young women yet. The Williscrofts were good friends of the Lancasters. Mrs. Williscroft was genuinely concerned about people. She was kind hearted and would do anything to help someone in need. She contributed a great many hours each week to charitable organizations. Unfortunately though, she could, at times, be a very nosy and gossipy woman.

Mr. Williscroft, probably feeling some of the pain Richard was experiencing with the inquisition, subtley suggested to his wife that they excuse themselves to visit with some other friends he had just noticed in the crowd.

It was a very elegant and formal affair, but yet not stuffy at all, Richard thought. This was probably because, as Lady Lancaster had explained earlier, the gathering was strictly a mixture of Lord and Lady Ashton's family members and many friends, as well as those of Jason and Monica. Richard recognized a few of Jason's friends scattered about and anticipated chatting to them when the opportunity arose.

After some mingling and introducing Richard to a few other friends, Lord Lancaster was tapped on the shoulder from behind and heard Lord Ashton say, "Ah, you are finally here James. I understand Richard was late getting in from Cape Town."

"Yes, but we've actually been here for a while. Joy Williscroft latched on to Richard and wanted every detail of his life since he left the hospital."

"Oh James," defended Lady Lancaster, "It wasn't that bad. You know she is a kind and generous woman."

"Well at any rate you are here now and I want you to come and see my daughter," said Lord Ashton. "She's been asking about you. She's just over there with her mother." Lord Ashton pointed to an area on the other side of a baby grand piano near a large bay window facing out onto a lighted pool and fountain. Lady Monica Ashton was the same height as her mother and had amber hair. She wore a black and white cocktail dress that was stunning. Richard wondered how he hadn't noticed her in the room before now.

As Lord and Lady Lancaster approached Lady Monica Ashton, she turned and almost yelled, "Uncle James, Aunt Muriel, it's so great to see you!" She lunged forward to hug Lady Lancaster before turning to Lord Lancaster and giving him a smack on the cheek. "I have missed seeing you both. I especially missed our rides into the hills."

"You look wonderful Monica," exclaimed Lady Lancaster. "I think this travelling business must have been good for you. You will have to come for a visit and tell us all about it."

"My dear girl," said Lord Lancaster, you look prettier every time I see you. I am glad to see you home safe and sound, as I'm sure your parents are as well."

"Oh my goodness," said Lord Lancaster in an apologetic manner. "Monica, I would like you to meet Richard." Lord Lancaster turned aside revealing Richard who had been standing hidden behind Lord and Lady Lancaster. Lord Lancaster presented Richard with a gesture of his hand. "Richard, this is Monica. Lady Monica Ashton."

Monica looked up at Richard and her natural smile left her face for a moment as it transformed into an expression of wonderment and confusion. The expression had not been noticed before she regained her engaging smile and said to him, "How do you do Richard. It's nice to meet you."

Richard's immediate thought upon seeing and hearing Monica was that he was happy he had not missed the party, Mrs. Williscroft notwithstanding. She was cute and outgoing. Her voice was endearing and her words seemed sincere. Richard extended his hand and said, "Hello Monica, the pleasure is all mine." After holding her hand perhaps a moment or two longer than necessary, he released his gentle grip and said, "Jason didn't tell me nearly enough about you."

With a hint of flush in her cheeks, Monica gazed directly into his eyes to say, "Well he has told me something about you." With sincerity in her voice she continued, "I'm sorry that you have endured so many tribulations. Has any of your memory returned?"

"Not really but I'm starting to think it might be soon."

"You are very fortunate staying with Lord and Lady Lancaster," suggested Monica, turning in their direction.

Lord Lancaster entered the conversation saying, "Actually, we think that we are the lucky ones to have Richard living with us. We are very proud of his quick recovery and of the accomplishments he has made in such a short time." Continuing to boast about his ward, Lord Lancaster asked, "Did your father mention that Richard is working for our engineering company and that he has already saved us a few million dollars? We think he might be a recent engineering graduate."

This time the expression on Monica's face did not go unnoticed. Her mother said with a caring voice, "Monica, is something wrong?"

Monica regained her composure and her smile once again saying, "No mother, it's nothing." Trying to deflect any further questions Monica responded to Lord Lancaster, "No I didn't know he was working with your company, Uncle James."

Richard was starting to feel uncomfortable once again as the conversation seemed to revolve around him so he quickly intervened and said to Monica, pointing to her neck, "That's an unusual looking pendant you're wearing." He paused for a moment then asked in a teasing voice. "Is it a mouse?"

Monica's face transformed such that everyone could see her surprised expression. Clearly she was stunned. "Adam?" she gasped with excitement. "Adam is that you?"

"Do you know this young man?" asked her father.

"It can't be a coincidence," Monica responded looking at Richard. "Even though I know your face as been altered by plastic surgery, the first time I saw you I thought I recognized you. Then when I heard that you might be an engineer, I was even more puzzled. Now you just asked me the exact same question, the exact same question about my pendant that a boy I met in Morocco asked me. He and you are the only two people who have ever known this was a mouse." She held the pendant up to show everyone. "I think your name is Adam Ramsey."

"Richard, does any of what Monica said mean anything to you?" asked Lord Lancaster.

"I'm sorry but it doesn't," apologized Richard.

"Do you remember travelling with two fellows both named Ben?"

Richard took time to think before saying, "That doesn't ring a bell."

"I know," she said in revelation. "I used the name Baily. Do you remember me as Baily? We met in Fez."

Richard shook his head.

"What about Christmas day at our villa? You were playing the guitar and we were all singing Christmas carols?"

"We know that he plays the guitar," said Lady Lancaster. "He came with me to a children's home and played for some special needs children."

"The Adam I met told me he used to volunteer with children with a mental disability. You see this must be Adam." She moved closer to him, looked up to his face and said, "Adam, I know it is you. We just need to prove it and help you regain your memory."

Observing her daughter's obvious emotions, Lady Ashton asked with a hint of a smirk on her face, "Monica, how well did you know this Adam fellow anyway?"

Moving back from Richard, Monica said, "We were just close friends Mother."

Lord Ashton broke in to say, "I am sorry to have to break up this intriguing discussion, but we need to attend to our guests. It's time for the formalities unfortunately Monica."

"Perhaps it is just as well that we sit and stew about these new revelations for a time. As Monica said, we need absolute proof," said Lord Lancaster. With that, the group disbanded. The Ashton's moved toward the temporary platform that had been erected in the great hall.

"I imagine this has been a great surprise for you," Lord Lancaster said to Richard.

"You can say that again," replied Richard. "But so much she says makes sense. Can it all be one big coincidence? I wish I could remember."

"Well let's leave this for now as James has suggested. We can mull it over in the morning and see if it sounds anymore reasonable," said Lady Lancaster.

For Lord and Lady Lancaster, Richard and Monica, the recent conversation and allegations would not easily leave their minds. Richard fought for sleep that night but he lost the battle many times. He played the evening's conversation with Monica over and over in his mind. He tried to remember any association with the things that she had mentioned about an Adam Ramsey. He wondered what kind of a relationship she had had with Adam. On the one hand he wished it was romantic and fun and that he was actually Adam. On the other hand, if he wasn't Adam he was hoping that they were just friends. In any event, he had plans to get to know her more. With those thoughts he fell asleep.

The next morning, Monica came rushing into the dining room where Lord and Lady Ashton were having breakfast. Hardly able to get the words out fast enough she said, "I can prove it, I can prove Richard is Adam."

"Calm down Monica before you burst something," said her mother. "What do you mean you can prove Richard is Adam?"

"I know how I can prove that Richard is Adam, or that he isn't," she admitted. "We need to go over to Lancaster Manor right away to find out. Daddy please call them to say we're coming."

"Now just hold on a minute Monica. I'm not going to disturb James and Muriel so early in the morning. And what kind of proof are you talking about?"

"I need to show you. I need to show everyone. I am so sure it is him. It must be and I have a way of providing undeniable proof. Daddy please call them," she pleaded. "I can't wait to know for certain."

"Alright," conceded her father. "I'll call now and ask if and when it would be convenient to visit today."

The Ashtons were invited for a late lunch, which was set for 1:00 PM. All four of Astons arrived in one car at 12:45 PM. Jason wasn't present in the evening when Monica revealed that she knew who Richard really was, so he wasn't going to miss the show today.

Reston opened the door and greeted the Ashton's then led them into the parlour where Lord and Lady Lancaster were seated on a sofa in front of a fireplace. There were greetings all around when Monica asked, "Where is Richard?"

"Here I am," Richard said as he entered the room behind everyone. "Good day Lord Ashton, Lady Ashton, Jason and Monica."

Monica turned to Lady Lancaster and graciously thanked her for allowing the Ashtons to visit today. Not wanting to delay any further, knowing that lunch was to be served at any time, Monica said to them all, "I can prove that Richard is Adam."

"What proof do you have?" asked Lord Lancaster. "You certainly have peaked our interest, my dear."

Monica turned to Richard and said, "Take off your shirt."

"Monica!" exclaimed Lady Ashton. "What's gotten in to you?"

"You know how to get down to business, don't you Monica," teased Jason.

"Oh mother, I'm just asking Richard to take off his shirt, not his pants." She turned again to Richard and said, "Richard please."

All eyes were focused on Richard. He was still standing close to the entrance to the parlour facing them. "Alright, if you say so."

Richard drew his jersey over his head to reveal a solid frame. He had kept himself fit since all the physical rehabilitation. He regularly used the home gym and the lap pool. He often swam laps with Reston in the morning, part of Reston's normal morning routine.

"Now turn around," Monica spoke more softly to Richard.

Richard turned himself to face the entrance to the parlour so that his back was clearly visible to the Lancasters and the Ashtons. A coordinated gasp was heard from Lady Lancaster and Lady Ashton, their faces expressing a sense of shock. In addition to a number of small scars distributed over his back, there were two trails of raised scars - four wavy lines on each side from shoulders to waist. It wasn't anything pleasing to look at.

Lady Ashton lashed out at Monica, "Monica, why are you being so cruel. You know very well what happened to Richard when he was attacked. Why must you make the poor boy show us his dreadful scars?"

"Those scars aren't from the beating mother," responded Monica. "They're from a Grizzly bear that attacked Adam over three years ago, when he was planting seedlings in the wilds of northern Canada."

Richard turned back around in confusion. Lord Lancaster said, "I don't know about a Grizzly bear, but I can attest to the fact that the marks on Richard's back aren't from the beating he suffered several weeks ago. Dr. Rogers told me about these. He said they pre-existed his beating."

"I thought of it last night." Monica looked at Richard with caring eyes. "It was Christmas night in our villa in southern Spain. Everyone had gone to bed except Adam and me. We cleaned up and then sat together in front of the fireplace all night and talked. I sat in front of him and Adam brushed my hair for almost an hour, so long that he complained of a sore back. I asked him to take off his shirt so that I could rub his back. At first he didn't want to. He said that his back was kind of scary looking and he explained what had happened with the Grizzly bear. A friend was with him when he was attacked. They were both mauled and probably would have been killed, except that someone had come by with a rifle and ran the bear off. I told Adam that I was a nurse and wouldn't faint. I was shocked when I first saw the scars, just as you were Mother. But it didn't take long for me to see past them. I've touched those scars."

Monica's eyes were wet and starting to overflow. Lady Lancaster and Lady Ashton too found themselves wiping back tears. It was unclear as to whether the tears were of joy in the discovery of Richard's true identity or in hearing the heart wrenching story.

Monica walked over to a confused young man and held him close. "I missed you," she managed. "I hope you will soon start to remember again. I'll help you OK?"

Richard was at a loss for words. Monica had laid out a convincing story. Surely this was proof that he was Adam Ramsey. But he wished so much that he could remember. He looked down at Monica and said, "Well Monica or Baily, now I have even more inspiration to recover my memory. I'm going to hold you to your offer and I'm going to enjoy spending the time it takes." He smiled and looked around at everyone. "So are we all in agreement? I am now Adam Ramsey?"

"It would seem so," said Lord Ashton. "I'd say Monica has given us the proof we needed."

Lord Lancaster had been sitting in silence yet fully aware of all the drama and excitement felt through Monica's story about her and Adam. His thoughts were now focused on the ramifications of knowing this information. The difficulty in giving Richard an official temporary name and identification was enormous and highly irregular. He had had to stretch himself very thin in calling for the favours required to make these arrangements and in such a short time frame. He pictured in his mind what it was going to be like now, not even two months later, to undo what has been done and convince the authorities, both British and Canadian authorities, that Richard Lion is really Adam Ramsey. Richard didn't even have his memory back to corroborate the details. They only knew about Adam from Monica's experience. In his mind he was certain that the whole mess could be sorted out, but it would take a great deal of effort. Sworn affidavits would have to be taken from everyone who has been involved with Richard since the car crash. That meant the police, the hospital staff, ourselves, he thought, our friends, and Monica of course. Lord Lancaster then imagined how it would be necessary as well to have his parents and family involved to substantiate these claims. But then another problem came to mind: Richard doesn't look like Adam any longer. His parents may eventually come to understand and be convinced, but any photos of Adam, such as on a driver's license or a passport would not be supportive evidence. And how do we find his family, Lord Lancaster thought again. We may know he is Canadian, but there may be several people with the name Adam Ramsey. Perhaps, he thought, that it might be best to keep the status quo for a time, until Richard or Adam regained his memory.

Finally Lord Lancaster interrupted the jubilant conversation. "Excuse me everyone, I'd like to say something." There was quiet and all eyes turned to him. "We are all very happy for …", Lord Lancaster hesitated, ". . for Adam in discovering his real name and some things about himself. But it's a bit of a dilemma at the same time knowing still so very little. What we all seem to want right now is to tell everyone that Richard is actually Adam and to start addressing him so. But that's not really as easy as it sounds. There are a number of complications. All of his proof of identity, the kind that any person requires on a regular basis and more so if one needs to travel as Richard, sorry Adam does with his work, is in the name of Richard Lion. He can't claim to be anyone else until his papers are changed. If he tried, say at an airport, or just simply using a credit card, what would he say his name was. If he said Adam Ramsey and his identification said Richard Lion, I wager the police would be called. And if he can't claim to be Adam, how can we address him as Adam in public."

"But surely the answer is as simple as arranging for new documents?" questioned Lady Ashton.

"But it isn't that simple," replied Lord Lancaster, a little surprised and irritated that someone could think so. "It was highly irregular for the government authorities to grant Richard his current documents. To now go back to them, and not only British authorities but more importantly Canadian authorities, to claim that Richard is actually Adam, there will be significant challenges. I'm certain it can be done, of course, but it will take a great deal of effort and a great deal of time. And the fact that Richard still has not regained his memory doesn't help us any."

Richard said, "I understand and agree with Mr. Lancaster. It would be very difficult during the interim period, while trying to arrange for new identity documents to be known as one person for some purposes and another person for other purposes. Tomorrow for instance I can be Adam to you but when I buy my lunch with a credit card I will have to be Richard. If I mess up with the credit card and sign as Adam, I'll have a lot of explaining to do."

"Yes, I see what you mean now, "said Lady Ashton. "I'm sorry for thinking the solution was so simple. I can see now that it is not."

Lady Lancaster asked, "Well, where does that leave us. What should we do?"

Lord Lancaster said, "I suggest that we keep this news to ourselves for now. We don't tell anyone. As far as anyone else is concerned, Richard is still Richard for the time being. I will discuss the situation with my lawyers early next week and get them to make some enquiries, hypothetical of course, in order to understand what will need to be done to facilitate a formal and official change in identity. Two major impediments we have currently are that Richard still has not regained his memory and can't help us with details that would help support his claim to be Adam. The second is that he doesn't look like Adam. Monica wasn't certain herself! Even if Canadian authorities can find photographs of Adam from a driver's license or an old passport, they will likely not believe he is the same person. I know this is difficult for you Richard, but I see no other way until we can get a plan together. In the meantime, let's hope Monica can spring free that memory of yours."

All in the room made a pact to keep this new information to themselves. It was also agreed that they would all continue to call Adam, Richard, so as to lessen the chances of slipping up in public.

CHAPTER NINETEEN

That night Richard experienced another nightmare. This time, with fire all around him, the huge bear was beating him and yelling: Richard, Adam, Richard, Adam, alternating his names over and over again. He woke up trembling and calling out, pleading with the bear to stop. Beads of perspiration hung onto his forehead, the chest of his t-shirt was wet and clinging to his skin. A voice outside his door called to Richard to ask him if he was alright. With no answer after a second request, Reston rushed into the room.

"Master Richard, are you alright?" Reston could see the panic still frozen upon the young man's face. "Master Richard, it's me, Reston, everything is fine now. Please calm down, I'm here with you." Reston moved to the night table where a glass sat half filled with water. He turned on the bedside lamp and then offered the glass to Richard. "Drink some water, it will help calm you. But drink slowly," he cautioned Richard.

Richard's breathing began to ease. He took the glass again and emptied the last of the water into his mouth. He looked around to be sure of his bearings and only then did he realize who was with him. "Reston, thank you. I'm sorry for disturbing you. I had another dream."

"You didn't disturb me. I was actually on my way to the kitchen. I couldn't sleep and thought some warm milk would help. You did give me a terrible fright though. I was passing right by your door when you cried out. How are you feeling now?"

After apologizing again for causing such a commotion, Richard said, "I feel much better now." He looked at Reston and said, "Reston, let's not mention this to Lord and Lady Lancaster, alright? I don't want to upset Lady Lancaster. Promise?"

"Alright, if you say so. What about Lord Lancaster?"

"Maybe I'll mention it to him myself, but don't you say anything."

Reston didn't expect Richard to speak with Lord Lancaster about his dream, but he would keep his promise not to divulge knowledge of the night's incident. "If you are sure you are alright, I'll continue on to the kitchen. May I fetch you something?"

"No Reston, thank you. You have been very kind and helpful already. I'll be fine now. Good night."

It took some time for Richard to fall back to sleep, but he did and he slept well until his alarm clock sounded.

Little pools of water were scattered randomly on the surface of the highway into London and Richard was trying his best to avoid them while fighting to keep in his lane of traffic. It had rained heavily overnight and the morning didn't seem to have brought much relief. The windshield wipers were turned up to the second highest speed and fog was building up on the glass all around him, causing him to switch the fan to full force. Richard cursed the van passing him for splashing up a wall of dirty water onto his front window, sufficient enough that his wipers could not dispose of the grimy liquid in one swipe, thereby leaving him blinded while the car following the van approached – a little too close to the centre line he thought. His position about a hundred feet behind the semi-trailer was bad enough without more water hampering his view.

Richard had not mentioned last night's dream to Lord Lancaster at breakfast. He could have, since Lady Lancaster had not appeared until just before he left for work, but he didn't want to burden the man with his problems any more than he already had. He would have to work them out himself. During breakfast Lord Lancaster asked Richard about what they had discussed the day before and if he still agreed with the plan to consult the lawyers before divulging his real name. Richard said to Lord Lancaster that he still thought it was the right course to take. Lord Lancaster then said he would try to contact his lawyers later in the morning.

Richard pulled into the underground garage below the office building and found his assigned parking space. He walked the hundred and fifty feet to the elevator and met George Casper coming from a different direction. "Ah, good morning Richard," said George. "I'm glad I ran into you. Can you meet with me right after lunch today, say 1:15? I need to speak to you about something regarding the South African project."

"Sure thing," replied Richard. "Is there anything I need to prepare?"

"No, but it won't take long."

Richard wondered what George wanted with him. He certainly wasn't volunteering any hint.

When they reached their floor, George went in one direction and Richard headed in another. Before he went too far down the hall a voice chimed out behind him. "Oh Mr. Lion," called a woman wearing a baby blue two piece dress. Richard only knew that she worked in Sir Loxley's suite of offices. He didn't know her name and they had never met. As she approached him she said, "Sir Loxley would like you to see him at 2:00 this afternoon, after you meet with Mr. Casper."

"Alright, thank you." Richard now wondered how she knew that he was meeting with George today. After all, it was Monday morning and George had just entered the building with him. He would just have to wait and find out. He would also take some time over lunch to brush up on the status of the project. He wanted to be prepared when he met with his boss and the CEO of the entire company.

The first thing that Lord Lancaster did when he reached his office was to return a call from South Africa's Minister for the Interior, Jacob Renjeu. He had missed Minister Renjeu's telephone call of late Friday afternoon. Lord Lancaster and the Minister had developed a strong working relationship over the past number of years since Lord Lancaster's company undertook its first project in South Africa and since they had each become members of an international advisory council on environmental issues. Due to their many dealings over the years, they also had many occasions to socialize and had eventually become good friends, both having a great deal of respect for each other.

Lord Lancaster knew exactly why the Minister had been calling. The Minister wanted to confirm that Lord Lancaster would be attending the upcoming meeting with the Minister and his staff concerning some issues with the South African project. He also wanted to strengthen his Ministry's negotiating position with Lord Lancaster's company by trying to influence the company's chairman to reign down his own staff from their rock solid positions on the issues to date. Lord Lancaster was all too familiar with Minister Renjeu's strategies. He had used them himself on several occasions. But Lord Lancaster had two surprises for his South African friend. First he would advise him that he would not be attending the meetings after all. Second, he would tell the Minister that the company would be sending only the Project Director to the meeting and that that person would be on their own with the company's total confidence and full authority to negotiate as they saw fit. Lord Lancaster had a smile on his face as he thought about how his good friend would react. After a few moments the Minister came on the line, "Good morning James, how nice of you to return my call so soon."

Richard was ushered into George's office at precisely 1:15. He had run down to the cafeteria to grab a sandwich and soft drink to take back up to his office, then spent the rest of the noon hour gearing up for any potential questions George might have for him on the South African project. He had arrived at George's office with only a pad of paper and his pen.

"Thanks for coming Richard," George said to him as he entered the office. "Have a seat. I've just been called to attend an emergency meeting over at Crenshaw's. It seems the buggers are wanting to back out of our contract, so I will have to come right to the point. I received a call from Jennifer on Saturday. Her pregnancy is not going well. She is having some complications and her doctor wants her to stop working now, rather than in another three months. Of course she has to do what is best for the baby and for herself. I've discussed the situation with John and Sir Loxley and we all agree that you are the most logical person to take over as Project Director. Jennifer agrees as well. She indicated that the rest of the staff would have no problem with you taking over. You have proven yourself many times over. So, do you accept the new position?"

Jennifer was five months pregnant. Richard knew that she had planned to begin maternity leave in about three months and he secretly hoped that he would be given consideration for the Project Director position when Jennifer left. While much of the planning work had been completed, including the enhancements he was responsible for, development and installation was still months away. His tenure as Project Director would be responsible for success or failure of the project.

This news came as a complete surprise to him. But he knew in his heart that he was ready. He had developed a great deal of confidence in himself over the past number of weeks at Regal, and so apparently had his bosses. "I'm sorry about Jennifer," he said first, and he meant it. "I really appreciate the offer and yes, I accept. Thank you very much."

"I hope you feel the same way in a few weeks," remarked George. "The position obviously comes with additional responsibility and challenges, but we think you are up to those challenges. Your pay grade will increase of course, but you will earn every penny." Searching for a piece of paper on his desk, George continued, "Ah, here is what I'm looking for. Jennifer is expecting your call. She said that it would be best to call her tomorrow after lunch. She wanted to speak to you about a few matters in order to help transition you into the position. Here's her number. After that, you will have to use your own resources. This is a relatively small project Richard, but in many ways it has challenges we don't always encounter. You are already aware of the huge potential for similar projects of this nature, possibly on much larger scales, if we are successful with this. This project could open many doors for the company."

Richard was nodding in agreement pretending that he was well aware of all the challenges. In truth he wasn't, but he also wasn't about to show his current apprehension in front of his boss. He would have time to figure things out.

George stood while gathering up some files from his desk and said, "OK then, congratulations Richard. I'm sorry I don't have more time to spend with you today. If you need to speak to me, just drop in. Otherwise, I'll see you next on Friday morning when I normally meet with the Project Directors."

Richard took the cue to leave. He thanked George once again and turned to exit the office. He paused and turned back to George to say, "Excuse me George, did you know that Sir Loxley wants to see me at 2:00 today?

"Yes," was all George replied.

"Do you know why he wants to see me? Does it have anything to do with South Africa?

Without looking up at Richard, George said, "Yes and yes, offering nothing further. Then looking up with a slight smirk on his lips he said, "You'll have to find out more from Sir Loxley."

Richard sat down at his desk still wondering what the mystery was about Sir Loxley wanting to meet with him. He had attended some meetings in Sir Loxley's office before of course, but only in the company of his bosses. This was highly irregular he thought to himself. Before he could think more of it, two heads appeared around the edge of the doorway. "Congratulations boss!" the two men said in unison. "We just heard the news. Too bad for Jennifer, but we're glad you got the nod."

Richard was surprised that the word had gotten out so soon, but appreciated the vote of confidence from two of his colleagues. "Thanks guys." With a bit of a tease he said. "You know of course that I'll have to fast track the learning curve which means you two will be working harder than I will to bring me up to speed."

One of the men said, "Bring it on boss." They all chuckled and agreed on a time for a briefing meeting.

Richard made certain that he would not be late for a meeting with the President and CEO of Port of Grace Enterprises, the parent company which oversaw Regal Engineering and many other subsidiary companies. He arrived at the executive suite of offices ten minutes before 2:00. At one minute to the hour, John Maxwell passed Richard heading to Sir Loxley's door. "We'll be with you in a minute Richard." Richard was at first surprised to see the Regal Engineering President, but then reasoned that it would be normal for the head of the engineering company responsible for the South African project to be at the same meeting.

At two minutes after 2:00, Richard was shown into Sir Loxley's office.

The two men rose from their chairs and greeted Richard by congratulating him on his promotion. There was some generous mention of his skills and his value to the company before Sir Loxley got down to the reason why he had asked Richard to meet with him and John.

"Late last week we were informed by the South African government that they may not be able to honour the agreement on our water/hydro project. They cited a number of issues that must be resolved to their satisfaction. Depending on how serious the South African government is about their concerns, this project could come to a crashing halt. A meeting has been scheduled in Cape Town two weeks from tomorrow. Lord Lancaster, John and I discussed the matter Sunday afternoon after hearing about Jennifer and agreeing on your promotion. We had already conceded before we had heard about Jennifer that you had the greatest knowledge of the enhanced project, even more than Jennifer had, and would be the most effective person to represent the project and the interests of both the company and Lady Lancaster's charitable organization. The problem was that, as a junior engineer, you wouldn't be respected or accepted by the African officials. That is no longer a problem; your new position will give you the legitimate authority to deal with the South Africans. As Project Director, you will be representing the company at the meeting in an effort to convince the South African bureaucrats, specifically officials from the Department of the Interior, that the project can still be a success for all concerned and that we can work through or around the issues."

John carried on with the briefing. "This matter is very important for us, yet extremely sensitive for the South Africans. The bureaucrats need to be on side as much as the political leadership if we are going to succeed with this project and many more we hope to gain in the country. The bureaucrats have to speak with someone they can understand and they must feel convinced that they have influence with the politicians regarding the direction of the project. That being the case, we have decided that only you will go to Cape Town. Only you will represent the company. Lord Lancaster spoke to Minister Renjeu this morning to advise him. He also told the Minister that you had the company's total confidence and full authority to speak to the South Africans and to try to resolve the issues before us. Apparently, the Minister was at first very annoyed that we were sending only the Project Director, but Lord Lancaster explained the strategy and the Minister could see the merit in this approach. So it's all set. We have two weeks to get you ready. But I'll be frank with you Richard, I truly believe that if you can handle yourself with the confidence, knowledge and passion you expressed when you first mentioned the hydro power enhancement to us, you will do fine. It may turn out that the South Africans have already made up their minds to kill the project and they are just going through the paces. In that case it wouldn't matter who we send."

Richard sat alert but in silence as Sir Loxley and John Maxwell generally described the nature of the mission on which he was being sent. The details would come in the next few days but he already had enough information to give him a clear understanding that his diplomatic as well as his technical skills would be fully tested. As he was listening to the two company executives he realized that the emotions building inside him were more of excitement than fear. On the other hand, he thought, the fear would come later. Not the fear he had experienced when the Grizzly bear attacked or when the three men started beating him, but the fear of being this massive company's sole representative to save an important project.

Suddenly, Richard gasped out loud realizing that he had just recalled two incidents from his memory – the bear attack and the beatings involving the Lancasters. This was the very first time any of his memory had come to life. Up until this point he was only aware of the attacks through his dreams or from Monica and the Lancasters telling him about them. For a moment he completely forgot where he was and the important topic being discussed with Sir Loxley and John.

Sir Loxley, obviously seeing what he thought was Richard's startled reaction to the information about his mission to South Africa said, "I'm sorry Richard, we know this is a great deal to throw at you all at once, but you need to know that we have faith in you and we wouldn't have made this decision if we didn't think you could handle it."

Richard stared at Sir Loxley and responded saying, "I'll admit that I am overwhelmed with this information, but I'll also admit that I feel really quite excited with the opportunity and the challenges. I'm about twenty-five years old. I have been with Regal Engineering for just a short time. You said yourself this mission could be for naught. I have very little to lose and an awful lot to gain if this goes the company's way. I am going to be trying my damned best to see that it does."

Richard took a breath before continuing. He had a wide smile on his face. "But what you saw and heard me react to was something I was thinking about that doesn't have anything to do with South Africa, or at least not directly. While I was listening to you I could feel anxiety was building up inside me but I was telling myself that it wasn't fear. I was telling myself about the real fear I experienced when the Grizzly bear attacked me and when the three men beat me and Lord Lancaster. Don't you see, my memory, I have regained some small part of my memory for the very first time." Richard was almost beside himself in jubilation.

"That's fantastic," remarked Sir Loxley. "Lord Lancaster had mentioned that you were experiencing snippets of memory. Maybe this is just the start of more to come."

"I'm sorry to get off topic, but I couldn't help myself," said Richard. "About the South African project, I'm anxious to start preparing for the meeting. It's not much time and already, as I was listening, I was formulating thoughts about some additional information I would like to have."

"That's what I wanted to here," said John Maxwell. "Get some thoughts together in the next few days and we'll convene a bit of a think tank before the end of the week. Get anyone you need involved in this. I'll talk to George as well."

Richard left the office ahead of John Maxwell, his head full of thoughts regarding South Africa, blended with his epiphany regarding his memory. He was anxious to speak to Lord Lancaster about both. He wondered if Lady Lancaster knew about the problems with her South African project. He bet not. He decided he would speak to Lord Lancaster alone first. In any event, the next two weeks were going to be extremely busy. And he was gung ho!

CHAPTER TWENTY

With Monica starting her new nursing position, interestingly, at Mount Royal hospital, but in the obstetrics ward, and with Richard's promotion and need to prepare for the South African meetings, the young pair didn't have much time to see one another during the next two weeks. Monica was elated of course about his memory recall, as were the Lancasters, although she wished it had been concerning something less frightening. But she did accept that it was a beginning. She was also extremely proud of Richard receiving not only the promotion but the vote of confidence from company executive regarding his mission to South Africa.

On the two occasions they did share during that two week period, they went for dinner to be by themselves. Monica would talk about their time together in Morocco and Spain in the hope that something she said would spark Richard's memory, but nothing did. After a while without any progress they could both feel frustrations rising and wisely agreed to switch subjects and not try so hard on the memory thing. Richard mentioned that Lord Lancaster and he managed to have his identification papers, including his passport extended, this time for six months. They were hoping that this would be the last time it would be required. He also mentioned that Lord Lancaster had spoken with his lawyers and that they would begin to look into the matter of having Richard's name officially changed back to his real name of Adam Ramsey. The lawyers indicated, as was expected, that it would be a challenge and especially difficult if Richard continued to suffer from amnesia. They told Lord Lancaster they would have a report for him within a couple of weeks.

As Richard had expected, Lady Lancaster was not apprised of the concerns in South Africa and Lord Lancaster emphasized the need for secrecy. He knew that Lady Lancaster would be furious with him once she found out, or if she found out. He had hopes, however, that Richard would be successful in resolving the issues and she wouldn't hear about them at all. Lord Lancaster repeated the confidence the company and he himself had in Richard to do his best. That's all they could ask for. They believed this strategy was their best chance for success. Lord Lancaster also mentioned that he told Minister Renjeu that Richard was the Project Director. He further mentioned that Richard's relationship with Lord Lancaster would not benefit him in his dealings with the bureaucrats, but that Minister Renjeu did give Lord Lancaster assurances that Richard would be treated with respect and would be given a fair hearing. Lord Lancaster didn't expect and didn't ask for anything more.

In the two weeks prior to the South African meeting, Richard and his new staff broke new overtime records for their unit. To his and their credit everyone pitched in without any complaints. Richard had been advised by John Maxwell and George Casper that the first issue the South African bureaucrats had raised was actually a series of logistical concerns. Apparently, even though they had been agreed to weeks ago, the bureaucrats indicated that they had not fully understood the critical plan involving the order in which certain aspects of the proposed work needed to be completed and could not authorize the previously agreed to government staff to participate at the times specified in the plan. These particular concerns in time-activity planning were stretched out over the life of the project. Richard would take these issues back to the drawing board and see what options his staff could come up with and what overall impact they would have to the budget and timeframe. The second issue concerned what only now the government bureaucrats say they fully understood was the on-going infrastructure operating and maintenance costs in the three communities once the project construction was completed. They indicated that they were not fully apprised of the full cost implications and that this would be too much of a burden for the communities to bear and that the government would then be called upon to subsidize the costs. Everyone at Regal Engineering recognized this issue for what it really was, an attempt to leverage more non-government funds for the project. Richard knew this matter would take some different thinking and some different strategizing. But he had a plan already formulating in his mind. He just hoped he and his staff had enough time to prepare the information Richard would need to make his case.

Because practically all of Richard's extra time was being consumed with work, he was excused from driving up to Coventry on one of the Lancaster's regular visits with Judith. On this occasion the Lancasters had Stewart behind the wheel of Lord Lancaster's new sedan. Lord Lancaster had replaced the town car lost in the fire with a full size Lexus. As always, Judith was full of questions, wanting to know everything new with the Lancasters and especially with Richard. Before the Lancasters departed from Judith's home, she felt that she had successfully interrogated the Lancasters into revealing everything about him.

When Edward had called his mother the day following the Lancaster's visit, Judith talked for a solid hour about Richard and his successes, as well as the fact that there were signs of him regaining his memory. She mentioned how the Lancasters on more than one occasion mentioned how proud they were of him. She remarked that they were talking about the young man as if he was their own son. She said she was happy that Richard had entered their lives. Listening to his mother carry on and on, Edward began to think that she was actually gloating over Richard herself. When he met with some of his buddies at the pub that night, Edward was not so kind in his description of his uncle's new fair haired boy. Being as ignorant as he was about the facts concerning Richard's rising success, coupled with his growing hatred for both his uncle and Richard, the boy who could do no wrong, the four pints of beer he consumed in record time only spoke of retribution and a mumbling about some plan that would have to move forward sooner than expected.

CHAPTER TWENTY-ONE

Richard was escorted into a large board room on the fifth floor of the Ministry of the Interior's office building by a young woman who he suspected was in her mid-twenties. She was short and plump, very friendly, very happy and very pretty. She introduced herself as Mary. It was 8:45 in the morning and the meeting was scheduled to begin at 9:00. Before leaving him, Mary offered Richard coffee, but he declined.

Richard had arrived in Cape Town on the afternoon before the meeting day. An assistant of Minister Renjeu's met him at the airport and delivered him to his hotel. The assistant indicated that he would be back at 8:30 the next morning to take him to the meeting at the government offices where he found himself now.

With time to spare, rather than doing some last minute cramming before the other meeting members arrived, which would only have increased his anxiety levels, Richard decided to walk about the room to look at the many pictures and maps that hung on the walls. Almost immediately he spotted a map of South Africa hanging on the wall opposite the windows. It was a large scale map showing town sites and roadways, rivers and lakes and elevations. A number of red and green dots were scattered almost equidistant from one another throughout the country. There were far more red dots than green. Upon further review, Richard saw the purpose of the map printed in the lower right hand corner. It read, Proposed Cellular Towers. The green dots represented towers that existed and the red dots represented towers that were planned. Richard was aware that the vast majority of South Africa was rural and remote land. Only a quarter of the country had electricity. Communication, while more of a necessity today, was made difficult and he surmised that building a series of state-owned cellular towers was being considered as an affordable solution. He also figured that it would take the government many more years before they could accomplish their plan. As he strolled over to look at a unique piece of art work standing on a pedestal in the corner, the door to the conference room opened behind him.

"Mr. Lion," boomed a deep voice coming from a tall dark man dressed immaculately in a crisp blue grey suit, starched white shirt and silk striped tie. "Welcome to South Africa."

Following the distinguished looking man into the room were three other gentleman, two white and one black. It was clear to Richard even before introductions, that the deep voice belonged to Minister Renjeu and that the three gentlemen not so crisply attired, were the departmental officials. Introductions confirmed this.

Richard had been briefed a little about the Minister before leaving London. He had been in office for many years and would likely continue his role, if not a more powerful one, for many more. He was considered to be a very intelligent man and very shrewd as well. He was said to have a great deal of important contacts in South Africa and beyond and walked easily among some very wealthy and powerful people. Somewhat surprisingly, he was also considered to be a fair man and was respected for this trait by most who knew him, Lord Lancaster for one.

The taller of the white officials was introduced by the Minister as Mr. Donald Bacon, the Assistant Deputy Minister for Infrastructure in the Ministry of the Interior. He was the most senior government official aligned with the project. Besides being tall, he was clean shaven, he had most of his sandy blond hair, he wore wire rimmed glasses and spoke softly and with confidence. He was in his late-forties or early fifties and he was friendly and outgoing. The same could not be said for the other two men, Boze and Shiring, the other white man. They were the antithesis of the Assistant Deputy Minister. They were introduced as being senior engineers responsible for the project working under Bacon. Both were extremely suspicious looking and cordial rather than friendly. It seemed to Richard that they were trying to purposely display an attitude and a message that he had better have come up with the goods if this project was going anywhere. They made a comment that it seemed strange for Regal Engineering to send only one delegate to this important meeting, especially one so young. Richard ignored the comment. He sensed the pair were salivating and eager for combat.

After the introductions had been made Minister Renjeu explained that he himself would not be taking part in the discussions but he would be auditing them, at least for a while. The officials must have already known about the roles to be played as there was no reaction from any of them. The Minister was actually a man of few words and ended by saying that he hoped that the morning's discussions would be successful. Richard was not sure what successful meant for the South Africans.

Bacon immediately took over from Minister Renjeu asking Richard if he was fully aware of the issues before them or if Bacon should spend some time to outline them to him. Richard believed he said this legitimately, wanting to be helpful.

Richard thanked Bacon for the offer but indicated that he had been fully briefed. "As a matter of fact, Mr. Bacon, I would like to begin our discussions by coming to an agreement right away on the purpose of this meeting and what we both hope to achieve." Richard did not allow enough time during his pause for anyone to speak. "I believe there are four major parties who have a great deal of interest in the outcome of this meeting: the three communities, the charitable organization that originally applied to sponsor the project, the Ministry of the Interior representing the South African government, and finally, Regal Engineering. The last two parties, represented by ourselves, have the controlling interest" He lifted his hands to indicate he meant the people in the room. "What we decide here today will have a significant impact on the other two. So it is important for us to be very candid about what we want from the meeting. I am assuming that we both want this project to go ahead and that while we both may have some concerns about this or that aspect of the project, we want to work together to resolve the issues so that the project can proceed. Quite frankly gentleman, if you are not in agreement with what I have just professed, we can save each other a lot of valuable time and leave now."

During his opening remarks Richard was sure to address each of the government officials, saving most eye contact for the Assistant Deputy Minister. While he was speaking, Richard had noted that one of the engineers, Shirling, was itching to say something. When Richard had concluded, Shirling did not hesitate but spoke right up. "Mr. Lion you speak as if you believe the parties are equal in this proposed project. Keep in mind that unless the South African government …"

Shirling's words were halted by Bacon who very calmly said, "Excuse me Mr. Shirling for interrupting. Mr. Lion, I believe you have outlined our common position quite well. The Ministry of the Interior has welcomed the proposal for this project and also wishes to be able to proceed. That being said, our Ministry has identified some significant issues that must be resolved to our satisfaction. I'm sure your company has been in similar situations in the past. Doubtless some of our own solutions to these issues will leave you with concerns as well. In short Mr. Lion, I believe we have sufficient cause to continue. But thank you for this introduction."

Richard had accomplished what he wanted from his opening statements. He knew who his adversaries were and who was more prepared to consider options. He also believed that the leadership of the Ministry truly did wish the project to go forward, but that it may require some give and take. That's all he could hope for. He was prepared.

Richard also had the opportunity to notice Minister Renjeu's reaction to the initial discussions. Actually there wasn't much to see. Only his eyes seemed to move, casually from one speaker to another with no change in facial expression. He must have seemed satisfied with the outcome, or if he didn't, he kept his word about not interfering.

Richard responded to Bacon as politely and as professionally as Bacon had to him. "I'm glad we are all on the same page Mr. Bacon. Thank you."

Richard pulled a bundle of paper and a pad and pen from his brief case saying, "I would like to address the series of what I will refer to as logistical issues first if that is alright?" Bacon nodded .

Richard handed out a set of papers to each of the officials as well as to Minister Renjeu. "What you have before you printed in bold type is a summarized description of the issues your Ministry has identified which are logistical in nature and present themselves at four different points along the original critical path we developed some time ago." Richard did not add that the original critical path had also been agreed to at the time. "For each issue we have developed two or three options for your consideration. Now the tricky part here is that the options presented are interrelated, in that approval of an option for the first issue may require a specific option from a subsequent issue in order to be feasible. I'd like to take you through them one at a time. If we can agree on a suitable option for the first issue, I will explain which other options are necessary down the line and which are still open for discussion. Any questions so far?"

Shirling said, "I can see that the first option for the first issue won't work already."

"Perhaps you'll allow me to make my presentation before you jump to a conclusion," Richard responded, still in a level tone. What an ass he thought to himself.

"Please continue," said Bacon as he gave Shirling a warning look.

"Alright, in developing some of these options we discovered that there may also be some cost savings depending on whether they are acceptable from a logistical point of view. In other words, there may be an option that does not at first glance appear feasible, but when looking at the potential cost savings, there may be room for further consideration. By the way, I am referring to cost savings for your Ministry."

"Very interesting, Mr. Lion," said Bacon. "Please continue." Boze looked at Shirling silently communicating for him to keep his cool.

After two and a half hours of a solid and gruelling examination of the options, the group was prepared to review what they thought might be workable solutions. Bacon called for a fifteen minute break before they proceeded. He also suggested that they order in lunch as it seemed clear they would be working through the noon hour at least. On the way to the men's room, Richard was replaying some of the morning's discussion in his head. Shirling had settled down early on in the presentation after the potential for cost savings to the Ministry were mentioned. From that point on, the presentation and requests for clarification went smoothly. He was feeling reasonably comfortable so far.

When Richard returned to the meeting room he found Minister Renjeu in conversation with Bacon. Minister Renjeu broke off with Bacon and signalled for Richard to join them. "Mr. Lion, Donald and I were just saying that we thought the meeting was moving along quite well. I must attend to some matters that have just come to my attention, but I expect to return before your discussions are concluded." The Minister moved through the doorway and Boze closed the door. Bacon asked everyone to take their seats so that they could continue.

During the next hour the advantages and disadvantages to both parties of the various options and their interdependencies were reviewed. A few options were easily cast aside early on by both Bacon and Richard, as neither found them workable. These included some of the options Richard's unit had prepared which were meant to be throw-aways, a strategy to make the Ministry think they were influencing the negotiations. Most of the remaining options were viewed as possible, with conditions. Clearly the Ministry's officials wanted to look good to their superiors and saving Ministry funds was a way to do it, while ensuring that the project went ahead. In the end, after the hour of give and take, Bacon announced that they agreed with the last proposal of options discussed. While it would put some strains on their resources, even with the cost savings identified, he indicated that he believed the Ministry could manage them. Richard could play the martyr game as well as his counterpart and left the three officials believing that Regal Engineering would take a hit with these changes, but that they could live with it if it meant that the project would go forward. In fact, Richard had ended up almost where he had hoped as far as a final negotiating position was concerned and far better than where he was prepared to go to ensure the project would proceed. He looked at his watch. It took three and a half hours, but they had made it past the first set of hurdles.

The second and last issue was straight forward, but possibly more critical an issue for the Ministry. The Ministry claimed that they were not made aware of the full costs for on-going operations and maintenance and that they were not prepared to commit to these costs. This was a joke back at Regal. Richard's unit could not believe that the government officials would pull a stunt like this when the preliminary agreement that they had signed clearly outlined all expenses in the budget. Richard would not make a big deal of the obvious ploy to again reduce the Ministry's financial exposure on this project. He had come with a plan that he felt would satisfy the Ministry and besides, his confidence level had increased substantially with the first set of victories.

Richard explained that neither the charitable organization nor Regal were in the business of operating a facility. The by-laws of the charitable organization outlined very clearly that they could only finance one-time capital costs for the development and construction of the necessary infrastructure. Richard further explained how the South African government was getting a better deal than originally intended since the hydro enhancement was going to allow for some much needed electricity to allow for three resource centres to be developed. And the capital cost was all being funded without South African dollars. Richard knew full well that the officials recognized the benefits of this project. They just wanted a better deal.

Richard shuffled a few papers to get himself organized before he spoke. He did not pass out any documents or proposals to the officials. "I am authorized to include the cost of building and outfitting the three resource centres in the communities as part of our contribution." Richard mentioned the proposed buildings, their dimensions and the materials that would be used to construct them, the number of computers, furniture, freezers and fridges that would be supplied. "In addition, funds will be provided to stock a medical clinic for six months, provided a medical practitioner is hired. This is what we will commit to in a revised agreement, if you agree to pay for the on-going operations as earlier described."

The three officials huddled together for a few minutes and whispered among themselves. It was evident on Shirling's face that he wanted to fight for more. He could not read Bacon's expression as he listened to his staff.

Finally the three bureaucrats separated. "Mr. Lion," Bacon said. "Your offer is very generous. Clearly we do see the benefits of saving funds for the one-time costs. However, let me tell you something that we must deal with on a regular basis. All governments, not just ours, are bombarded with these types of proposals from similar organizations who I believe truly want to help a population in need. If the government had the funds it would do this work themselves. Part of the reason they can't is because government cannot afford the entire costs. It must look at the total costs of funding a project, which includes long term operating and maintenance costs when it reviews such projects. These costs, as you must know Mr. Lion, can amount to much more than the original capital costs over time. I'm sorry but we cannot accept this offer. The on-going operating costs are too much of a burden."

As Richard was thinking of something to say that wouldn't be antagonistic, the door opened and Minister Renjeu walked in. "Excuse me for interrupting, please continue." He sat at the end of the table in his former chair.

"Actually Minister, perhaps now would be a good time to take a short break. Do you agree Mr. Lion?" said Bacon.

Richard did not have a great deal more to throw on the table but he knew he could use a little time to formulate an alternative or additional proposal. He was prepared to offer a greater amount of hydro power to the three communities using slightly larger generators. They were still based on the same new technology for small systems but were more efficient. Again, it would only require some additional capital. Lord Lancaster would just have to hit on more contributors. The question that Richard didn't have an answer to was why the Ministry would want to agree to the increase in power? How would this benefit them enough to change their minds about funding operating costs? "Yes, I agree, Mr. Bacon. A few minutes would be appreciated."

Bacon motioned to the Minister indicating that he wanted a word with him in the hallway. Bacon's two staff followed behind them.

Richard drummed his pen on the table staring out the window searching the blue sky for an answer, something he could work with. He swivelled around on his chair as if an answer might appear from somewhere within the room as the sky wasn't yielding any ideas. His eyes drifted to the wall map he had seen earlier in the morning, the one that depicted proposed cellular towers. An idea started to form in his head. He leaped from his chair and walked over to the map. After studying it for a few minutes he noticed that two proposed cellular tower sites were positioned very near two of the three communities in the project. He thought to himself, near enough!

Richard managed to find his way back to his chair as the four men entered the room.

"Are we ready to proceed?" asked Bacon.

"Yes, I believe so," replied Richard. His confidence had suffered a blow a short while ago, but now he was newly invigorated. He was also certain that Bacon had briefed Minister Renjeu on the current state of affairs with respect to the negotiations. He most likely told the Minister that he had Richard cornered and that he expected the only way out was for Regal to sweeten the pot further so that the Ministry would not have to pay on-going costs. Richard wondered if Bacon also told the Minister that Regal could just as well give up on the project. He also wondered if that would matter to the South Africans. But something led him to think that the Minister wanted this project, even if the officials didn't. Richard would first play some hardball.

"At the beginning of the meeting, some five hours ago, I believe we had agreed that we both wanted this project to continue. We worked diligently together to successfully resolve the first series of logistical issues. In attempting to resolve this final issue, I have outlined a significantly enhanced offer. Your response, Mr. Bacon was simply that you can't accept it. You haven't even attempted to contribute to a way around this barrier. Frankly, I am not certain that we are operating under the same principles we had agreed to earlier and further I am getting tired of a process where we seem to agree on something only to be refuted later by your Ministry's officials." From the corner of his eye Richard thought he could see the slightest smile upon Minister Renjeu's face. But the Minister said nothing.

Before Bacon could respond Richard continued. "Before you tell me again about how government works and its battle to find money for all the projects thrown at it, Mr. Bacon, let me toss you one more carrot." Richard was on a roll and he was a little pissed off as well, but he still knew he was in control of himself. "We will invest additional funds in our generators in order to provide a greater amount of hydro power to two of the three communities. The surplus power can then be sold to the Ministry. The revenue to the communities can be used to offset the operating costs for the resource centres."

This time the Minister actually shifted his weight in his chair and looked directly over to Bacon. He still remained silent. Richard was not finished yet, but he held back for the reaction from Bacon or his underlings. He secretly hoped that Shirling would speak out again.

After a short huddle, Bacon said, "Well Mr. Lion, you have given us a great deal to think about. I applaud your resourcefulness in coming up with a means to generate surplus electricity for these communities, but we are uncertain how that will help. Do you also have some idea as to how the Ministry could use this surplus energy and why we would wish to pay for it?"

"Yes Mr. Bacon, I do and I believe you will come to realize that it is a good one. But since I am the one who has thought of it and not your staff, the idea is going to cost you more than a partial operating cost. I have gone overboard to try to gain your support on these issues. I'm afraid this is my last shot. Take it or leave it. The fate of this project is in your hands."

"What is this big idea of yours," blasted Shirling.

Richard first spoke to Shirling then returned his attention to Bacon. "You will pay the two communities for the hydro needed to power two cellular towers. Regal Engineering will fund the installation of the towers and the Ministry will give Regal a contract to undertake a feasibility study and costing of installing further cellular towers on your grid there up on the wall near communities that could benefit from small system generators similar to the ones we are talking about here. Just a cursory look at the map leads me to believe that there could be enormous opportunities. Finally, if the feasibility study is acceptable, Regal gets first option on contracting for the hydro and cellular tower installations."

Silence prevailed in the room. Boze looked at Shirling trying to figure out what was just said. Bacon was writing notes on his pad. A few more moments held the silence before Minister Renjeu said, "Mr. Lion, I wonder if you will excuse us for a few minutes."

"Of course," Richard replied, hardly able to contain himself from giving out a cheer.

Nearly thirty minutes had passed before Bacon re-entered the room. He apologized for taking so long and indicated that Minister Renjeu would not be returning, nor would the other two officials. He asked Richard if he was prepared to put his most recent offer in writing before he left for London. Richard said that he was prepared to do just that, if the Ministry was prepared to agree and sign the agreement. Still trying to test Richard, Bacon asked him if he had the authority to sign such an agreement on behalf of Regal Engineering. Richard said that he did and that Minister Renjeu was aware that he did.

It took Richard and a secretary loaned to him over two hours to document the morning's resolutions as well as the new proposed agreement which included additional hydro power and cellular tower installations. The secretary had to work overtime but she said that it was alright with her; she could use extra pay. Richard was not concerned about having to catch any particular flight as he had come to Cape Town on the Port of Grace Enterprises company jet. With a half hour notice, the jet would be ready for flight.

Once the documents were completed, Richard read them thoroughly and made a few amendments. He read them over two more times before they were passed on to Bacon. A half hour after having received the documents, Bacon came out of his office to speak to Richard. "This looks fine, except for one minor point that I think you will agree with." He showed the document to Richard and Richard indicated that he agreed with the revision proposed. Bacon asked the secretary to make the revision as quickly as she could and then to make two originals for signature. While they waited, Bacon said to Richard, "Should I expect to see you in the future with respect to this project?"

Feeling more casual now, Richard said, "I assume so, but the way things have been going for me over the past couple of months, who knows."

"I was told about the incident involving Lord and Lady Lancaster and yourself and how you had been in a coma for so long. I hope I am not being too personal in asking you this question, but your situation is most interesting. Is it true that you still suffer from amnesia?"

"Yes, unfortunately, although there have been signs lately that suggest to my doctors that my memory should come around soon now."

"Well, I hope it does. And I also hope that I will have the opportunity to work with you again." The secretary came back, but without the agreements. "Mary will take you to Minister Renjeu's office. He will have the agreements ready for your signature. Have a safe trip home Mr. Lion."

"Please call me Richard. And thank you. I too look forward to meeting you again."

"It's Donald. Good bye then." Donald Bacon turned and walked briskly down the hall in the direction opposite to where Mary guided Richard.

"Come in Mr. Lion," boomed Minister Renjeu, as Mary opened the Minister's office door for Richard. "Please, have a seat." The Minister gestured with his hand for Richard to sit at the large working table to the right of the Minister's desk. Richard noticed right away that two original copies of the agreement had been placed on the table, ready for signature. "Please take a final look at the agreement and sign both copies if you are satisfied."

Richard examined the agreement carefully for the last time, then went to sign both copies. He paused for a moment, looked up at Minister Renjeu, then proceeded to place his signature in the space over the name Regal Engineering. While he tried not to show it, Richard was surprised to see that the agreement had already been signed for the Ministry and that the signature was that of the Minister himself.

"Thank you Minister. This has been a long but successful day for all concerned." Richard took one of the copies of the agreement and placed it in his brief case.

"It is I who owe you the thanks Mr. Lion. You came with a purpose of resolving the issues before us and you proved very resourceful in achieving that goal. We want very much for this project and many more like it to be undertaken in our country, but wanting something, even when it makes all kinds of sense and you believe you have the budget, is not always enough. Mr. Bacon was quite correct about how government works. Our Ministry must satisfy the larger government on several matters before we can proceed to commit funds. This was one of them."

The Minister paused and looked down at his hands as if considering whether he should continue to say what was on his mind. As he lifted his head again he said, "I'm afraid we mislead you somewhat today Mr. Lion. Mr. Shirling, who you were clearly not impressed with, is not a member of Mr. Bacon's staff as you were told. He actually represents the government's Treasury Board and was present to determine whether there was merit from a central government perspective to proceed with the project. The plan for the cellular towers happens to be a priority for government and your proposal opened up a potential low cost means of accelerating installations. I don't know how you came up with the concept on the spur of the moment as you did, but you sold Mr. Shirling and you certainly impressed Mr. Bacon and me. So you see, Mr. Lion, this is why it is I who owe you the thanks. I will be passing on these sentiments to Sir Loxley and Lord Lancaster as well. I expect that they will be very pleased with your performance here today."

Richard was stunned that the Minister trusted him enough to reveal what he had about Shirling and the Treasury Board. At the same time he was just bursting with self-pride. He knew now that he did well today.

Minister Renjeu and Richard said their good byes. The Minister said he hoped that Lord Lancaster would bring Richard along with him on his next visit.

On his way down the elevator, Richard called the jet's captain to say he was on his way back to the airport. The captain indicated that the plane would be ready and waiting. The estimated time for departure was 8:00 PM.

CHAPTER TWENTY-TWO

Richard had called Lord Lancaster from the jet on his way back to London and gave him an abridged version of the day's discussions and outcomes. Lord Lancaster was extremely pleased with the results and congratulated Richard for thinking on his feet the way he had. A more formal briefing with Sir Loxley and John Maxwell had already been arranged for 9:00 in the morning.

At 9:55 the next morning, Richard had completed his briefing. For the most part, Sir Loxley and John Maxwell did not say or ask anything unless it was for clarification.

Sir Loxley looked up from the signed agreement and said, "Well Richard, you not only carried out the plan successfully, you also pulled off a minor miracle to secure the cellular tower contract. And possibly more importantly, you established a working relationship with Minister Renjeu and his Assistant Deputy Minister that could provide Regal Engineering, maybe even Port of Grace, with a stronger presence in South Africa in the future. Well done young man!"

The meeting ended with Richard acknowledging that the positive outcomes of yesterday's meeting now required additional work for his unit, in accordance with the new agreement. Richard indicated that they would get right on it.

As Richard was leaving the room, Sir Loxley asked John Maxwell to remain behind. "This is outstanding news, John. I don't know how he came up with the cellular tower idea, perhaps luck as much as cleverness, but you have to give Richard credit for his creativity and negotiating skills. I think it is a forgone conclusion that Richard will continue to lead the fresh water/hydro project, but I think we should also consider him to take the lead with the cellular towers as well. One, he thought of it and two, the South African's like him. But I'm also thinking, while the iron's still hot, that we should use his relationship with the South Africans, particularly with Renjeu's Ministry, to go after other projects in the country. As I said, there may be avenues open for other sectors of Port of Grace – resort development or mining, for instance. The benefit of having a good relationship with the Ministry of the Interior, is that they are almost always involved in every major project."

"That's an awfully large plate," John said in response.

"I know it is. Can you give it some thought, at least in terms of Regal? He would need to be freed up from some of the hands-on work. We may have to elevate him a rung and get him some more staff. How will this go over in your department? Will the staff accept him? Miracle or not, he's very young and inexperienced. Hell, we still don't really know that he's an engineer!"

"He's well liked. His unit is solidly behind him and George Casper has been a real supporter. George has also got too much on his plate." John stared at the ceiling for a moment organizing his thoughts. "I'm thinking that if I were to split Richard's unit off from George's area and create a separate South African Project Group with Richard at the head, it would work. Some pressure would be taken off of George and Richard could lead an area that he has clearly proved himself in. I would have him report directly to me." Facetiously he continued, "I can always use more work."

Sir Loxley said, "That sounds fine with me."

"I'll have to give it further thought though. We can bring Jennifer back to her old position when she's finished maternity leave, but we will have to find someone to replace Richard or at least assist him so that he can manage the larger portfolio and direct at least the two projects now on the books. But he will need to be freed up to promote other projects as well. It is going to have to evolve, I'm afraid. Richard will have to adapt as we go, not that I don't think that he can."

Sir Loxley interrupted John to say, "And we don't know what Richard's reaction will be. He could say thanks but no thanks; that he's already bitten off more than he can chew. You think this through some more John and we'll meet again. I better bounce the idea off of Lord Lancaster as well before we make any final decisions. In any event, we have a huge opportunity in South Africa that we do not want to let escape. I'll see you later."

Monica met Richard in the stables just as the sun was rising. They had planned this early morning ride a few weeks ago. It was the first free weekend for the both of them since Monica declared that Richard was Adam. It had been a cool night following a warm July day and fog was still hanging in the air as they cinched up their saddles. The combination of dawning light and a thick fog presented an eerie outlook and a sense of being alone – which they were. Normally during the week there would be more staff on the property, but on Saturday early in the morning, they had the grounds to themselves. Once saddled, they went on their way. Richard had a small duffle bag strapped around the saddle horn carrying a thermos of coffee and some donuts. They were both wearing sheep skin jackets that they hoped to shed later in the morning. Richard wore a ball cap and Monica had a woollen hat on her head.

By the time they reached the hills, the fog had lifted and was no match for the sun that started to send warmth from its higher placement in the sky. It was a slow trek to the hills as the fog in the low land made it dangerous to gallop. The slow pace made it easier for them to chat along the way. They made the most of it catching up on two busy lives. Monica was saddened after witnessing her first still birth earlier in the week. Fortunately the seven normal births thereafter had brightened her spirits somewhat and made the tragedy that much less disturbing. She had also taken extra shifts to help out a friend, which meant she had to forgo a chance to have seen Richard Thursday night. That was another reason this ride was so important to her. Richard, of course had told her all about the South Africa meeting and Monica said how happy she was for him.

Richard and Monica dismounted close to a fallen tree at the top of the hill they had climbed. They tethered the horses and sat on the tree trunk. Richard opened the duffle and poured a steaming cup of coffee for them both. Monica said, "Richard, have you thought any more about changing your name? Have Lord Lancaster's lawyers said anything further about the process and how long it will take?"

Richard swallowed his mouthful of coffee and replied, "Apparently the lawyers are having difficulty getting some information from the Canadian officials and don't expect a report to be ready now until sometime next week. Frankly I have been so busy with this South Africa matter that I haven't really thought a lot about it. I mean, I've only known the name Richard Lion. At first I was excited when you told us what my real name is, however, over time that excitement has faded. Everyday people call me Richard. The staff at Lancaster Manor, the office staff, the customs people in South Africa and the officials I met all know me as Richard. Most of what I've been thinking about is how weird it would be to tell everyone to call me Adam."

"But your whole family and all your friends know you as Adam. It will be more weird for them to call you Richard."

"I've thought of that too. You know what the big question is for me?

"What? replied Monica.

"When I finally regain my memory, then what am I going to do? I'll call my folks, I know that, but will I go home and if I do will I stay in Canada or come back to England? I know I have a job, a fantastic job here and new friends, but maybe I have a job waiting for me back home."

Monica hadn't thought about how complicated Richard's situation was getting the longer his memory was being kept from him. And she had not really considered that he wouldn't return to England after a visit back to Canada. Monica had her own feelings about the decisions Richard would have to make, but she also appreciated how rough it was for him. "I suppose time will tell, but I for one hope you will stay in England. You have established yourself here now. It's not so unusual for someone to take a job in another country. You had even told me that your goal was to be able to work your way into a position where you could undertake international work. Well, you are doing that right now, here." Monica moved nearer to Richard and linked her arm through his to draw him closer. She liked being in this cozy position and it brought back memories of times in Morocco and Spain. She looked up at him, their faces only inches apart and said in a caring tone, "Besides, I want you to stay."

Richard slowly lowered his head until his lips were hovering over Monica's. He could see crystals of sugar from a donut in the corner of her top lip. He smiled and said softly, "You have sugar on your lip, let me fix that." Before she could respond he pressed his lips gently to hers. Eyes closed they both savoured one another for only a few seconds. Richard gently broke the union and said in a teasing voice, "There, I got it." He smiled down at her and hugged her close and said, "I want to stay too. I just don't know if that will change when I learn more about myself."

"Alright, that's good for now. Let's wait and see how things go."

They decided it was time to return to the Manor. They packed up what was left of their coffee and donuts and mounted their horses. As Richard was leading his horse around to change direction, a rabbit jumped out of a hole buried behind the fallen tree and startled his horse. The horse rose up on his back legs taking Richard by surprise. Richard lost his balance and fell hard to the ground, bouncing from his hip to the side of his head. He didn't move. Monica cried out to him as she dismounted. She rushed to him and collapsed to her knees. "Richard, are you all right?" She gently probed for blood. She didn't see any. "Richard, can you hear me?" There was more concern in her voice. Richard did not respond to Monica's questions. "Richard," she said again. Still no response. Monica went to the horses to retrieve the two sheep skin jackets and returned to Richard's side. She very carefully raised his head enough to stuff the left sleeve of one of the jackets under Richard's head. She did not want to move him any further in case there was a spinal injury. She then hung the torso part of the jacket over his shoulders. The other jacket was placed over his side and hips. That was the best she could do for now to keep him warm and comfortable. Monica contemplated making a stretcher to pull behind a horse from limbs and small branches of the fallen tree, but dismissed the idea almost immediately. She checked him again but Richard was still unconscious. She thought to herself, "not again", then took her cell phone from her jeans pocket and called emergency services.

Lord Lancaster was in his study at Lancaster Manor speaking on the telephone with Sir Loxley about the South Africa meeting. Both gentlemen had received a telephone call from Minister Renjeu on Friday and both heard the same unsaid message, that as a result of the successful meeting, a door to South Africa has been opened to Regal Engineering. "I was telling Maxwell, following our briefing with Richard, that a huge opportunity has landed in our laps and that we can't ignore it," said Sir Loxley.

"Agreed," said Lord Lancaster.

Sir Loxley continued, "Maxwell and I were considering how we could best utilize Richard's skills and working relationship with the South Africans. I'll have more details to share with you next week, but the gist of it is that we create a new branch for South African projects, headed by Richard." Sir Loxley took another fifteen minutes on the telephone to summarize his discussions with John Maxwell on Wednesday morning. Lord Lancaster agreed in principle with the idea, but was concerned about Richard being able to handle all this so soon. They agreed to speak later when Sir Loxley had more information from Maxwell.

Before entering into a discussion on another matter concerning the company, Reston burst into the study holding a cordless phone outstretched for Lord Lancaster to see. With a note of panic in his voice he blurted out, "Excuse me Lord Lancaster, it's Lady Monica Ashton. Richard has had an accident."

Lord Lancaster asked Sir Loxley to hold on his private line while he took the phone from Reston. "Monica, what happened? Is Richard alright?"

By this time Lady Lancaster had heard the commotion and came to see what all the fuss was about. Reston whispered to her about the accident and that Lord Lancaster was speaking with Monica.

Monica explained how Richard had fallen off his horse and hit his head, that she had called emergency services and that a helicopter was on its way. She told Lord Lancaster that the fall had occurred approximately twenty minutes ago. She mentioned that there was no bleeding but that he had been unconscious up until a few moments ago. Then her tone of voice changed from being all business to enthusiastic excitement. "Lord Lancaster, his memory is back!"

Lord Lancaster covered the mouth piece of the phone with his hand and yelled over to Lady Lancaster and Reston who were anxiously awaiting any tidbit of news. "He had a spill off his horse and hit his head. But he's conscious now and Monica says that his memory has returned. It must have been the blow on the head." He turned back to the phone. "Monica does Richard feel alright now?"

"He says that he is sore from the fall, but we don't know if there is any significant damage. I expect the doctors will want to give him a battery of tests when he reaches the hospital." She paused for a moment before speaking again. "I hear the helicopter coming. Yes I can see it now. I will call you again when we reach the hospital."

"We will meet you there," said Lord Lancaster. They broke off their conversation.

Lord Lancaster took his private line again and said to Sir Loxley, "Did you hear any of that John?"

Sir Loxley replied, "Enough to know that Richard's memory seems to have returned. You get on to the hospital. I will catch up with you later. Give Richard my best regards."

Only minutes before she called Lord Lancaster, Monica was shaken from her trance by groans coming from the still body beside her. She had been thinking of the ferry from Ceuta back to Spain and hiding away in a corner with Richard sharing some tender moments. "Richard, can you hear me now? How are you feeling?"

Richard moved at a snail's pace to right himself onto his back. He grimaced in pain, but it didn't stop him. This was a sign to Monica that no major damage had been done to his spinal column. "Ouch, that was quite a fall," he said. My head aches like crazy. How long have I been out?"

"Only for about twenty minutes," Monica told Richard. "That's a good sign. But I was so afraid that you would slip back into a long term coma again." With tears beginning to show in her eyes, Monica said, "Oh Richard, I was so worried about you."

Monica adjusted the jackets to keep him warm and said, "Now don't move any more than you have to. I'm going to ask you some questions." She held up four fingers. "How many fingers do you see?" He answered four. She held up two fingers. "How many now?" Again he answered correctly. "What day is it today?" Richard answered Saturday. "Good, you are doing fine. Now what is my name?" Richard took a moment to look at Monica, then said, "Baily. No, Monica. Actually both."

Monica was initially enthusiastic about the last answer thinking that perhaps Richard had regained his memory and was referring to his first association with her as Baily. Then she realized that she had provided all that information to him when she first met him at her party. She thought of another question to test her secret hopes. "Tell me your mother's name." Richard said Joan. "Tell me your father's name." Richard indicated that it was Ed. Monica was thrilled with these answers and finally said, "Now tell me your sister's name." Without hesitation he told her that his sister's name was Joy. "Richard," she said more lively now, "It appears that your memory has come back! Do you sense it?"

As they waited for the helicopter to arrive, Richard began telling Monica some recollections of his past, including how he broke his leg when he was six. A larger friend and he were rolling down a hill on their sides when the larger boy rolled right over Richard. He recalled the day he left home for Europe and how concerned his mother had been. Monica was so happy, tears were now streaming down her face in joy. She said, "I better call Lord and Lady Lancaster."

After a few minutes on the phone with Lord Lancaster, Monica heard then saw the helicopter approaching and broke off the call. "They will meet us at the hospital," she said.

CHAPTER TWENTY-THREE

All tests conducted on Richard, including an MRI and x-rays concluded that no damage had been done that a few days of rest wouldn't cure. He had suffered a mild concussion but Dr. Rogers was not concerned about it. As a precaution, Dr. Rogers asked Richard to stay overnight in the hospital for observation. Richard agreed but insisted that he not be required to wear hospital gowns or eat hospital food. He would wear his own clothes and lounge around the private hospital room and eat pizza that Monica said she would bring him. The compromise was agreeable to Dr. Rogers. The most exciting news for everyone was that Dr. Rogers confirmed Richard had, in fact, regained his memory. Richard said that he wanted to call home as soon as he could.

"Still no answer," Richard said to Monica, after his third attempt in an hour to reach his parents. "The strange thing is that there isn't a voice messaging system. That doesn't make sense."

"Maybe it's the time difference. It's 3:00 in the afternoon here which would make it about 9:00 in the morning in Winnipeg, right?"

"Even so," admitted Richard, "Someone should still be home to answer the phone and why isn't there a messaging system." Richard indicated that he would try again on Sunday evening.

It was 9:00 PM Sunday in England and 3:00 PM in Winnipeg. On the third ring a voice answered, "Hello."

Richard thought he recognized his sister's voice. "Joy," he said. "Joy is that you, it's Adam."

There was a moment of silence before his sister cried out, "Adam?" Then with fury in her tone, Richard heard, "Adam where have you been? Why haven't you called?"

All Richard could say before his sister continued her inquisition was, "I'm sorry I've not been able to call until now, but …." He didn't have time to explain and his sister wasn't listening.

"No one has heard from you since Christmas and you haven't been able to call home any time since then? Damn you Adam, I've been here by myself looking after things and you didn't have time to call home? You have no idea what it has been like for me."

Richard was beside himself. He didn't have a clue about why his sister was so upset. "Joy, what are you talking about, what's wrong?"

"Mom and Dad are both dead, that's what I'm talking about and you weren't here when I needed you."

Richard had been sitting straight up in his bed. His face turned pale with an expression of disbelief as he fell back against a pile of pillows. Monica could clearly see that he had received some devastating news. "What's wrong?" she asked.

Richard heard Joy's voice yelling in the phone and sat up again saying to her, "Joy, let me explain." He kept talking over his sister's cries hoping she would hear and understand some of what he was saying. "I had a bad accident and was left in a coma for several weeks then amnesia. My memory only came back yesterday. I tried to call yesterday but there was no message system to leave a voice message." Joy seemed to have heard some of what Richard was saying because she stopped ranting herself and listened. "When did they die, how?" he managed.

Joy ignored what Richard had just told her about himself for the moment and explained that their mother had had cancer and died soon after Christmas, before the end of January. She said that their mother had known about the cancer for some time but didn't reveal anything to anyone until just before New Year's Eve. After that, the cancer accelerated. It had been in her liver. She then told Richard that their father had had a heart attack just two months ago - in May. He was at work and just collapsed in the hallway. He died before reaching the hospital. Aunt Trina had gone to Winnipeg to assist Joy with funeral arrangements but had to return to Montreal soon after to care for her sick special needs child. Joy was staying with her best friend Jill's family. Jill's mother and father had been very kind to Joy in helping her deal with the legal matters subsequent to their father passing away.

Joy began crying again as she said, "Adam, please come home. I need you. I can't do this by myself."

"I'm still in the hospital but will be discharged tomorrow. I'll be home in a few days. Don't worry, I will see you in a few days, I promise and we can work through the rest of this together."

Richard had finally gotten his sister to calm down, at least enough that she was listening to what he was telling her about his situation. He summarized everything but left out the horrific details. He didn't mention Lord and Lady Lancaster by name and didn't talk about his job. That could wait he thought. Since Jill's parents were waiting for her in the car, Joy said that she should go, but made Richard promise again that he would come home in a few days. Richard said he would. Before he hung up, he said to his sister, "Joy, there's something else you need to know. You may not recognize me when you see me at the airport."

Joy answered Richard in a way that suggested he was crazy. "What do you mean I may not recognize you?"

"Well, I got beaten up quite badly and the doctors had to reconstruct my face a fair amount, you know, plastic surgery kind of thing. I don't look the same."

"Do you mean you have all kinds of scars on you face?" Joy asked with definite concern.

"No, no scars at all actually, at least not that you would notice. I just look different, good, but different. As a matter of fact, yesterday, after I regained my memory, was the first time I was able to compare myself with how I had looked. I was a bit shocked at the difference, of course, but I don't look bad. Maybe even more handsome than before," he said trying to make a joke.

"OK, I'll be looking forward to seeing the new you then," she said. Richard could detect a hint of levity in her voice and he was happy for it. "I've got to go. Adam, I'm so glad you called."

Richard was grief stricken as he told Monica about his parents. He was particularly concerned for his sister, having to go through a second parent's death all alone. He felt guilty for not being with her despite Monica telling him that it was not his fault. He called Lord and Lady Lancaster and broke down on the phone telling them all over again what had happened. At one point Monica had to rescue the phone from Richard as he could not talk through his crying. Lord and Lady Lancaster were understandably distraught with this news and extremely concerned for Richard's wellbeing. When Richard regained control of his emotions and was ready to talk again, Lord Lancaster told him that when he was ready to go to Canada, the company jet would be at his disposal.

Richard convinced Monica to finally go home, as it was already close to 11:00 PM and she had to be at work for 7:00 in the morning. He assured her that he would be alright and really needed the rest. Monica said she would speak to the nurse on duty and see if Richard could be given something to help him sleep. Monica kissed Richard good bye saying that she would see him tomorrow.

The next morning, Lord Lancaster arrived at the hospital at 10:00, forty minutes after Richard had called to say that he could be released. Lord Lancaster had brought Richard some fresh clothes, for which Richard was grateful. Lady Lancaster had not accompanied her husband as she would have liked, because Lord Lancaster and Richard planned to go to the office for a good part of the day. Some arrangements would have to be made to cover for Richard while he was away. Richard thought that a week would be enough for now to help clear matters up in Winnipeg. While he didn't say anything to Lord Lancaster, he secretly wondered how he would feel about returning to London after being home, especially under the present conditions. During the night, before he asked the nurse for some sleeping pills, Richard kept thinking about what he and Monica were discussing Saturday morning with regard to changing his name and whether he would settle in Canada or England after his memory returned. Could he leave his sister alone again? He vowed that he would return to England after a week's time. He would have to convince Joy that he had responsibilities here as well. But at the same time, he would promise her that he would not abandon her. He simply needed time to think things through. It was all very complicated and emotions right now weren't helping.

At Regal Engineering, the management were supportive of Richard and assured him that they could handle a week without him. Richard met with his unit to outline what he wanted them to do during the week he was away. He would meet with them all first thing upon his return. With that out of the way, Richard and Lord Lancaster headed for home.

During the ride back to Lancaster Manor, Lord Lancaster mentioned to Richard that he had heard from the lawyers. They would have a report for Lord Lancaster concerning the process for changing Richard's name, on Wednesday. Richard hoped that Lord Lancaster would not take this opportunity to question him about how he thought about changing his name, given the new set of circumstances in his life. He didn't.

"You know Richard, last night after you called us about your parents, I spent a great deal of time trying to understand how you must feel. After all that has happened to you since we first met, you have been challenged time after time and you have overcome these not insignificant challenges with strength, grace and character. I can only imagine how you feel of course, but I also have come to realize just how special a person you really are. I am very proud of you," he said tensing up his stomach muscles to keep control of his emotions. "Both Lady Lancaster and I are very proud of you."

Richard was having his own control problems with his emotions and he hesitated before saying, "After the incident and I came out of the coma, I felt so alone. I never knew who my parents were or where they were. I was frightened. When you and Mrs. Lancaster introduced yourselves and offered to take me in, I was very grateful. And I have been grateful ever since as you have guided me and encouraged me during the evolving process of recovery, making friends, landing a job, leading pretty much to where we are now. For all intents and purposes you were fulfilling a parental role for me, someone I could turn to. I may not have said this to you before, it was too awkward knowing that somewhere out there I had natural parents, but I have loved you like a son."

Lord Lancaster put his hand on Richard's forearm as a gesture to calm him. With great emotion he said, "Richard, we have felt the same way about you. Muriel and I have often said that if we had been blessed with a son, we would have wanted him to be just like you." Lord Lancaster paused to relax before saying, "With your parents dead, we want you to know that you have a home with us for as long as you want. And if ever there is a time where you would have gone to your father for advice or counsel, I want you to know that you can come to me. I will always be there for you."

The two men hugged each other as a father and son would and said little more during the rest of the drive.

CHAPTER TWENTY-FOUR

The Lear jet owned by Port of Grace Enterprises touched down at the Winnipeg International Airport at 3:45 in the afternoon on a hot and sunny day, typical of Winnipeg summers, thought Richard. It was a long flight, just over nine hours, with a stop in St. John's Newfoundland for refuelling and customs. Richard was able to sleep for a few hours, catching up on the rest he sorely needed. He spent another three hours doing work related business: reading reports, answering emails, writing emails to his staff asking for further information he would need upon his return. The remaining time was spent thinking about his family and his friends in Canada.

He recalled the many family vacations up at Gimli on Lake Winnipeg, the time they all went to Disney World when Joy was five and he was eleven. He could still hear the words "it's a small world after all" roaming around in his head. He remembered his Mom's love for entertaining and her wonderful cooking. He remembered golfing Sunday mornings with his Dad and some of the life skill discussions they would have. There were so many fabulous memories of the life they had together. He would miss his parents very much, but he knew in his heart that they would be proud of him for securing an important position in a large international engineering company and for his work in South Africa, just as Lord Lancaster was proud of him. But unlike with Lord Lancaster, he couldn't share these times with his parents and that is what made him so very sad.

Richard also spent some time thinking about the pros and cons for living and working in Canada versus England. He made a list in his notebook and each time he reviewed the list it overwhelmingly pointed to England as making the most sense. Eventually after a headache overcame him he decided that he would need the week at home at least, before he could really decide. And Joy was a major factor he had to consider.

After the jet taxied to position and the engines were shut down, the cabin steward helped Richard retrieve his bags, consisting of one large case plus his carry-on bag and computer. After thanking the captain and his crew for a smooth flight, he wished them a safe flight back to London. It was Tuesday, July 6th. The plan was for them to return next Wednesday, unless he advised of a change. In the interim, the jet would be used by Lord Lancaster and Sir Loxley for two day-trips that Richard was aware of, to Frankfurt and to Bern. It occurred to him at that moment that he, Richard Lion, lowly Project Director in a large engineering company, one of several large companies comprising Port of Grace Enterprises, had had exclusive use of the company's jet on two occasions within the past two weeks. He smiled and shook his head as he proceeded to the terminal entrance.

Richard realized something late in the flight that he neglected to mention to Joy about meeting him at the airport. He had forgotten to mention that his plane would not be disembarking at the same locations as the normal commercial planes and that she should ask an airport attendant where to wait for him. It was not surprising then for Richard not to see his sister at the door when he passed through it. Accepting this, he made his way to the luggage claim area for the commercial airlines, already having his own luggage in tow, to try and find her. His plane was on time so he was sure she would be waiting for him somewhere in the airport.

Seeing the crowd of people ahead of him, many hugging and kissing their friends and relatives presumably, Richard surmised from the sign atop the luggage conveyer belt that an Air Canada flight had landed at about the same time as his plane had. The escalator transferring people down from the second floor was full of travellers eagerly wishing to meet up with loved ones or business associates, or maybe just a taxi driver when they reached the ground level. Richard scanned through the crowd seeking young women looking up at the escalator hoping to spot Joy. After a couple of minutes several more travellers descended and left the area with those who came to meet them. The crowd shrank but still not enough to make it easier to find his sister. Then after yet another scan, he was sure he had spotted her. From the side he recognized a tall, athletic looking girl, who now looked more like a young lady he thought. Her hair was brown and drawn back into a pony tail, the way she would normally wear it, sunglasses propped on top of her head. He called out, "Joy." No response. "Joy," he called again. She turned her head in his direction. He called again, waving his hand above his head, "Joy, over here." Another girl accompanying Joy turned in the same direction she was looking. That looks like Joy's friend Jill, Richard thought. "Joy, over here," he called again to be sure they saw him, again waving his hand in the air. Richard had a smile on his face to reflect the excitement he was feeling to meet his sister.

Joy looked up in the direction of a man who had hailed her. She thought she found the man in the crowd who was calling her name but he didn't look familiar, so she looked at faces standing near the person. When the first man called out again, Joy glanced at her friend with a mystified expression. When she looked back up the man was smiling directly at her and waving his hand in the air. Joy and Jill cautiously plodded their way through the crowd, as did the man. The man wore a big smile, Joy did not. When Richard was within five feet of his sister and her friend, he dropped his bags and was preparing to step ahead to give Joy a hug. He hesitated, seeing confusion and apprehension on her face. He looked at her and said, "Do I really look that different?"

"Adam, is that really you?" responded Joy, not yet revealing any excitement to see her brother.

"Yes, it is really me, your big brother." Richard did not move toward her. He would wait until Joy was ready.

With a gentle nudge and a whisper from Jill, Joy released the grip on her face and mustered a familiar smile, then charged ahead into Richard's waiting arms. With her head resting on his chest and tears forming in her eyes, Joy blurted out "Oh Adam, I'm so glad to see you. You don't know how much I have waited to hear from you and for you to come home." She pushed back and looked up at him saying, "You do look very different you know. I recognize it's you now, but I wouldn't have if you hadn't called out. And from a distance I couldn't tell either." She reached up with both hands and held his face. "Only if I look closely can I see any hint of scars. You look older. I think your eyes are the same but your smile is different somehow. I don't know, maybe ..., are those new teeth?" She stepped back and looked at the whole of him before she remarked, as if she hadn't really taken much notice of him, "You know, you look really good!"

From behind Joy, Jill said, "I think you look like a real hunk."

Richard took Joy's hands and said to her, "You look great too. It is so nice to see you." He turned to Joy's friend and said, "Hi Jill, thanks for coming with Joy to the airport."

"I can't wait to catch up," said Joy, now with excitement in her voice. "I have so much to tell you and I have so many questions to ask you." She changed tone and asked, "By the way, where did your plane come in? I didn't see any flight from London or from Montreal or Toronto on the arrival boards."

"I actually came in on a private jet. It's parked at the other end of the terminal," said Richard.

"A private jet!" exclaimed Joy. "How did you manage that?"

"It's a long story," replied Richard, not wanting to get into any details. "Let's get going and get me settled, then we can have a long talk. Where do you have the car?"

"I've got Mom's van," said Joy. She then immediately transformed from a bubbly young sister to a girl crippled with emotional pain.

Richard reached out and took her into his arms and held her tight. "Don't cry any more Joy, I'm here now. I'm so sorry I wasn't able to be with you when Mom and Dad died, but I'm also very proud of you for managing the way you have. Don't cry now," he repeated.

After a few more moments, Joy released herself from her brother. Her tears wiped away, she said with a sniffle, "I'm alright now. Let's go."

The car ride to their parent's house took about twenty-five minutes and both Joy and Jill had all kinds of questions for Richard. He answered in generalities, wishing to wait until he and Joy were alone before sharing details about his past eight months away. He also wanted to ask his sister many questions about his parents, but for the same reason he controlled his interest. Joy dropped Jill off at her parent's house and thanked her for coming to the airport. She reminded Jill to tell her mother that she would be staying at her own house with Adam, until other plans were made. Three minutes later Richard and Joy pulled into their driveway and Joy pressed the remote to raise the garage door. Stepping through the garage door leading into the house, Richard was struck with the feeling of an empty house, not of furniture but of life. He fought with everything he had within himself not to break down in front of his sister, but inside he could imagine himself falling to the floor and crying like a baby. He told himself that he had to be strong for his sister now.

After Richard had unpacked his bags, he suggested ordering in pizza and just staying at home and talking. Joy was totally in favour of his idea. They sat themselves down on the sofa in the family room just off the kitchen, their pizzas placed on the coffee table before them. It wasn't a large room in and of itself, but coupled with the open kitchen, the combined rooms appeared quite spacious. The furniture comprised a sofa and a large matching arm chair, three tables and a television. On the mantle of the fireplace stood picture frames bordering photos primarily of Joy and Richard. Looking at the pictures, Richard was reminded of the time his father told him how he had been at a business conference in Alberta on an Indian Reserve and had taken part in a Sweat Lodge ceremony. Mr. Ramsey had said that he survived the lodge's unbearable heat by focusing on the pictures of the kids on the mantle. They and their parents spent a great deal of their time between these two rooms, especially in their younger years. In the winter, Mr. Ramsey would often have a fire blazing in the fireplace. It was particularly nice and cozy after coming in from an outdoor hockey game or from cross country skiing. The whole family enjoyed the outdoors together, in both summer and winter.

Richard first wanted to talk about their Mom and Dad. Joy spoke for almost two hours and only once really broke down and cried until the comforting by her brother calmed her again. She told Richard about how quickly the cancer had spread in January and how strong their Mother had been through it all. She talked about how depressed their Dad had been after her death. Richard almost broke down himself when Joy told him how much his Dad had wished he had been able to be home for his Mom. Finally Joy told Richard about their Father's death. Unlike their Mother's, his was swift. He keeled over at work, didn't suffer a great deal of pain and died on the way to the hospital. She then talked about the funeral and how nice and helpful all their Mom and Dad's friends had been at that time and afterwards until she had gotten settled in with Jill's parents. She mentioned how she would come back to the house a few times a week and then more often when school finished. Richard was reminded that Joy had just finished high school, which prompted the question of what she would do now. Joy said that she really hadn't thought much about it. She mentioned how she had met with their parent's lawyers and how she insisted that she only wanted to deal with matters that had to be dealt with. She had wanted to wait as long as possible until Adam had called home. She started to talk about a list that was made of things still to be done, but Richard suggested they wait until tomorrow to talk about it. At that point they both agreed it was time for a break. They took their empty dishes and pizza boxes into the kitchen, then both disappeared for some personal space.

Fifteen minutes later Joy arrived back in the family room. Richard was already sitting there thumbing through an old photo album. Joy asked if Richard wanted any coffee. He declined. Joy decided she didn't want any just then either and sat down beside him, linking his arm into hers and holding him close. She said to Richard, "So, now you've got to tell me all about your trip and how you ended up in England and how you managed to fly home on a private plane."

"It's a long story," said Richard.

"We've got all night. If you can stay awake, so can I."

With that emphatic statement urging him on, Richard began at the beginning. He took Joy through Portugal and told her about the fellow he had met from Montreal and how they hung out together for a while. He told her about meeting some younger kids who spoke English and were interested in Canada and had invited him to their home for dinner. Their mother was surprised but was agreeable and had prepared a simple but delicious meal. The father never showed himself. He took her on a tour through Spain mentioning crazy Fred and Jed from Madrid, the old city of Toledo, the wonders of Cordoba, Seville and Granada. He told her about meeting up with the two Bens and their grand entrance into Morocco. When he talked about the days in Morocco and then back to Spain, he only used the name Baily, not wanting to introduce Monica until later.

"So you had a little romance going on over there eh," Joy said in her best teasing tone. "Did you ever contact her again?" Richard said that he hadn't.

From the phone call home at Christmas, Joy was aware that Richard had met up with TJ and was headed to Barcelona and southern France. Richard picked it up from there, talking about the wonders of Italy, the ancient buildings and culture and the food and wine.

Joy interrupted often to ask questions, not only about what Richard saw, but also about process and how he did things, how he travelled. Joy was still very much interested in travelling herself.

"After I left Oxford…, well, the rest of my life changed," Richard said in a slower and lower voice. "It was later that day when the incident occurred."

"Is this when you got hurt?" asked Joy. Until now, Joy had been told only the barest of details concerning the incident and the attack Richard had suffered.

Joy had come to tears several times during Richard's recollection of that terrible day, but insisted that he continue his story. She was both shocked and sickened by how premeditated and scary it was, yet at the same time she was completely intrigued for the same reason.

"Did they ever catch these people?"

"No, there was virtually no evidence and I couldn't help because of being in a coma or with amnesia."

"So you just happened to be in the wrong place at the wrong time?"

"In a way, yes. On the other hand, the Lancasters could say I was in the right place at the right time. They would have been killed otherwise." Richard had not yet revealed who the Lancasters were.

"So you were rushed to the hospital, then what?"

Richard continued his story and what he had been told about his stay in the hospital up until the time he had awakened from the coma. He eventually told his sister about Lord and Lady Lancaster, Lancaster Manor and the Lancaster Estate.

Joy was overwhelmed with excitement. She quickly became more interested in Richard's living in an old English manor than with his injuries and surgery. "This is incredible," she said. "You couldn't make up a story like this." She urged her brother to continue.

At the point in his story where Richard was talking about meeting Lady Monica Ashton at her homecoming celebration, Joy blurted out, "She was really Baily, the girl you met in Morocco, right?"

Richard continued to tell his sister about Monica proving who he really was. Up until this time, Richard had not told Joy that his official name was Richard Lion.

He explained how he received the name and how Lord Lancaster had managed to arrange for official documents. He further explained the complexities of changing his name once he knew that he was Adam. "So you see, officially my name is Richard Lion. At this point, I can't prove to anyone that I am Adam Ramsey." He explained that lawyers were looking into the processes necessary to make the change.

Another two hours had gone by and Richard was feeling the weight of the day. He had finally completed his story, bringing Joy completely up to date. He had taken particular delight in telling her about his position with Regal Engineering and the South African projects.

Richard had begun to suggest an agenda for the next day when Joy interrupted saying, "You're going back to England aren't you?"

Richard replied, "Well yes, in about a week. I told you that earlier."

"No I mean you're going back to stay. You're not going to live here, am I right?" Joy had the look of someone afraid of hearing the answer to her question.

Richard had difficulty saying, "Joy, I really don't know. I thought a lot about it on the plane coming over and I decided I couldn't make a decision like that right now. There are too many things to consider, you being one of them. I don't think we should talk about this now. It's really late."

"If you return to England next week, when will you come back again?" Joy took a moment before continuing. "We won't have time this week to take care of all of Mom and Dad's business, then I'll be left with the rest of it on my own again. Adam, I need you here."

"We'll make sure that everything that needs to be done will get done, I promise, even if we need to contract with the lawyers to do it. I can come back later and we can finalize things. From what you've told me, you and the lawyers have managed to do most of the work already. All the funds of Mom and Dad's estates have been identified and assembled and you have paid off any debts they had. It seems like all that is really left to do is decide on what we want to do with the house and cars. They can sit here for a while until we can think about this some more. In fact, I have an idea. Why don't you come back to England with me for a while. We can talk more about the future at our leisure and you can get to know all the people I have met."

Joy was certain that wrapping up her parent's business in accordance with their Wills was much more complicated than what her brother just said about it, but he had expressed himself so genuinely and convincingly that she began to wonder. She said back to him, "I can't just go back with you."

"Why not?"

"In the first place, who's going to look after the house? In the second place, where would we live and what would I do there when you will be working all day?"

Richard smiled now that he had his sister's interest. "The house can sit. Friends can look in on it from time to time." He came closer to his sister and put his hands on her shoulders then said, "Lord and Lady Lancaster actually invited me to bring you back before I left. They would love for you to visit or stay as long as you wanted. And yes, I would be working a lot, but you could do some sightseeing. I know that Lady Lancaster would love to show you around and take you shopping. If you find yourself bored, you can come home earlier and I'll come back when I can. But I think it would be great. Joy, you could even consider going to university there."

"What? Are you crazy? University?"

"Why not? You often told Mom and Dad that you would like to go away for university to take law. Here's your chance. Remember I told you about my friend Jason, Monica's brother. He just finished his third year of law."

Joy was confused. She hadn't ever considered the possibility of going to England with Richard. "I can't think about this now. You're right, let's wait until morning."

They concurred with the decision to go to bed and start fresh again in the morning by making a to do list.

CHAPTER TWENTY-FIVE

Richard was up and around before his sister the next morning and had to wake her in time to eat the breakfast he had prepared. While sharing scrambled eggs, bacon, toast, orange juice and hot coffee, they created their agenda for the day that included picking up more groceries. All they bought the day before on their way from the airport was being consumed as they wrote their list. When Richard spoke to Joy after his amnesia had broken, he asked her to make an appointment with the lawyers. They would meet with them first, at 10:30 that morning. Much of the rest of the week's activities regarding their parent's business would result from that meeting. They would wait until the weekend to visit with some of their own and some of their parent's friends, but they would make some calls ahead of time. Richard also wanted to try to call Professor Hitchcock, hoping he would still be in his office at Queen's University. He would call later in the week

"I couldn't get to sleep right away last night," Joy said to her brother, just before taking a sip of her coffee. "I was thinking a lot about going back to England with you, at least for a little while. Maybe it isn't such a bad idea."

Richard completed his swallow before responding. "It would be good for you to get away from here for a while. You will be treated like a princess if Lady Lancaster has anything to do about it. Those people have been so kind to me. I have to tell you Joy, during the past few months when I didn't know who I was and didn't know who my parents were, I came to think of the Lancasters as being my parents. I don't know what I would have done without them. After the incident and coming out of the coma, it had seemed like I had been reborn."

"We'll keep talking about it, but right now I better go have a shower. The meeting with the lawyers is in less than two hours."

Joy had earlier provided all the documents that her parent's lawyers had asked for, including life insurance policies, the name of her father's employer, bank accounts and investment statements, as well as utility and other home service accounts. They told Joy at the time that they would contact the various institutions and confirm the transfer of property and any on-going payment responsibilities into Joy's and Adam's names as joint owners. Fortunately, Joy had turned eighteen and was of legal age prior to her father's death, since Richard was nowhere to be found.

The meeting with the lawyers began on time. The first several minutes were taken with introductions and very brief explanations why Richard had not been available following his Father's death. The lawyers confirmed that they had received all financial contributions that were expected given the various policies and investments identified to them. They further confirmed that they had paid all debts owing. Finally they reminded Joy that the house was now in her and Adam's name and that all utility bills and taxes etc. would be addressed to them. They were in fact regular home owners. It was at this point that Richard explained the issues concerning his name. The lawyers listened with interest. They understood his dilemma but had to advise him that, under the current circumstances, Joy was therefore the only child of Mr. Edward Ramsey legally entitled to share in the inheritance. For all intents and purposes, Adam Ramsey did not exist. Richard assured them that his lawyers in England were looking into the complexities of having his name changed. His parent's lawyers were happy to hear that and were appreciative of knowing the situation ahead of time. One of the lawyers submitted that if for some reason Richard were to keep his current official name, there would need to be a petition drawn up and approved by the courts acknowledging that any property of Adam Ramsey's or any property or funds that were entitled to become Adam Ramsey's, like the inheritance, belonged to Richard Lion. Richard indicated that he understood the ramifications his name presented. He admitted that for these reasons and many others, he was having difficulty deciding what he should do about his name. He left them saying that he would advise them as soon as he made his decision and asked that they represent him in Canada, whichever decision was made. The lawyers indicated that they would be pleased to represent him.

Joy had come away from the meeting feeling less of a weight on her shoulders. Just having Richard by her side made her feel more comfortable. She was relieved to know that, just as Richard had predicted, all matters were taken care of. The house and cars and all other property belonged to them jointly and they could do whatever they wanted with them, whenever they wanted. Most of the funds from the life insurance policies were placed into short term investments giving the two siblings time to consider longer term investments or how else they wished to use their inheritances. Much of the total value of their inheritances was tied up in the house and property, but they had time to decide what they wanted to do with it. Sufficient enough funds were placed in a bank account to pay for on-going expenses, primarily related to maintaining the house for several months. In short, there was no reason why Joy could not take some time and go to England with Richard. She was starting to warm up to the idea more and more.

On Friday morning Richard finally connected with his old mentor, Professor Hitchcock. The professor was delighted to hear from him. When Richard told the professor an abridged version of his story and about his position with Regal Engineering, the professor was full of pride for his former student.

"This is an amazing story, my boy, and you have certainly landed squarely into a plum position. I knew you would of course. I always had confidence in your talents, but what a stroke of luck to be given such opportunities at such a young age. I will be certain to mail copies of all the proper documentation concerning your graduation and credentials to your employer as soon as I can next week."

"Thank you very much professor." Richard broke off their call promising to keep in touch.

Much of the weekend was filled with visits to family friends. Many tears were shed at the homes of Richard's parent's friends, reliving the deaths and funerals. They were all completely astonished by Richard's adventures and all wondered when he was going to return to Winnipeg, or if he was. Richard indicated that he had a great deal to think about. Joy confirmed that she was going to go to England for a while and help him decide on his future.

Richard also gathered up a few friends for drinks Saturday night, but came away feeling like he hadn't missed out on much while he was away. Jeff was still in Toronto with the basketball team and Richard had not been able to get a hold of him. His friends told Richard that they had heard from his parents that he was doing fine. But Jeff himself had not kept in touch. Apparently he had met a girl and they were going to have a baby in the fall. No one knew if or when there might be a marriage.

On Sunday morning Richard called Lord and Lady Lancaster to tell them that Joy would be accompanying him home. They were ecstatic at the news and Lady Lancaster didn't hesitate to say that she would start lining up places where she could take Joy. She also said that she would arrange for a small party to celebrate Richard's return and to welcome Joy. After Richard's stated concern over too much fuss, Lady Lancaster promised that the party would be small and informal. When Lord Lancaster indicated that he had some business to discuss with Richard, Lady Lancaster graciously left the room, more anxious to start planning for Joy's arrival. At the other end of the phone call, Joy also excused herself.

Lord Lancaster said, "Richard, you sound good. The tone in your voice indicates to me that you are in a comfortable frame of mind and in your decision to come home. And we are so happy to hear that your sister will be coming as well. I hope you told her that she is most welcome to stay as long as she wishes."

"I do feel good sir. This has been a week of mixed emotions for certain, but my sister and I have had time to sort out many things and to talk about some matters still to be decided. We hope that her coming back to England will help in this process." Richard took a moment before continuing. "Sir, I think I better tell you something. I think Joy has already sensed this but nothing final has been said."

"What is it my boy," asked Lord Lancaster, clearly concerned by Richard's tone of voice.

"I've been thinking of it continually since I left for Canada and I am all but certain that I not only want to continue to live and work in England, but also I want to keep Richard Lion as my name. The latter also makes more sense if I go with the former. Do you know what I mean?"

Lord Lancaster had secretly wished that Richard would make this decision. He hoped now that he would follow through with it, after discussing the matter with his sister. "I'll be honest with you Richard, after you had informed us about your parents, I had hoped that you would come to the decision to stay and live here. As for the name, yes, if you stay in England it makes a great deal of sense as you say, to keep Richard as your name. I will help you with whatever choice you make."

"Alright then, we can discuss it more when I get back."

"So, are you still planning on coming home on Wednesday?" asked Lord Lancaster. If you are ready, I could send the jet for you sooner."

"I was actually going to ask you about that. We could be ready on Tuesday," said Richard.

"I'll have it arranged and you will receive an email with all the details by this time Monday." Lord Lancaster paused before asking, "Richard, would you mind making a short stop in Toronto on yourway home?"

"Toronto, what's in Toronto? Richard asked.

Lord Lancaster explained, "Sir Loxley and John Maxwell have exchanged some emails and telephone conversations with the President of Dorset Dynamics over the past several days. It's a small firm that manufactures components for cellular tower operation. We are considering the benefits of buying such a company, in the event we were successful in contracting for the towers in South Africa. Sir Loxley asked if you would be able to drop in and take an on-site look at what they had to offer. He could call first thing on Monday to pave the way. It would give us an opportunity to have an initial inspection of the operation since you are practically next door and it would save the cost and time of having to send someone eventually."

"Well, if you can set it up and send me some briefing material, that will be fine."

"Good, I'll call Sir Loxley now. Alright Richard, we will get you all the information you need about flight times and on Dorset Dynamics as soon as possible. Have a good trip and we will anxiously await your arrival, you and your sister. Good bye now son."

After hanging up with Lord Lancaster, Richard shared the news with his sister about an earlier flight and the stop off in Toronto. Joy was full of excitement, but suddenly aware that she had to think about packing.

CHAPTER TWENTY-SIX

As it turned out, Richard and Joy didn't return to London until Wednesday after all, although it was very early in the morning. The Port of Grace jet was late arriving into Winnipeg and the crew required some minimum amount of rest time before flying out again. The later than planned take off and the stopover in Toronto ultimately delayed their original estimated time of arrival. Richard had been impressed with the operations at Dorset Dynamics and had spent a couple of hours during the flight preparing a report for Sir Loxley and John Maxwell. While he was at Dorset, Joy enjoyed a few hours of shopping in Toronto accompanied by the cabin stewardess, Miss Sommers, who Richard had asked if she wouldn't mind keeping Joy company. Miss Sommers jumped at the chance.

In between naps brother and sister talked about London, Maidens Green and Lancaster Manor. Richard hadn't yet told Joy about discovering the Firebird and he was giddy with excitement telling her about that story. It occurred to Richard again as he was talking with his sister that she seemed to look older than her eighteen years. He first made this observation at the airport when he arrived in Winnipeg. He wasn't surprised though, given her experiences over the past several months helping their Father deal with their Mom's death and then being all alone to deal with their Father's death. She had grown up in many ways during this time and she had aged physically as well. Not that she looked old, he told himself, but she did look like she could easily pass for twenty-one. In fact he had to remind himself that she was only eighteen. She would be younger by five or six years than his new friends, who were primarily Jason's and Monica's friends, many of whom had begun university or were working. It dawned on Richard that he was considering how Joy would get on hanging out with him and his friends. This is not something he would have promoted back home. Truth be told the opposite would have been the case. But he was obviously seeing her in a different light now. She had always been outgoing, never shy. She blended well with his friends in Winnipeg and when his water polo team was shorthanded for a few games, they welcomed his younger sister to fill in. Of course, she could swim circles around most of them. Joy was actually an elite swimmer and had competed in swimming meets all over North America since she was ten years old. However, due to the deaths of their parents she couldn't maintain the gruelling training and swim meet schedules and had to quit the team. This was another of the many things Richard felt guilty about.

Due to the early hour, it was 5:00 in the morning in London, Lord and Lady Lancaster decided against meeting the plane but sent Stewart to retrieve Richard and Joy from the airport on their behalf. Stewart passed on the Lancaster's apologies and indicated that Lord and Lady Lancaster would be waiting to greet the pair upon their arrival back at Lancaster Manor and that an early breakfast would be waiting for them if they were not too tired. As she got into the limousine, Joy was once more impressed with the treatment afforded them, first a private jet, now a long black limousine. She was anxious to see the Manor that Richard had described to her and to meet the Lancasters, who she had heard so much about already. Joy was not disappointed, the Manor was more glorious than her brother had described and the Lancasters were truly welcoming.

"Thank you so much for inviting me into your wonderful home," said Joy, addressing Lady Lancaster's initial greeting. "Adam has told me so much about you and Lord Lancaster and you both look just as I pictured you would."

"Well, I hope that is a good thing," gestured Lord Lancaster.

"Oh, it is, I didn't mean to …."

Lady Lancaster interrupted Joy saying, "We know what you meant Joy, James is just teasing you." She put her arm around Joy's shoulder and started to lead her away. "He's like that with all the pretty young ladies. Poor Monica was tortured by his antics growing up. He still likes to needle her. Now come with me and we'll talk more over a little breakfast before we get you settled in." They all moved in the direction of the family dining room.

Just as Richard had anticipated, Joy was instantly liked by everyone who met her and Lady Lancaster enjoyed showing her off to her friends as often as Joy was willing to accompany her. The party that Lady Lancaster had mentioned was held on the second Saturday following Richard and Joy's arrival. True to her word only close friends had been invited and it was a casual affair. Reston had even arranged for a barbeque dinner to be served on the patio next to the swimming pool behind the Manor. The day and evening weather had been meant for it. Joy thought that Monica was a terrific young woman and she was instantly smitten with Jason. Other than the expected expressions of sympathy on the deaths of their parents, the conversation was very friendly and uplifting. For Joy, she genuinely felt welcomed and not out of place.

It was at the party that Richard's name was divulged for the first time in public. It couldn't be hidden any longer now that his sister, Joy Ramsey had arrived. Lord Lancaster did most of the explaining within the various small groupings that formed around the pool. All were a little curious as to why he was still being called Richard by everyone except his sister. When Richard was asked directly if he was going to change his name, he only said that he wasn't yet certain, but that he would decide soon and that there were many things to consider. No one except Edward Bolden wished to pursue the question further.

Judith had been invited to the party of course. She would never have forgiven Lady Lancaster if she had not. And if Judith was to be invited, it really left no choice to the Lancasters but to invite Edward. While Edward might have otherwise declined the invitation, he was not about to pass up a chance to see the fair haired boy's little sister who Judith had been gushing over, even though she had only spoken to Lady Lancaster about her.

Edward was standing on the outer edge of a small gathering around Richard when he commented, "I would think that you would be jumping at the chance to reclaim your real name. Why is it such a difficult decision?" The faces in the gathering all turned toward the voice behind them, then to Richard.

Richard said to Edward, "It may seem simple enough to you, Edward, but please just accept that there are reasons, personal reasons." Richard, as well as the rest of the gathering expected the topic to be concluded and all turned back to their earlier conversations, but Edward would not be halted in his quest.

"Surly you must be proud of your real name, your Father's name, how complicated can it be .... ." Before Edward could finish his sentence, in that portion of a second before Edward could utter another word, Richard's body went tense, his temperature surged and he was grabbing hold of Edward's shirt lifting him on to his toes, his determined jaw clenched inches away from Edward's face. The smaller Edward was startled by the sudden fury and the surprise just as suddenly turned into fear as he peered into eyes burning with rage.

"Richard," came a calm and familiar voice over his shoulder. "Richard, let him be. Don't do something you'll soon regret. It's not worth it." The voice was getting closer. Richard started to relax his hold on Edward, as did the grip on his face. When the man with the voice put his hand on Richard's shoulder, Richard released Edward, mumbled something that sounded like, "I'm sorry," then lowered his head and walked quickly away.

"Well you should be," cried Edward after Richard. "What the hell's the matter with him?" Edward said to no one in particular. The gathering turned away and disbanded.

"I should have allowed him to throttle you," said Lord Lancaster, now with an anger he had hidden to this point. "Are you so dense that you don't know when to leave well enough alone? You are one of the most inconsiderate and rude people I know. If you expect to be invited to this house in the future you will change your attitude Edward or so help me…"

Lord Lancaster couldn't finish his warning, but it didn't matter as Edward was already turning to walk away. He looked back at Lord Lancaster with a sneer, but didn't say a word. He kept on walking not paying attention to and not caring about the other party members who were watching him leave. He passed by his mother without noticing her and she didn't try to stop him. Judith felt humiliated and wanted to hide. A few minutes later a sound of a car skidding away on loose stones could be heard even from the other side of the Manor.

Both Monica and Joy ran to Richard, who by this time was standing in the entrance way to the stables. He was leaning against the wall breaking pieces of straw with his fingers. He saw the girls approach and held up his hands to say, "I know, I know, I shouldn't have lost my temper."

"Well, you livened up the party," Monica joked. Then she said, "You did what anybody would have done. That Edward is such a jerk."

"I thought you were going to throw him in the pool," added Joy.

"I should have been able to keep my cool. I know Edward is an ass, so I should expect him to say these things." Richard paused then said, "But when he insinuated that I wasn't proud of my Dad, I lost it."

"Are you alright now to go back to the party?" asked Monica. You don't have to worry about what people are going to think. They know Edward better than you do. Come on let's go."

Edward burst on to the main highway leading away from the estate's winding entrance road, scattering stone and leaving traces of rubber on the pavement. He was furious after yet another bout of humiliation from his uncle and as well from Richard Lion, the boy who could do no wrong. Edward had not been drinking heavily at the party but he felt intoxicated with hate towards these two men, two men with whom he vowed to get even. He continued to race his car down the highway and through the village of Maidens Green, leaving angry pedestrians in the wake. Fortunately his reckless driving hadn't hurt anyone. Even after driving hell bent for nearly twenty minutes, Edward was still fuming. He kept on thinking about how close a relationship Richard was developing with Lord Lancaster and how far his own relationship with his uncle had drifted, not that he was ever very close to him. He was jealous of Richard: Richard the mechanic, Richard the guitar player, Richard who taught special needs kids, Richard the fencer, Richard the engineer. Richard, Richard, Richard. Edward's mind was so absorbed with his disdain for Richard that he wasn't watching where he was driving. He narrowly missed an on-coming car and then over compensated with his steering adjustment causing him to lose control of the car. The next thing he knew he and his car had careened into a ditch and stopped up against a large fir tree. An air bag was flattening his face. Edward escaped serious physical injury, but his car and his emotions were terribly scarred.

It was such a pleasant night that after the guests had departed, Joy decided to go for a swim in the outdoor pool. She had been taking advantage of the two pools at the Manor, swimming every day in one or the other or both and had even gotten up early to pace Reston in the lap pool on a few occasions. Reston was quite impressed with Richard's sister and more so since she could outswim him over short distances.

Lord Lancaster waited until all the guests departed, including Judith and Monica and her family, before discussing the matter of Richard's outburst with him. He found Richard in the library, a book on medieval history in his hands.

"I dislike violence," Lord Lancaster said to Richard, as the older gentleman entered the room, "but I can't blame you for feeling the way you did toward Edward. People like Edward are fools. There are many of them in this world and you will undoubtedly meet many more like him, but it is how you choose to react to them in that brief instant that will help shape your character for a lifetime. How are you feeling now?"

"Like a bit of a fool myself," said Richard. "I apologize for causing a stir out there this evening. I shouldn't have lost my temper. I should have known better, especially with Edward. I'm sorry."

Lord Lancaster had not sought out Richard to belabour the interruption to an otherwise nice party. "Well, I said what I came to say. I'm off to bed. Have a good sleep yourself my boy."

The next morning, Richard and Joy joined Lord and Lady Lancaster on a Sunday ride into the hills. The evening and night before yielded to a bright and cloudless sky, warm sunshine and a gentle breeze. It was another perfect day. Joy was much more comfortable on a horse than Richard had been when he first arrived at Lancaster Manor. She had enjoyed two summers as a camp counsellor primarily teaching swimming, but she had also taken advantage of the many opportunities to go horseback riding as well at the camp. At the top of their favourite hill, the four riders dismounted to enjoy the view of the country side. While it was something the Lancasters had seen thousands of times before, they still marvelled at the splendour of the green meadows, the winding creek that this year overflowed its banks, the random stands of birch trees and the thick forests of oak and fir. They were happy to be able to share this little bit of nature with Richard and Joy.

Breaking the silence, Richard declared, "I did a great deal of thinking last night and I have made up my mind." He turned first to Joy and then to the Lancasters. "I am going to stay in England and I am going to keep Richard Lion as my name, actually, Richard Adam Ramsey Lion. I will take Adam and Ramsey as my middle names. I'd like to begin the process as soon as possible, if that is alright with you Lord Lancaster." Following Joy's arrival, Richard declared to the Lancasters that he would feel more comfortable calling the Lancasters by their title as everyone else did.

Lady Lancaster asked, "And you are very sure about this decision?"

"Yes," replied Richard, a definite sense of resolve in his voice.

"I want you to know that you have my support in this decision," said Joy. "Even though I have been here for just under two weeks, I have come to understand that this is your home. And for all practical purposes," she said as if with the wisdom of a sage, "you have been reborn here and you are known as Richard Lion." Joy closed the distance between them and hugged Richard's arm to say, "As your loving sister, I may still call you Adam though." They all chuckled.

"I will arrange a meeting with my lawyers as early as possible," said Lord Lancaster. "I'm glad you have come to a decision Richard. I know it has been weighing on your mind and now you can start to take that weight away."

"On an entirely different subject," said Lady Lancaster. "Did James tell you that he has a meeting with the Queen next week?" Lady Lancaster wasn't bragging about the meeting, she simply thought it would be interesting for the young people to know.

"You know Queen Elizabeth?" exclaimed Joy.

"I actually know her quite well as a matter of fact," Lord Lancaster responded quite casually. "I have known her for many years, even when we were children, but we don't see her or Prince Phillip socially very often any more. But this is not a social visit next week. No, you see, I am a member of one of her many councils, this one being for International Relations. We meet with Her Majesty four times a year. The Prime Minister also attends."

Late that same night, the phone on the wall at the Old Squire Inn rang five times before the barman answered. Sarge was not here yet, the barman told the voice on the other end of the phone. "I guarantee he'll be in within the next half hour though; it's darts night."

"I'll call later," said the voice.

CHAPTER TWENTY-SEVEN

Joy was genuinely convinced that Richard had made the correct decision for himself to stay and live in England under the name of Richard Lion. And after a period of four weeks into her stay with her brother and the Lancasters, Joy was equally convinced that her home and future were back in Winnipeg with her friends. She would delay university for a year and travel with her friends Jill and Tony, as she had always hoped she could. Richard, while concerned for his sister, gave her his support, saying that he was only a phone call away. They decided that they would sell the house and property and invest the proceeds. A call to a family friend in real estate and to their lawyers would begin the process. If neither Joy nor Richard were available to close the transactions, the lawyers would be given authority to do so on their behalf. As soon as Richard's official identification documents could be finalized, including the petition to convert property of Adam Ramsey to Richard Lion, which was expected within another three to four weeks, he would fly to Winnipeg to finalize any loose ends. Presumably, by then, Joy would be somewhere in the Australian outback.

Four weeks and a day after she had landed in England, Joy was about to board the Air Canada flight back home. Richard and Lord and Lady Lancaster were at the airport to see her off. "Thank you for inviting me into your home and making me feel so welcome," Joy said to the Lancasters, as she gave Lady Lancaster a hug and Lord Lancaster a kiss on the cheek. "I'll miss you very much but I will treasure the memories."

"You will always be welcome here," returned Lady Lancaster. "Remember, if your travels ever take you into the UK, you must stop by and bring your friends too."

Lord Lancaster added, "You take good care now Joy. Be safe. If I may be of assistance in any way, please do not hesitate to contact me."

"This past month with you has been so wonderful," Joy said to Richard. "I will miss you very much."

"I'm going to miss you too," said Richard, "but I want you to keep in touch, alright. Call me if there are any problems with the arrangements regarding the house and the lawyers. I'll handle the rest from here or if I have to, I'll go back to Winnipeg when you are travelling. I'm sure everything will work out fine."

Joy said reluctantly, "Well, last call, I better get going."

With a final hug all round, they said their good byes and Joy disappeared down the walkway toward the plane.

Richard's new promotion had been approved and an organizational change under John Maxwell had been made to accommodate the new South African Projects Branch. Richard would be responsible for the development of business and the management of projects generated with the South Africans under Regal Engineering. Further, he would be a consultant to the other companies under Port of Grace Enterprises that might wish to do business in that country as well. One of Richard's unit engineers had been selected to take over most of the South African project until Jennifer returned from her maternity leave. However, Richard still insisted on having a major hands-on role. He had also been given approval to hire additional staff to round out the new branch. Donald Bacon had contacted Richard to begin work on developing a feasibility study of cellular tower development. Here too, Richard planned to be fully engaged along with his project managers. He knew that he would be over taxing himself somewhat, but he was not about to give up control until he was comfortable operations were able to be run smoothly. If future work grew beyond their projections, he had been assured by John Maxwell that further staff would be available. Richard's own position title was changed to Director and Special Liaison, South African Projects Branch. Not surprisingly, the office was firmly supportive of these organizational changes. As expected, no one could argue that they had as much success or as much influence with the South African government as Richard. Because Richard's branch was moved under John Maxwell from George Casper's department, no one in George's department could complain that they were being overlooked for a promotion in the department. And George was more than pleased that he could go home a little earlier each day after work to spend more time with his family.

Even while he was extremely busy, all was going well with work. Richard couldn't have been happier. On the home front, Monica and Richard were still trying to figure out where they stood with each other. There was certainly the attraction but the romance had not flourished. The primary reason was clearly related to the on-going changes in events and the relatively few hours available to them to promote their relationship.

Early one evening when Richard was on his way home after a long day's work, he found himself trying to think of something special he could do for Monica, something different and romantic. He was driving his Firebird slowly through Maidens Green when he spotted the florist shop. He parked but didn't get out of the car. An idea, a series of ideas was beginning to spawn in his mind. Whenever Richard had something to prepare for, such as a business meeting or going to a social function or even preparing a fancy meal, it was his habit to try and visualize the event or activity in his mind, almost like walking through a virtual simulation. He was doing this now. Fifteen minutes later he knew what he would do for Monica. He first had to check her schedule and then make certain arrangements so that she wouldn't suspect anything and she would be free to enjoy the day he was planning for her.

Over a late dinner with the Lancasters that same evening, Lord Lancaster mentioned how tied up he had been all day and hadn't been able to talk to his wife or to Richard about an upcoming visit to Cape Town. Lord Lancaster said, "Minister Renjeu called me today to invite us, that includes you too Richard, to be his guests at an upcoming celebration honouring a number of South African artists. September 16th, I believe. Apparently this is supposed to be a very big annual event, very VIP so to speak, and it raises hundreds of thousands of dollars in funds for impoverished children. He also said we should come a day early so we could visit. I told him that I thought we could attend, at least Muriel and I, but couldn't speak for you Richard. I said I would get back to him within a few days."

Richard put down his glass of water and said, "I would have to check my calendar, but offhand I can't think of any reason I couldn't go. I'll let you know tomorrow." He paused for a moment of inspiration then said, "You know, if we could manage to stay an extra day and arrange a business meeting with Minister Renjeu and Donald Bacon, we could have a preliminary discussion about the feasibility study design. I will have it ready by then."

"Splendid idea. You let me know and I'll arrange it." He turned to Muriel and said, "You won't mind a surprise shopping trip will you dear?"

"I'm sure I can keep myself occupied for a few hours," replied Lady Lancaster. Over the years she had enjoyed many surprise shopping trips when she accompanied her husband on business trips. On as many occasions she would do some sightseeing, if the city appealed to her. Lady Lancaster could be very independent when she had to or wanted to be.

The next morning, the trip had been confirmed, including the business meeting. They would leave September 15th, the day before the Arts celebration.

Also that morning, Richard had heard from Lord Lancaster's lawyers who indicated to him that all the discussions with appropriate authorities had been completed and all the documents necessary for his official identity change, both here and in Canada had been prepared and that signatures were being solicited. They said that by this time next week he would officially become Richard Adam Ramsey Lion, on a permanent basis.

Joy had called later in the day to tell Richard that she had sold the house already, including much of the furniture and one of the vehicles. She said that three couples had been engaged in a bidding war and in the end one of the couples paid twenty-five thousand dollars more than the asking price. She said that, as agreed, she would put selected items in storage and sell the rest of the contents of the house. Whatever didn't sell would go to a charitable organization. She said that she was happy she was able to handle this business before leaving for Australia on September 5th. She also said that she couldn't wait for her trip to begin. Richard told her the news about the final documents for his name change. They broke off their phone conversation agreeing that everything seemed to be falling into place for them.

On Sunday afternoon, Judith had called Lady Lancaster for a brief sisterly chat. She had also heard through the grape vine, not from her sister, that Joy had returned to Canada and she wanted to know why. They spoke for a half hour about many different things including the upcoming visit to Cape Town on September 15th. Lady Lancaster was excited because all three of them would be going, almost like a family. They ended the conversation with Lady Lancaster saying that they would see each other again next month on their next visit to Coventry.

On Tuesday of the next week, Detective Inspector Giles called Lord Lancaster and asked for a meeting that afternoon. It was concerning an urgent matter. "Nice to see you again Inspector," said Lord Lancaster as he welcomed the Inspector into his office. Your call this morning certainly peaked my interest. What can I do for you?"

Inspector Giles took the seat offered to him in front of Lord Lancaster's huge walnut desk. "I appreciate you seeing me on such short notice, Lord Lancaster, however, I have something important to discuss with you. I never mentioned this to you back when we had been investigating the attempted murder because we really did not have any evidence to support it, but now we are wondering again …"

Lord Lancaster interrupted the inspector saying, "Please say what you came to say Inspector."

"Right. Well the thing of it is that we may have uncovered plans for a possible attempt on your life. And we are now thinking that the earlier attempt may have been related."

"Good God," said an astonished Lord Lancaster. "Are you certain? Who are these people and why would they want to come after me?"

The Inspector shuffled his position in the chair and answered Lord Lancaster. "We are not one hundred percent, but we have been working with the boys from MI5 on some recent death threats and during the investigation your name had come up. I won't say who, but two of the people that received the threats are members of the Queen's International Relations Council, the same council of which you are a member. It is our understanding that the council will be voting on a certain recommendation at its next meeting that may trigger the use of economic sanctions against a certain country. This could be the connection."

"I've not received any threats."

Inspector Giles looked directly at Lord Lancaster and said, "You may have had more than a threat, Lord Lancaster. This is why we are now thinking of the possibility your attack could be linked to these other threats."

Lord Lancaster rose from behind his desk and looked out at the window, before turning back to the Inspector. "So now what? Should I be arranging for security protection? I won't have our lives disrupted unnecessarily."

"Until we know more for sure, I can only suggest you consider some form of protection, or at least take some extra precautions. If we discover that we are wrong, we will advise you immediately. At this point we don't want to take any chances."

Lord Lancaster stepped in front of his desk closer to the Inspector and said, "I will take this all under advisement for now, but I thank you Inspector for coming to see me about it."

The Inspector, taking the hint that the meeting was about to end, said, "Alright Lord Lancaster, but please do not hesitate to contact me if you have any questions or if you would like us to assign someone to watch out for you." After the Inspector left his office, Lord Lancaster asked his secretary to send in his next appointment.

CHAPTER TWENTY-EIGHT

Monica was leaning lightly on her arms that lay folded on the white linen, as she looked directly into Richard's eyes from across the table. A small candle lamp provided just enough light to enhance the romantic ambience surrounding them in the quaint Italian bistro. Although the light was dim, her face was aglow and she was shaking her head in disbelief as she said, "I can't believe you were able to plan this wonderful day for me and still keep it a surprise."

The last secret envelope Monica opened earlier in the afternoon was an invitation to dinner. She was instructed to "dress to kill" and told that a limousine would call for her precisely at 7:00 in the evening, plenty of time for her to get ready. The envelope was accompanied by another red rose.

The Saturday morning first began for Monica with a mysterious telephone call at 8:00 from a woman whose voice was not familiar. The call woke her from a pleasant sleep and she was a bit groggy when she first heard the voice on the other end of the phone. The woman said that Monica should look for an envelope on the steps leading up to her front door and follow the directions. The woman then promptly hung up. Naturally curious and wondering if there was any truth to the call, Monica threw on her dressing gown and went in search of the envelope. Somewhat surprised, she found an envelope just where it was supposed to be. More to her surprise was the red rose lying across it. The envelope was periwinkle blue in colour with sculpted borders. Monica's name was the only word upon it. Still standing on the steps, the red rose between her fingers, she rushed to open the envelope, retrieving the one page letter inside. It read, "Dear Monica, a special lady deserves a special day, and one is about to begin for you. A limousine will call for you at precisely 8:30." The note was unsigned. Monica stood on the steps not knowing what to do. She reread the note trying to decide whether to take it seriously or not. At the same time, she was intrigued by the mystery and secretly hoped that it was authentic and that Richard was the author.

"What was your first reaction when you received the call? That was my secretary Margaret by the way," Richard said to Monica.

"At first I was mad because someone woke me up. I had planned on sleeping in and having a real casual morning. Then I wasn't sure what I was hearing. My curiosity won out so I went looking for the envelope."

"It's a good thing you were willing to play along without question, otherwise it wouldn't have been as special. But I knew you would. I knew you would be up to the challenge."

"When the limo arrived at 8:30, I was ready, but still a little surprised. The driver would not tell me where he was taking me and that started to freak me out a little." Monica broke into a wide grin and said, "I had my cell phone in my hand with my finger on speed dial to my father, just in case. But the spa treatment was glorious and so soothing. The light breakfast of strawberry crepes they served while I was having the pedicure was delicious. What a way to spend the morning!"

At the conclusion of her spa visit fifteen minutes to noon, Monica was given another secret envelope by the receptionist. It came with another red rose. The receptionist was as excited as Monica, as she lifted the note and began to read. "I trust you feel relaxed and ready for a visit with friends over lunch. The limousine is waiting for you outside. Enjoy."

Monica placed her fluted crystal glass on the table and asked Richard, "How did you manage to have Sam and Mary meet me for lunch? We were supposed to hang out today but Sam told me just yesterday that she had to go visit her folks this weekend because her Mom had had a bit of an accident.

Richard just smiled an all-knowing smile and said, "I started planning this day over two weeks ago. Sam and Mary were in on it from the beginning. Sam was supposed to keep your day free for me by suggesting you two spend the day together. When she told you she had to go to see her parents, your day suddenly became mine."

The limousine dropped Monica off at her favourite café where she found Sam and Mary seated in the corner wearing two very broad smiles. After the girls finished their lunch and their visit where Monica had told them all about the mystery envelopes and the spa treatments, the owner of the café came to the table to announce that their lunch had been paid for and that a limousine was waiting for all of them outside. She handed Monica another envelope and red rose. Inside the note read, "Yes Monica, you as well as Sam and Mary are leaving together. Enjoy your afternoon. I hope you didn't eat too much."

The waiter placed their desserts before Richard and Monica asking if they would like anything further, coffee perhaps. They both nodded that they would. Both black. Monica said, "That was so special to spend the day with Sam and Mary. The three of us haven't been together for a few months now. I kind of felt bad though when they were sitting there watching me try on all those gorgeous outfits you had picked out. This one I'm wearing was the first one I tried on."

Richard had arranged a private shopping spree for Monica at a shop that Sam had told him Monica liked. He had approached the shop owner a few days ago telling her about his surprise day for Monica and asked for her help. Richard had picked out a dozen outfits that he thought would look good on Monica. They were then put aside for her special day with her two friends. Sam and Mary were treated with champagne as they watched Monica deliver her fashion show. The young women had a hoot helping Monica make decisions and Monica walked away with three fabulous outfits all thanks to her mystery person.

"You know of course that Sam and Mary's boyfriends will hear about this and come looking for you," said Monica with a grin on her face. "When I read the girls the last note about going to dinner, they said this was the most romantic thing they had ever heard of and said that I am very lucky." Monica took a moment to reach across to Richard's hand before continuing, "I am very lucky you know. This has been such a special day, I don't want it to end."

Richard produced a final envelope from inside his suit pocket and handed it to Monica. "I was hoping you would feel that way."

Monica looked suspiciously up at Richard then back down as she opened the envelope and unfolded the note. She smiled as she read in silence and when she finished she looked up again and said, "You devil, you must have been reading my mind. She then retrieved a golden key card pass from the envelope with the words Embassy Hotel emblazed upon it. "What are we waiting for?" They left the restaurant hand-in-hand laughing and giggling as they walked in the direction of the lavish hotel down the street.

The next evening Sarge was in the middle of a throw when his name was called from across the room. He missed the dart board all together and gave out a roar of profanities. After another earful to the barman, he grabbed the phone and spoke into the mouthpiece still irritated, "Yeah, what do you want?"

The voice hesitated, hearing that Sarge was obviously pissed off at something or someone. The voice finally said, "It's me, do you have everything you need?"

While Sarge would normally change his attitude when he heard the familiar voice, this time he didn't at first. "Yes I have everything. I told you there wouldn't be a problem," he said, clearly still annoyed that he had been interrupted.

"I just want to be sure there won't be any problems this time," the voice responded.

"Don't you worry, the bloody car will blow into the clouds," Sarge promised. "Just tell me when and where and be sure to put the money where we agreed."

"Alright, they are leaving on Wednesday, September 15th, got that, Wednesday, September 15th. Their flight leaves at 11:15 in the morning. They will leave by car for the airport at about 8:00. Do you need any further information?"

Sarge answered in a normal tone, "No, that's all I need to know. I'll handle it. Just make sure the money is there. I want to get away from here as quick as possible after it's done."

"It will be waiting for you," said the voice. Then the voice added, "This will be the last time I contact you." The line went dead.

CHAPTER TWENTY-NINE

The plan was for Stewart to drive Lord and Lady Lancaster and Richard to the airport in the limousine. They would leave around 8:00 in the morning in time to reach the airport and board their flight at 11:15. Plans have a habit of changing at the last minute. At dinner on the night before they were to leave, Richard announced that an urgent matter had surfaced during the day that demanded his attention and that he would not be able to leave with Lord and Lady Lancaster in the morning. Lord Lancaster responded to Richard's news saying that it was unfortunate Richard couldn't fly out with them but that he understood and he was certain Minister Renjeu would as well. He also said he was glad that Richard could still make a later flight in the week to attend the business meeting that had been arranged.

The next morning, another situation was presented to Lord and Lady Lancaster that further altered their original plans. Stewart had come down with a terrible flu and would not be capable of driving Lord and Lady Lancaster to the airport. "No need to apologize," Lord Lancaster said to Stewart. "You just get yourself better as quickly as you can."

With that news, Lord Lancaster asked Reston to move their luggage from the limousine to Lord Lancaster's new sedan. It was too late to make alternate plans. He would drive the forty-five minutes to the airport and leave the car in the airport parking area. "It will only be for a few days," he said to his wife. At 8:13, Lord and Lady Lancaster pulled off the winding stone road from the estate on to the main highway in the direction of the airport.

Sarge had received word that the Lancasters were on their way. He was waiting at a pre-arranged location where two of his men were getting prepared to create an interruption in traffic that would leave the Lancaster car stranded and out of sight from other drivers for five minutes, giving Sarge time to scramble under the vehicle and attach the device without being seen. Ten minutes later it would all be over and Sarge could collect his money and get out of the country.

Sarge was starting to worry. The Lancaster car should have appeared by this time, he thought. He looked over to his men and shrugged. Another ten minutes passed and no car. Sarge placed a call to his man that had informed him that the Lancaster's had left the estate. The man assured him that the Lancasters had left and had driven off in the direction of the airport. He could not explain why they hadn't shown up at Sarge's location.

As the Lancasters pulled on to the main highway, Lord Lancaster felt his body jerk, enough that he momentarily lost his grip on the steering wheel resulting in the car edging off the pavement onto the gravel shoulder. The car fish tailed slightly on the gravel but was soon brought under control. "What happened?" asked a startled Lady Lancaster.

"I don't know," Lord Lancaster replied. "I had a little flinch, like a spasm. I've had them from time to time over the past month. They're nothing to worry about dear."

Lady Lancaster asked again, "Are you sure? Are you are alright to drive James?"

"Yes, now don't worry," he replied.

After a few minutes, Lord Lancaster had regained control of the car as well as his wife's confidence in driving and began to accelerate to the maximum cruising speed allowed for the highway. At that time of day, mid-week, the traffic was heavy. The person driving behind Lord Lancaster was in a hurry and leaned on his horn to try and coax Lord Lancaster to move faster. Since Lord Lancaster was already driving at the maximum limit he didn't feel as if he had to accommodate the man with the horn so he waved him to pass. The next thing he knew, the car blasted out from behind him and was soon several car lengths ahead. A few more minutes went by and Lord Lancaster found himself in the same position as the earlier gentleman had. Now he was caught behind a slower vehicle. When he determined that it was safe to pass the slower car, Lord Lancaster pulled out of his lane and accelerated. A large semi-trailer was in the distance heading in Lord Lancaster's direction, but he knew that he had ample time to pass the other car and pull back into his original lane, which he did.

When the semi was five hundred feet away from Lord Lancaster's car, the truck driver pulled hard on his blow horn while at the same time placing his foot lightly onto the brake pedal. Three hundred feet away and the truck driver pressed hard on the pedal and cranked his steering wheel to the left. It was not enough and it was not in time.

Just prior to the horn sounding, Lord Lancaster's car had veered into the truck's lane and stayed there. Lady Lancaster was screaming at her husband to turn back into the lane, but her cries were of no use. Lord Lancaster was not responding. He couldn't, he was dead. It was learned later that Lord Lancaster had suffered a massive stroke and died before he even saw the truck in his path. The collision into the semi-trailer obliterated the Lancaster's car killing Lady Lancaster instantly. Her terror and pain lasted 3.4 seconds, the time it took for the two fast moving vehicles to close the five hundred foot gap. The truck driver survived the crash, but had several broken bones and a concussion.

Richard was seated around the conference room table with Sir Loxley and four senior managers representing Port of Grace's mining and hospitality sectors. Both sectors had new and on-going interests in South Africa. At 9:35 Sir Loxley's secretary entered the room and walked over to Sir Loxley to whisper in his ear. Sir Loxley's face went pale, his expression showed horror. He looked up at his secretary with disbelief and said, "Are they sure?" The secretary nodded. Sir Loxley turned his head to Richard and with great pain uttered the words, "Lord and Lady Lancaster have been killed."

Richard was simply stunned by the words that had been spoken, not really believing that he had heard correctly. "Oh my God," he said, "they can't be."

Richard searched Sir Loxley's and then his secretary's face for a sign that he had misunderstood, that this couldn't be happening. Sir Loxley said, "I'm sorry Richard. Apparently they died in a crash with a semi-trailer halfway between Lancaster Manor and the airport. They died instantly."

Richard closed his eyes and covered them with his hands, not believing that this tragedy could have happened. After several moments of silence, Richard started up out of his seat and said, "I've got to go." Looking at the secretary he asked, "Have they been taken away yet?"

The secretary spoke softly and replied, "Yes, they have been taken to the hospital, Mount Royal."

Richard turned to Sir Loxley and said, "That's where I'll be. I'll call and inform Reston on my way. I better contact Judith as well." Richard stopped and leaned on the table. He put his other hand over his face to shield his emotions and said, "I can't believe this. I was supposed to go with them today. If I would have gone with them, this may not have happened."

Sir Loxley jumped up and slid over to Richard taking him by his shoulders. With a firm tone he said, "No Richard, you cannot blame yourself for this accident. It was not your fault. Do not think that way, do you hear me?"

Richard nodded, but he didn't feel any less guilty.

Sir Loxley backed away and said, "Richard, I can't let you leave here in this condition. You must accept this for what it is. Can you do that?"

This time Richard nodded and said that he could. He said he was fine and he would be alright to drive. Before he left the room he said to Sir Loxley that he would call him later.

Edward Bolden was getting into his car to leave for work. He had a late night and he was slightly hung over. He turned on the ignition and heard the last few words from a news cast, "…. I repeat, the top story this morning concerns the tragic death of Lord and Lady Lancaster of Maidens Green. Stay tuned for more details at the top of the hour." A smile appeared on Edward's face. Underneath, he felt no pain or grief. He put the car into gear and headed out of the parking lot on to the street. He wouldn't be expected at work today, or for several more days. He had better call his mother, he thought. Judith answered on the third ring. She hadn't heard the news. Unlike Edward, his mother broke down on the phone unable to speak through the crying. He eventually hung up.

After Richard had called the Manor to speak with Reston, he tried Judith. The line was busy. Ten minutes later the line was still busy. When he pulled into the hospital parking area he decided to try Judith one more time. She answered on the second ring. In a weak voice she said, "Hello."

"Judith, this is Richard"

"Oh Richard," she cried, "I just heard. I can't believe this has happened." Richard could barely make out her words, she was sobbing so much.

Then suddenly Judith gasped and exclaimed in a clearer voice, "Richard, I thought you were dead."

"No, I wasn't in the car. I couldn't go with them after all."

With a sense of confusion Judith said, "But Edward said that James, Muriel, you and Stewart were all killed. He said that the bomb totally destroyed the car."

"Stewart wasn't in the car either. And what's this about a bomb. I didn't hear anything about a bomb."

Judith remained confused and said, "Well that's what I thought I heard Edward say. He said he caught it on the news."

Richard spoke to Judith for a few more minutes trying to console her. It was apparent that she was not thinking clearly and that she had been confused about what Edward had told her. He broke off the call saying that he would call her in a day or two.

The bodies of Lord and Lady Lancaster had reached the hospital long before Richard had arrived. While the autopsy had not yet been performed on Lord Lancaster, the doctors still strongly suggested to Richard that he would not want to see Lord and Lady Lancaster in their current state. The doctors assured him, however, that neither of them suffered before they died. Thanking the doctors for their sensitivity, Richard left the morgue. He decided to call Monica on his cell phone, but to do that he had to first exit the hospital before turning his phone back on. Outside a side entrance door, Richard waited for Monica to answer; she did on the second ring. Her caller ID showed that it was Richard who was calling and she was expecting him.

"Oh Richard, I'm so very sorry," said Monica, her voice full of sorrow.

Richard's emotions set in as he was making the call and by the time Monica answered, he was already distraught with grief. He was sobbing and crying uncontrollably, hugging the wall for support. When he tried to say something, to explain to Monica what he knew, he broke down even more. He couldn't get the words out. In those few minutes Richard knew he was balling like a little kid, but he didn't care. It was alright to cry, Monica said to him. He hadn't had the opportunity to grieve in this way for his own parents and now he was grieving for them as well as the Lancasters.

Monica waited patiently, hurting from the pain that Richard was experiencing. She tried to comfort him with soothing words but she knew that he couldn't really hear her. Finally, after several more minutes Richard regained some control. He apologized over and over for breaking down, but he also realized that he needed to cry, to cry long and hard, before he could start accepting what had happened and to help others as well as himself to carry on. He told Monica that he would be returning to Lancaster Manor to be with the staff and that he would see her in the evening.

On the way to the parking lot, Richard was hailed by someone getting out of his car. At first Richard did not recognize the man. When he came closer Richard saw that it was Detective Inspector Giles.

From fifteen feet away the Inspector called to Richard saying, "I'm glad I caught you Richard. Your office told me that you would be here. Please accept my condolences. I'm awfully sorry about Lord and Lady Lancaster. They were two very fine people."

"Thank you Inspector."

The Inspector said, "I know this is a bad time, but I wonder if I could have just a few words with you."

THE ROAD TO LANCASTER MANOR

"Sure, what can I do for you," Richard replied, not really caring.

"We're pretty certain now that it was an accident. From what the witnesses have said we suspect that Lord Lancaster probably had a heart attack or stroke then lost control of the direction of the car. It would have happened in a matter of seconds. We'll know for sure after the autopsy."

Richard looked up at the Inspector and said, "I just came from the morgue. They wouldn't let me see them. Apparently their bodies were pretty much destroyed."

"I'm sorry," the Inspector said again. But there is another reason I wanted to talk to you. I told Lord Lancaster just a few weeks ago that we suspected a death plot against him and …"

"What do you mean by that," asked Richard, now more attentive to the Inspector.

"We think it had something to do with his role on the Queen's International Relations Council. We also think that last February's attempt on his life may have been related." The Inspector paused before proceeding. "In any event, when we first heard about Lord and Lady Lancaster, even though the initial report claimed it was an accident, we still acted as if it could have been a terrorist plot and took action according to our established protocol. Road blocks were set up essentially establishing a net around the whole county. Five miles up the road from where the accident occurred, our men stopped and searched a car and found a bomb. The men in the car were taken into custody and interrogated. When the men were separated, the weaker of them pleaded for a deal and eventually admitted that they were waiting to plant the bomb under Lord Lancaster's car. And get this, he admitted to the February incident as well. I want you to come down to the station and try to identify them if you can. It doesn't have to be right away. They are not going anywhere."

Richard could not believe what the Inspector was saying. That even if there hadn't been an accident, Lord and Lady Lancaster would still have been killed from a terrorist bomb. "This is incredible, who would want to do this?" asked Richard.

"That we don't know," replied the Inspector. "Once the leader of the group realized he had been betrayed, he claimed that he didn't know who had hired him. He said if he did, he'd make a deal, but he didn't. He said he only spoke to him on the telephone. He said he didn't need to meet with him as long as he received his money. I expect he's telling the truth."

"I'll try to come down to the station tomorrow or the next day, if that is alright Inspector."

"That will be fine. Again, I'm sorry for disturbing you at this time, but I thought you would want to know."

Richard extended his hand and said, "I appreciate you tracking me down Inspector."

Richard and the Inspector said good bye to each other and headed to their respective cars. As Richard opened his car a thought came to mind. He turned in the direction of the Inspector and yelled for him to wait. They walked toward each other again and Richard said, "I just remembered something. It's probably nothing, but I thought I should mention it. When I called Lady Lancaster's sister Judith earlier to tell her about the accident, she told me that she had already heard the news from her son, Edward, Edward Bolden. According to Judith, Edward told her that Stewart, Lord Lancaster's driver, Lord and Lady Lancaster and I had all been killed by a car bomb. I told her that she must be mistaken since Stewart was not in the car and obviously I wasn't either. But how could she have been confused about people and about a bomb?"

The Inspector asked, "Do you know this Judith very well? Is she often confused about things?"

"I wouldn't say confused, but certainly manipulated by Edward," said Richard.

The Inspector was curious now and asked, "What about Edward, would there be any reason he would want to have Lord and Lady Lancaster killed?"

"He was definitely on the outs with Lord Lancaster, me too for that matter. Just a short while ago at a party at Lancaster Manor, Lord Lancaster practically threw him off of the Estate. Edward was furious. But I can't believe he could do something like arrange for someone to kill the Lancasters."

"Why would Judith believe Edward when he allegedly told her that you had been killed too?" asked the Inspector.

Richard replied, "I suppose she knew somehow, probably from talking to Lady Lancaster that I was supposed to have accompanied the Lancasters to Cape Town. But at the last minute, actually the night before, Sir Loxley asked that I stay behind to discuss some urgent business. I was going to meet them Friday. Why do you ask?"

"Well, it is possible that Lady Lancaster had mentioned the trip to her sister and that her sister mentioned it to her son, Edward. If so, he would have known that you too were going to be in the car. If he did have something against you and Lord Lancaster, this was his chance to get rid of both of you."

"Edward is a complete jerk, but I still can't believe he could go this far to seek revenge," Richard said. "Besides, I thought you were suspecting terrorists. Surely you don't think Edward is a terrorist."

The Inspector said, "Right now we are considering any and all possibilities. You may be right that Judith simply misunderstood what her son had told her, but on the other hand, you have also suggested a motive for Edward to have plotted to kill the Lancasters and yourself. I'll want to look into this a little more. Can you give me a list of the guests who were at the party where Lord Lancaster and Edward had words?"

"You can call Reston for the names," said Richard.

"Thank you Richard, I'll be in touch," said the Inspector. Both men returned to their cars and drove off in separate directions.

CHAPTER THIRTY

Edward was on his way to put the money in the hiding place he had arranged with Sarge. It was well worth it, he thought to himself. It took longer than he had expected, but at least he finally took care of both his uncle and Richard. It wasn't until Edward heard the full news cast on his car radio that he learned Lord and Lady Lancaster were killed in an accident and not by a bomb. And further, that Richard was not in the car with them. Edward pulled his car to the side of the road. His first reaction was disbelief that, once again, a well-designed plan had gone wrong. But just as suddenly he realised the beauty in this news. It was an accident. It wasn't murder and there wouldn't be an investigation. Besides he just saved himself a pile of money. He acknowledged that Richard had not been killed but accepted that the real target was his uncle, the man who he fully expected to replace at Lancaster Manor, if not directly as his only living relative, through his mother, who both Lord and Lady Lancaster were fond of. His smile brightened, he felt relieved. Then it hit him. Judith. He had told her that Richard had also been killed and that a bomb had been the cause. The horror lasted only a moment before Edward's calm and confidence returned. "What am I worrying about? Even if she had told anyone, they will think she was under stress and confused." He would deny what he had told his mother, suggesting that she was distraught. "Nobody will believe her." Edward had his smile back on his face as he moved his car back into traffic. "Yes," he said to himself again, "Everything was working out just fine."

The Lancaster's funeral was on Monday. It was now 8:05 of the following Wednesday morning and Richard was having breakfast in the family dining room of the Manor when Reston entered carrying a portable telephone. "Master Richard, I am sorry to disturb you, but you have a telephone call from Detective Inspector Giles. He seems to wish a meeting with you this morning."

"Thank you Reston, I'll take the call." Reston handed Richard the telephone and politely removed himself from the room. "Inspector Giles, what can I do for you?"

"I hate to bother you at this time Richard. I am sure you would prefer not to be disturbed right now, but I have some news about Lord and Lady Lancaster's deaths that I would like to discuss with you. May I call upon you this morning, say at 10:00?. I will try not to take up too much of your time, but I believe you'll want to hear what I have to say."

"That will be fine Inspector. See you at 10:00 then."

Richard stood from the table and began gazing out the bay window facing the rising sun. The coffee cup was set upon his lips as if ready to drink, but instead he simply froze in his position, as if in a trance. He wondered what news the Inspector wanted to share with him.

"So you are saying that Edward has become a legitimate suspect in an attempted bombing plot?" Richard said in disbelief to Inspector Giles. "Have you questioned him yet?"

"No, he doesn't yet know we suspect him. At least we hope he doesn't. We don't have any solid evidence to link him to the attempted murders, the information is all circumstantial. We interviewed a number of people at the party who witnessed Edward taunting you. You never mentioned that you went into a rage and nearly punched him out."

"I wasn't proud of it," Richard admitted.

"The witnesses also confirmed that Edward appeared livid at Lord Lancaster when the Lord spoke to him. "If looks could kill," they said. That was a quote. And when I spoke to Reston about the names of the people who were invited in the first place, he told me about a conversation he overheard between Lord Lancaster and Edward not so long ago where Lord Lancaster threatened to withhold Edward's inheritance if he didn't stop stealing from his mother. So you see why he has become a suspect. He has motive and he has the means to pay for a contract killing. But we still need to investigate further and I don't want to spook him, if he is guilty. I have men looking into his bank accounts for any large sums of money being taken out in February or recently."

Richard asked the Inspector, "Well, is there anything I can help with in the investigation?"

"No, I don't think so," said the Inspector. "But Richard, in the event Edward is the person we are looking for, you best be careful. He may still want to kill you as well."

"Thank you for coming," Richard said to the Inspector as he led him to the Manor's main entrance. "I'll keep that in mind. I've been informed by Lord Lancaster's lawyers that the reading of the Wills is to take place on Monday afternoon. I'm supposed to attend."

After saying good bye to the Inspector, Richard walked back to the library. On his way he accepted a fresh cup of coffee from Reston. He sat in the large leather arm chair, one of two facing on an angle to the fireplace. The fire had settled over the past half hour so he reached over to the logs and placed three small pieces of birch wood on to the dying flames. The dry wood quickly ignited and before long the fire was alive again.

Richard knew in his mind now that it was entirely conceivable for Edward to wish his uncle, and he supposed himself, dead. It was possible that Edward figured Lord Lancaster had not had time to follow through on his threats to erase Edward from his Will and if so, Edward would think that he needed to act quickly before that change was made. Richard did not know if Edward had been invited to the lawyer's office for the reading on Monday. "But there was no proof, at least nothing that a good lawyer couldn't dispense with," he said to himself. He sat staring into the fire allowing his mind to drift back, to recall some of the events that had transpired over the past number of months and particularly of the Tales of Ivanhoe.

CHAPTER THIRTY-ONE

The reading of the Wills was scheduled to take place in the law offices of Mr. Franklain J. Lester. Richard heard that Mr. Lester had been Lord Lancaster's lawyer since the early years, but when he first met the man that afternoon, he admitted to himself that he must have misunderstood. Mr. Lester was forty-five years old at most. He couldn't have been practicing when Lord Lancaster first started his businesses. Later he learned that Franklain J. Lester was the son of James R. J. Lester, who had passed away two years ago at the age of seventy-eight. His son had taken over Lord Lancaster's file.

Judith and Edward had been the first to arrive, although not together. Edward had made up a story to give reason why he couldn't drive with his mother, but the real reason was that he wanted to be alone to dream about the windfall he was expecting from the combined inheritance he as well as his mother would receive, both of which he expected to control. They sat beside one another at the centre of the meeting room table facing the windows. The table was large enough to seat twelve people comfortably. There would only be six seats required today.

Sir Loxley was the next to arrive and he entered the meeting room with his cell phone to his ear. He ended the call soon after and switched the sound to vibrate. He took a seat at the far end of the table after nodding to Judith.

Richard and Reston were the last of those invited to arrive. While Edward was not surprised to see Reston, the long-time servant to Lord Lancaster, he was not happy to see Richard. He had fought thoughts about Richard benefiting someway from the old man and in the end conceded that he would likely receive some token cash as his uncle's fair haired boy. Now that he actually saw Richard, his worst fears surfaced again.

Richard followed Reston into the room and sat beside him at the opposite end of the table from Sir Loxley but on the window side. Moving to his chair he nodded to Sir Loxley and Judith but only starred at Edward. Richard knew there was still no hard evidence tying Edward to the attempted murder of Lord and Lady Lancaster, but in his mind at that moment he was cursing the man.

Everyone sat in silence, some still in mourning and respectful of the circumstances that brought them to this place, one because everyone else was. Mr. Lester must have been informed that all those invited had been ushered into the meeting room, as he appeared through the doorway a few minutes after Richard sat down. He was holding a black three ring binder under his arm. Moving around the table he introduced himself to each person one at a time. When he came to Sir Loxley, Richard heard him say "Nice to see you again." After the brief introductions, Mr.

Lester took his seat at the centre of the table across from Judith and Edward. He placed the binder in front of him on the table, but did not open it.

"Since everyone is here I'll begin," Mr. Lester said, always giving each person equal eye time. "In spite of what you might think, the Will of Lord and Lady Lancaster is actually fairly straight forward. It is not necessary to read the entire Will, but rather I have prepared a short summary of the bequests. As such, I do not anticipate this to be a long meeting. For the record, everyone named in the Will is present except for, it is not really a person, rather, it's a foundation. The Lancasters have directed that a foundation be established to support the on-going work of two charitable organizations Lady Lancaster had been involved with and that Mr. Lion here be appointed the Chairman and Chief Administrator. A sum of fifty million pounds has been set aside to initially establish the foundation."

So that's why Richard was here, Edward thought to himself while concealing his smile. His expectations for a larger chunk of the pie had just surged.

Mr. Lester carried on. "The balance of the joint estate of James and Muriel Lancaster is to be disbursed as follows." Edward was the only person at the table who appeared anxious. The others either simply looked down at their hands in their laps or directly at Mr. Lester with no particular expression. "To Reston Phillips, our long time and loyal friend, we provide the sum of five million pounds." Reston gasped at hearing Mr. Lester's words and quickly whisked a handkerchief from his breast pocket to stifle his sobs and his tears. Edward shuffled in his chair trying hard not to show his reaction, thinking that the lowly servant had received far too much.

"To Sir John Loxley, a dear friend and business partner, we provide twenty shares of Port of Grace Enterprises." Sir Loxley's expression did not change. He had known that he would be given controlling interest in the company. He and Lord Lancaster had discussed the matter a month after Richard had come home from the hospital. Essentially his and Lord Lancaster's shares had been reversed. Sir Loxley now owned fifty-five per cent of the company, thirty-five shares were left in the estate, and two original employees, retired for many years now, each still owned five shares each of the company making a total of one hundred.

Edward was having difficulty keeping still. The lion's share of the estate was still available, he thought. He practically threw up at the use of the unintentional pun.

The next beneficiary Mr. Lester named was Judith Bolden. Her inheritance was in the form of a monthly allowance until her death, sufficient for her to live quite comfortably. But there was a condition. In order to receive the allowance, Judith had to agree to have Lord Lancaster's accountants manage her funds. Lord Lancaster had kept his word. He made certain that Edward could not control his mother's money. Edward tried to object, but for the first time Judith spoke up against him and cautioned her son not to interfere. Edward was clearly agitated at this point. There was no way the old man would leave Edward the majority of his estate, he thought. And if not, that only meant that Richard was going to benefit. "How could this happen?" he shouted in his head.

"To Edward Bolden, our nephew, we provide sufficient funds to retire all debts owing as of this date, as well as a monthly allowance of five thousand pounds until his death." There were no conditions attached to his allowance. Edward was incensed at what he believed to be a meagre amount, compared to what he now anticipated Richard could receive, but somehow he managed to contain the rage inside him. His mother tried to show a positive front by discretely congratulating him, but he would have nothing to do with her. The others around the table tried to ignore him.

"Finally," Mr. Lester said, still in a flat and sober tone, "to Richard Lion, the young man we have come to love so much and of whom we are as proud as any parents could be, we leave the balance of our estate, including all land, all buildings, all property, all remaining shares in Port of Grace Enterprises, and all investments."

Richard closed his eyes, bent his head and placed his hand to his forehead as if to pray. He could not believe what he had just heard. Reston put a friendly hand upon Richard's arm as his body quivered in shock and tears formed in his eyes. Edward was about to lunge out of his seat in protest when Mr. Lester said, "In addition, I, James Lancaster, Earl of Lancaster, under the authority and with the approval of Her Majesty Queen Elizabeth II, do hereby declare Richard Lion as the new Earl of Lancaster."

"I protest," shouted Edward as he jumped out of his chair, knocking it to the floor. His face was twisted in rage, his hands pounded at the table. "This is a sham! How can someone leave a fortune to a stranger he's only known for a few months? This ..., this con man has weaseled his way into the Lancaster's home and taken advantage of them. Can't anyone see that? Lord Lancaster must have been crazy or somehow forced to write this Will. It isn't legal I tell you. I'll take this to the courts and then we'll see who the real beneficiaries will be." Edward paused long enough to gasp for air before continuing. "And how can he be named Earl, he isn't even a legitimate heir? Am I the only one who understands? The old man wasn't mentally competent when he made this Will."

It was difficult to try and ignore Edward's outburst, and for Judith it was total humiliation. She attempted to calm Edward but he was not paying any attention. Finally she rose from her chair to separate herself from him. At the first sign of Edward's protests, Mr. Lester turned to him to explain that the Will was indeed legitimate and that Lord Lancaster was of sound mind when the Will was written. Mr. Lester's explanations, however, were drowned out by Edward's constant shouting. At that point, Mr. Lester chose to sit back and wait for Edward to finish his ranting. By the time he finally wore himself out, Edward also realized what a scene he had made and how a quick exit might be the best option at this point. Still the idiot he demonstrated himself to be, Edward left the room saying to Richard, "This isn't over. If I were you I would watch my back."

Richard moved around the table to try and console Judith, who repeated over and over how ashamed she was of her son saying such awful things about Lord Lancaster and Richard. Richard could only feel sorry for her to have to put up with a son like Edward and extended an invitation for her to contact him if she ever required assistance in any way. Richard knew that Lady Lancaster would have wanted him to do this. Judith thanked Richard and made her way out of the room.

Reston walked over to Richard to congratulate him on becoming the new Master of the Manor. He added that he was prepared to carry on serving the new Earl if Richard so wished. Richard wrapped his arms around Reston and said, "Thank you Reston, I don't know what I would do without you."

Mr. Lester called over to Richard, "Excuse me Mr. Lion, I wonder if I may have a brief word with you and Sir Loxley." Reston indicated to Richard that he would wait in the outer office for him.

"I won't keep you long but there are some things I must tell you about your inheritance, Mr. Lion," said Mr. Lester, "some things that the others did not need to hear. I have included Sir Loxley since Lord Lancaster had already shared the contents of the Will with him. Please sit down, won't you."

Mr. Lester first advised Richard that they would require several more meetings to go over all the details and implications of his inheritance. While it was simple to state that Richard inherited the balance of the estate, land, buildings, property, etc., it was another matter altogether to comprehend what that entailed. It was also recommended that Richard consider retaining his own legal and financial consultants.

What was primarily on Mr. Lester's mind, however, were the conditions attached to Richard's inheritance. Mr. Lester explained that the title of Earl had been approved by the Queen and the Prime Minister under a letters patent. Apparently, according to Sir Loxley, Lord Lancaster had approached the Queen following the last International Relations Council meeting. The Queen was more than happy to grant Lord Lancaster's request. Mr. Lester explained that since Richard was not a legitimate heir of Lord Lancaster, the title of Earl could not be passed on beyond Richard, in other words to Richard's son, if he were to have one.

The last thing Mr. Lester wanted to make clear was that if Richard decided not to live at Lancaster Manor and run the Estate, or for that matter if his children inherited the Estate and decided that they would not live at the Manor and run the Estate, he or they, as the case may be, would not be allowed to sell it. The lands of the Estate and the Manor, as well as a fund that had been set aside for such a purpose if required, would be transferred to a non-profit organization to operate it as a park and heritage site. This had always been Lord Lancaster's wish. All other property, funds and investments, etc. were Richard's to do with as he pleased.

Richard told Mr. Lester that Lord Lancaster had actually shared these wishes with him one day when they had been riding in the hills, so this did not come as a complete surprise.

Richard and Sir Loxley left Mr. Lester with Richard saying that he would be in touch very soon to begin the debriefing meetings. Reston continued with them out of the office building. Once outside, Sir Loxley said to Richard, "We need to meet as well Richard. Lord Lancaster hoped that he would have been able to groom you to take over leadership of the company someday. That responsibility now falls to me, if that's what you wish. You are still young and you have much to learn, but he and I both agreed that you have the potential. When you are ready, we'll discuss it more. In the meantime, you have a branch in Regal Engineering to run, not to mention a fortune and the Lancaster Estate to administer." Sir Loxley took a moment then said in a sincere voice, "Richard, you have a great deal to think about and you have lost, for all intents and purposes, two sets of parents to whom you could have gone to for

THE ROAD TO LANCASTER MANOR

council. I want you to know that if you would like my assistance or advice on any matter, I will be happy to help."

CHAPTER THIRTY-TWO

Even though the skies were overcast and rain was threatening, Richard and Monica still had sunshine in their hearts as they looked forward to two precious days alone at the Old Country Inn and Resort up in the lake district. It had been twelve tiring days for Richard Lion, the new Earl of Lancaster, since Mr. Lester announced his inheritance. His position at Regal Engineering alone demanded long working days, including a postponed trip to Cape Town. Often the work days spread into work nights when he also had to find time to attend to meetings with Mr. Lester, who became his lawyer, and his accountants in order to fully appreciate and make sense of his new holdings and his new responsibilities.

Many of those new responsibilities fell outside the boundaries of his job with Regal or Port of Grace Enterprises for that matter, as he was now a significant owner of the parent company. Richard also met several times with Lord Lancaster's personal assistant who agreed to stay on with Richard until he could hire and she could train someone to replace her. Mrs. Johnson was almost as old as Lord Lancaster and was ready to retire. During the meetings with Mrs. Johnson, Richard learned about several boards and committees that the Lancasters had been involved with, and the many groups that often requested the attention of the Earl of Lancaster in terms of speaking engagements or fund raisers or grand openings, many wanting him to confirm the Earldom's continued participation in one form or another. In most cases Richard had to say to Mrs. Johnson that he would have to get back to them. He soon understood how necessary and valuable an assistant like Mrs. Johnson would be to help him manage his responsibilities outside his business interests.

Richard met Monica early enough to take her to breakfast before heading out on their road trip. They had not spent more than a few hours with each other since the reading of the Will and longed for this quiet and undisturbed time together. Richard had decided to take the Firebird rather than one of his new cars from Lord Lancaster's garage. He was after all, still a young man who enjoyed the feel of the powerful car he had brought back to life. Besides, the bright red Firebird, even on a gloomy October day, felt more appropriate than a black sedan on their romantic weekend retreat.

Richard had told Monica how these past days at Lancaster Manor had been difficult emotionally, not just for him, but for all the staff of course. His spirits had been uplifted though when Reston confided in him about how happy the staff were that Lord Lancaster had appointed him as his successor and the new Master of Lancaster Manor. Richard allowed the staff to call him Lord Lion, mostly because they seemed to insist on it. On the very first day he returned to work, however, he made it quite clear to everyone that he was to be called Richard. He told his own staff in a private meeting that just because he was now a major share holder in Port of Grace Enterprises, his authority at work was still limited to being Director of the South African Projects Branch. Jokingly he reminded them that he didn't need to be an owner to hire or fire them, he already had that authority. They had all laughed and appreciated his candour.

Both Sir Loxley and Inspector Giles, on two different occasions, asked Richard if he had heard anything further from Edward. He told them that he hadn't. Mr. Lester suspected that Edward's claim he would challenge the Will in court was just talk. He suggested that once Edward had time to cool down he probably realized what an ass he was and felt embarrassed about his whole outburst. Richard didn't believe that Mr. Lester knew Edward very well.

"I can't wait to sit in the hot springs pool and soak my stresses away," Monica said to Richard, as they were passing the time cruising along on the highway. "The last time I was up to the resort, I was with Sam on a Christmas break during nursing school. We totally pampered ourselves that weekend. It cost us a fortune with the spa treatments, but it was worth it."

"That sounds like a plan," said Richard. "And after that we can have a nice romantic dinner and who knows, maybe dessert in bed," he said with a mischievous grin on his face.

"Just like a guy, the first thing they want to do is hit the sheets," she returned with a tease.

"At least I said after the hot springs and dinner, didn't I?"

They both laughed and Monica leaned closer to Richard taking his arm in hers. She stretched to give him a kiss on the cheek and said more seriously, "I'm really looking forward to this weekend."

Being too busy enjoying the drive with Monica, Richard hadn't taken particular notice of the cars following him on the highway. Before he made his turn off of the main highway he now noticed that several cars had actually been behind him but that only one car turned with him on to the secondary road. While the car remained several car lengths back on the main highway, it now began to close the distance between them. Richard expected that the other driver would pass him momentarily. As anticipated the car drew parallel with his own. What he didn't expect was to see Edward's grinning face appearing through the passenger window. Before he could say anything to Monica, he was shaken in his seat from the sudden jolt applied from Edward's car purposely smashing against the Firebird's right side, in front of the door. As Edward's car swung back into his lane still running beside the Firebird, Richard regained control of his car. "What the hell is he doing?" yelled Richard.

Monica reacted to say, "Did he do that on purpose?"

"It's Edward," Richard called out. "I think he's trying to run us off the road."

Bash! Edward drove another glancing blow to the Firebird's side, this time with more force. Richard looked over his shoulder after he steered off of the shoulder on to the road again and saw that Edward's grin had turned to an evil sneer. "That's it, I'm not taking any more of this crap," Richard yelled and in defence he turned the steering wheel hard toward Edward's car. Edward was doing the same thing at the same time resulting in the two vehicles bouncing off each other similar to two like-poles of a magnate repelling each other. The metal clanked and scraped and both drivers had to fight to maintain control of their cars. Still travelling at a high speed on a two lane road, Edward took another swipe at Richard's car sending Richard to the far edge of the shoulder kicking up loose stone and gravel as he brought the car back on to the pavement. Monica was screaming for Edward to back off but he couldn't hear her and he wouldn't have cared if he could.

As the two cars raced ahead and approached a bend in the road, Edward made another and more direct hit on to the Firebird, this time with greater force. His much heavier car kept clinging to the side of the Firebird, pushing rather than ramming the frame. The screeching of metal on metal was horrible to the ear and Richard realized that Edward was trying to force Richard and Monica over the side of the road. In response to Edward's assault, Richard turned hard in the direction of Edward's car and floored the accelerator. The powerful engine was losing the battle with the much heavier car and Richard could feel the Firebird slowly drifting further on to the shoulder. Both Edward and Richard were concentrating completely on controlling their vehicles and did not notice what Monica was seeing when she screamed, "Richard look out!"

Out from around the bend, a long flatbed truck carrying a full load of cement blocks was barrelling forward. A second before the two cars could be seen, the truck driver dropped a piece of his sandwich on to his lap and looked down to pick it up. When he raised his head again and his eyes saw what was in front of him, he threw his sandwich aside, automatically stepped as hard as he could on his brake pedal and yanked the steering wheel towards the ditch. The truck fish tailed. With the front end surging over the edge of the shoulder and into the small ravine, the back end slid right into Edward's oncoming car, rubber squealing from the tires moving sideways on the road.

At the same time Monica had screamed, Edward let up on the pressure to Richard's car and returned to his lane before attempting another and what he hoped to be his last attack on the Firebird. Edward was drunk with fury and determined to end this now, to rid himself of the fair haired boy. When he looked up at the truck's flatbed charging toward him he yelled out, raised his arm in front of his face and experienced the longest two heart beats of fear he could have imagined. The momentum of the heavy flatbed crushed the much lighter vehicle like a bug under foot, rolling it over before spraying cement blocks on top of it to emphasize the destruction.

When Richard heard Monica yell he looked up in horror and just as the pressure was released from the side of his car, Richard instinctively turned the car to the opposite direction choosing whatever harm laid before them from a run into the ditch on his side of the road over the likelihood of being caught up in the inevitable collision between Edward's car and the flatbed.

"Are you alright," Richard said to Monica, after the Firebird came to rest with its front fender buried into the clay side of the ditch more than two hundred feet from the point they went over the side. Richard was able to control the skidding enough to remain in the ditch and right side up. While Richard and Monica were bounced and jostled around a great deal, their seat belts kept them from flying out of the car and receiving more significant damage to themselves. Other than some hard knocks on the head and a few scrapes, they were relatively unscathed. Monica's biggest problem seemed to be from shock. Once Monica was able to calm down, they managed to crawl out of the car through his door. Even though it had received extensive damage from the impact in the ditch, at least it would open. Monica's door was sealed to the frame from the constant bombarding Edward had given the car. They were both stiff and sore as they climbed out of the ditch to witness the flatbed wrapped around the mangled car.

By the time they had made their way over to the pile up, they had given up any thought of Edward living through the collision. A car with two male passengers stopped at the scene and asked Richard and Monica if they were hurt. They informed Richard that they had already called for an ambulance. All four then went to inspect the wreckage for survivors. The two men went to find the truck driver. Richard and Monica learned later that he had survived the crash but that he had suffered an assortment of broken bones as well as some internal bleeding that the medics were gravely concerned with.

Edward's car or what was left of it was hanging over the edge of the road, a front tire still spinning from the crash's momentum. The car was resting on the driver's side and Richard could see an arm hanging out of the broken window. The body was deformed due to bones and spine being rearranged. Blood was everywhere. But much to their amazement, Edward was still alive, barely. He had only a few breaths left as he managed to whisper his final words to Richard, "I was supposed to become Earl. I had it all planned. Why did you have to …?" Edward never got to finish. His eyes rolled back and starred out into the grey sky. Rain drops started to tap the metal on the car. A siren could be heard in the distance.

Richard and Monica rose to their feet and moved away from the devastation to wait for the ambulance and police. Monica kept close to Richard, still overcome by the ordeal they had experienced, that was now over. The rain fell harder as Richard stared back at the pile of steel and cement. He was reminded of another car wreckage and another couple who had escaped a planned attack from the same man. He tried but he could feel no remorse for Edward. The man was evil and had brought his eventual death upon himself. Richard comforted Monica in his arms, sheltering her as best he could against the driving rain and cold air. There would be no resort or hot springs pool this weekend. There would only be another funeral to plan, then Richard and Monica could get on with the rest of their lives, together.

ACKNOWLEDGMENTS

My travels through Europe, North Africa and the UK in the early 1970's inspired me to write this book. I still have fond memories of the many young people I met along my journey.

A number of friends and family members have generously shared their time and comments during the writing of this, my first novel, and for their contributions and encouragement I am most appreciative. A special thanks to Marge Wright, Dan Milne, Matt Henderson, Laurie Andersen, Eleanor Chornoboy, and finally my extremely supportive wife Rosemary, who graciously accepted my passion for writing, even while on vacation.

The Corkscrew Inn is not a figment of my imagination; it is real, although not in England. The Corkscrew Inn thrives in the Kitsilano area of Vancouver BC, Canada. Check it out at www. corkscrewinn. com